A Shot of Irish

WORKS BY GORDON BREWER

Ray Irish Occult Mystery
A Shot of Irish
(Ray Irish Occult Suspense Mystery Book 1)
Die If You Want Praise
(Ray Irish Occult Suspense Mystery Book 2)
Drink with The Devil at Midnight
(Ray Irish Occult Suspense Mystery Book 3)
No Remedy Against Death:
(Ray Irish Occult Suspense Mystery Book 4)
Ray Irish Occult Mysteries: Omnibus Edition
Death Stalks the Runway: Ray Irish Mystery Case File #1
Reaper Walks the Garden: Ray Irish Mystery Case File #2

Paranormal and Fantasy
Beowulf: Curse of The Dreygurs
Infinite Loop
The Curse of Blackbane

Clovel Sword Chronicles Series

Shield of Skool (Book 1)
Battle for Three Realms (Book 2)
Downfall of the Gods (Book 3)
Clovel Sword Chronicles: Omnibus Edition

Clovel Sword Saga Series

Clovel Sword Saga: Volumes 1 - 2
Skeletons of Nilgava: Clovel Sword Saga 3
The Bleeding Mountains: A Clovel Sword Saga 4

A Shot of Irish

GORDON BREWER

Brewer Internet Publishing LLC
2023

This book is a work of fiction. Any references to historical events, people, or real places are used fictitiously. All characters in this book are products of the author's imagination, and any resemblance to actual persons, living or dead, is entirely coincidental.

Third Edition

Brewer Internet Publishing LLC

Cover Illustration Design: https://www.fiverr.com/oliviaprodesign
©Gordon Brewer

ISBN-13: 978-1-945590-58-0

Visit the series website at

www.gordonbrewer.com

Dedication

To my family and friends, thank you. Without your support and patience, none of my books would be possible.

Special thanks to Breonna for her invaluable help as my beta reader.

Contents

Chapter 1: Welcome to the City 1

Chapter 2: A Trail of Death 41

Chapter 3: The Gumshoe 78

Chapter 4: Sucker Punch 117

Chapter 5: Backtrack 148

Chapter 6: The Tail 188

Chapter 7: The Fall................................... 221

Chapter 8: Death on the Bay 247

About the Author................................... 275

Chapter 1: Welcome to the City

A slumped figure moved along with several hundred souls on the cold sidewalks of Oyster City that morning. A gray sky hid the sun, making the buildings' colors appear muted. Raymond Irish moved slowly, unlike the surrounding people. His head was down and his fedora pushed low. The man with his hands stuffed in his worn brown pants scanned the pavement for anything useful. His left pocket had a hole that he kept putting his finger through. While probing the hole would not return his last quarter, it kept him from overthinking. When left alone with his thoughts, his worst memories crept into full view.

No, the hole in his pocket reminded him of his current situation.

Ray was out of cash—road stake, as the hobos called it. Never a good idea to be in a hobo situation, let alone in the dead of winter and stuck in some city where nobody knew your name. Oyster City looked like many of the other medium-sized towns he recalled before the war. But it still wasn't home, and he was sure that he hated the place's name. He wasn't a fan of oysters, anyway. Sure, the town had some elements that Irish might consider his city. The dim neon lights and signs hanging in front of the diners, bars, and different stores along Broadway where he wandered.

On the street next to him, noisy vehicles belched fumes and smoke as they rushed every few feet in a line to the next busy intersection. Red, yellow, and green-colored lights, along with the occasional traffic cop, all tried to keep the downtown chaos from becoming full anarchy.

While Irish walked next to multistory buildings lining the street, Ray thought about the lost souls who walked inside, ready to fulfill another day in return for a few bits of cabbage. He could picture the throngs herding into elevators which lifted them into the sky, where they remained chained to a desk, toiling amid paperwork while silently urging the weekend to arrive faster. He had been there, enduring a soul-crushing job trying to sell trinkets to another person in a similar building somewhere in another part of the country. It was a rat race of collective struggle for the multitudes who watched the clocks on the walls before returning to their homes, sitting among the laid-out grids where the street names all had a familiar look, like Maple or Oak. Shivering, Ray suddenly felt his belly growl angrily. His last breakfast came from spending yesterday's dime on an orange in a nameless town before he hopped a train. He might not envy their downtrodden life, but at least those pushing past him had money to stave off hunger and keep warm at night.

The hole in his pants now forgotten, Ray mentally counted the number of places he'd been through since returning to civilian life. This gray town where he woke that morning made it stop number seven in the last year.

Good ol' lucky seven!

Irish ruefully tried to remember some of his travel. Mostly, one town appeared the same as another, especially for a guy who lived hand to mouth as he drifted across the states. Spending nearly three years of hell in the Pacific, jumping from one island and the next, the man followed a shiftless pattern. However, his wandering was something he controlled. Even cold and hungry, Ray Irish believed he was in charge of his destiny, not waiting for some damned moron to order him around.

As he stooped to pick up a cigar stub lying next to a lamp pole, Ray could not shake the unease drifting through him about his entrance into this particular town. The entire last year remained unsettled in his mind. Since he did not smoke, he placed the cigar into his jacket pocket that did not have a hole. It would be useful later for trading with other hobos.

Ray pushed away thoughts about his recent past hardships, which bothered him more than he liked to admit. Irish did not return to the appreciative and adoring crowds he read about in *Stars and Stripes*. The thongs who lined the docks after VJ Day never saw him. Instead, Ray Irish arrived weeks later and carried on a stretcher to a truck that took him to another hospital. It was the start of his tedious existence, which required a guy to forget thoughts of a future.

Well, that isn't the whole truth.

Haunting memories of the Canal and Okinawa remained. Some of it contained patches of images muddled in his mind, but one date stood out. Easter Sunday in 1945 etched into his memory like blasted concrete. He did not hear the explosion, but Ray remembered the winds he floated upon as his mind came in and out of a fog of pain and nothingness. Dragged through rocks for what seemed like miles, he remembered a tent where he watched a man with intense blue eyes and wearing bloody white clothes. The nurse said something, but they glanced at each other with knowing looks. He saw in their expressions that he would not survive. The eyes he saw pissed him off.

I'll live just to shove it in your faces!

Ray was never sure if he said it out loud. But he'd proved them wrong. Days of endless boredom came that went along with intense agony from multiple surgeries. Then, another round of countless days involving rehab when he got to a hospital near San Francisco. Weeks went by before they took his casts off, and they taught him to walk again, primarily by a big man in white who barked orders like a Marine. Still, he kept his recent past locked up, buried deep like his friends buried on those cursed islands.

In many ways, Ray Irish woke up to his new reality somewhere between Kansas and Missouri inside a smelly cattle car on a train heading east. That morning, he stared at the back of a wristwatch. Engraved on the watch were the words, *To Ray from Amy, '42*. In that cattle car, he decided he had to hock the once treasured heirloom. For the first time, Ray realized that all the booze might have given Irish liquid forgetfulness, but he put himself into the bottom of a barrel. There would be no returning to a sold ranch in Wyoming. His girl, Amy, had other plans. She was already married to someone who had returned from the war earlier. He sold the watch on the streets of Chillicothe for a grubstake to the next town.

Now Ray stood on the street of a place he couldn't find on a map. Oyster City might be a fair-sized town along the Chesapeake Bay coast, but the area looked to be on its last legs. Just north of the Mason Dixon Line, the port used to carry rust-red iron ore and lumber from Maryland out of the small harbor to places worldwide. The city took on a weary resignation, with the war ended like it expected to dry up and blow away with the next recession.

Ray came by this information from a thin, black man who called himself Pappy, running a newsstand on the corner a couple of blocks back. Being a drifter meant learning to get information from those who knew the area. A barrelful of information, the newsy kept his smile despite the hobo's questions. Pappy continued selling his newspapers to those passing by while telling Irish to look for jobs down at the docks. Encouraged by the tip from the only friendly person he had met, Irish followed the sidewalk on his way down to the port. He kept his eyes down to get hobo valuables along the street.

The chill of the air pressed on his clothes as another shiver shook him like a malaria fever. He just could not get warm. Hell, it remained a surprise to him that Ray had woken up at all that morning.

Irish heard yells and screams from below him as the railroad police rousted the hobos out of a nearby freight car on another line. Ray lay behind the observatory windows of an empty Pullman car. It was the only place he could grab when the Capitol Limited came to a stop in a small town called Garrett, back in Indiana. Somehow, during the night, Ray rode through Pennsylvania and nearly all of Maryland on the moving train.

While Irish ached to his core, barely able to move, the icy wind failed to kill him during the journey. Nobody noticed his prone form as he slept on a moving train, even after it stopped to discharge all the passengers. Ray always guessed he could sleep through anything, and now he had proved it. Irish caulked it up to his Irish luck. It took him some time to leave the car and slip into the town to dodge the railroad police.

Poking his index finger in the pocket hole again reminded him to keep moving. As Ray walked along, he mostly kept his eyes on the sidewalk. Bitter experience focused him on finding loose change that occasionally showed up on the concrete. More valuable were the cigarette butts or matches used for trading with others like him who were down on their luck. Unconsciously, he followed the traffic flow of legs, trying to avoid running into those who hurried past him. Each person trying to get out of the frosty morning air helped move the crowd along briskly.

"I don't have enough for a damn flophouse," Ray told himself.

In his difficult position, he needed to find a mission and battle the other tramps for a place to eat and sleep after hearing sermons against alcohol and drugs.

Well, at least I might get a bath and a shave, he thought while rubbing the few days' growth of beard on his face.

A gust of wind made Irish reconsider the possibility of a warm place, although he wasn't sure what was worse, the flophouse or the cold freight cars. Either way, he hoped lady fortune would come back to him soon enough.

Suddenly, the drifter noticed the tired, brown luster of a penny lying on the pavement. Even better, there were a couple of half-smoked butts near it as well. Ray made a beeline to the money and abruptly stopped, bending to get the coin. He felt a weight strike into his side when the woman fell over him, sending them both to the rough pavement.

"Watch where the hell you're going," Ray fumed, talking to the back of a stylish, tan wool coat while he grabbed his injured knee.

Quickly, he checked his trouser pant leg to ensure there were no rips.

"Skin can regrow, but not my pants," he grumbled to himself.

"Put on a stop sign next time," a woman's flustered voice replied indignantly. Ray looked over and saw her striking hazel eyes dancing with annoyance. The attractive woman sitting on the ground then gave him an uncertain grin, causing her slightly upturned nose to wiggle. Irish immediately liked her face, and her gesture reminded him of a rabbit-a cute little rabbit.

"Touché," he told her, as he smiled.

They burst out laughing at how silly they both appeared.

Ray let out a startled cry as a hand grabbed his collar and lifted him from the pavement. The tight grip on his coat and shirt began choking him as he scrambled to keep up with his elevating body. Soon he stood face to face with a bulky man wearing a too-small, gray wool suit. The undersized ape sported a chauffeur's hat on his head.

"I'll teach you to hurt a lady," the driver snarled as he twisted hard on Ray's collar. Ray's face turned a couple of shades of blue as he tried to breathe. He slammed one fist into his attacker's arm and thought he struck a steel column.

"Quincannon, let him go. It was an accident," the lady ordered the man in gray. The goon in the suit eyed her, cocking his massive head to one side skeptically, then released the drifter.

As he fell back among the gawking onlookers who gathered to witness the spectacle, Ray coughed and hacked for air. He noticed the disappointed crowd quickly broke up, returning to their monotonous routine.

Between gasping breaths, Irish listened as the lady told the brute to leave. She stepped over him, offering her apologies.

"Thanks, I guess." He forced out the words with another cough.

"Quincannon's pretty defensive about my welfare," the lady explained.

Her concerned expression helped Ray stop an upcoming sarcastic comment. He heard the almost abandoned tone in the woman's husky voice that caught his attention as well. He joined her when she glanced over at her ape protector, who continued to stare at Ray.

"Here, open your hand." Ray held out his fist, and she hesitated, then opened her palm. "It was supposed to be a lucky coin. The first one I found today. You take it."

He dropped a penny into her hand, and her puzzled look made him smile.

"I only appear like a bum in times like these. Good luck to you," Ray said before he kneeled to retrieve the cigarette butts.

They're worth more anyway.

Just as the drifter started to depart, the lady stepped in front of him with an outstretched hand.

"Here, this might bring you some luck as well." She smiled with perfect teeth. Irish instinctively held out his hand, and the lady placed two items into his palm before she spun back to the large vehicle at the curb. Ray liked the look of her long legs as she slid into the open door of a black Packard Clipper. He felt the staring eyes of the gray ape as the driver shut the heavy steel door before racing around the car to the driver's seat on the other side.

The large car drove away, leaving Ray inspecting the five dollar token and business card in his hand. The coin showed the emblem of a flower and the words *Stanley Rose,* while the business card revealed her husband's name.

"I guess Mrs. Henry La Spina of Terrace Court must take in strays for a hobby," Irish thought aloud as he caught the last glimpse of the car as it disappeared into traffic.

~~~

Greye La Spina pulled out her compact mirror, then glanced back through the window to catch another glimpse of the stranger staring at her car. His manner was unlike most of the drunks and vagrants she occasionally saw inside the mission. Despite his outward appearance as a bum with a scruffy beard and dirty face, he carried rugged self-confidence. The intense gaze of his brown eyes reminded her of someone in her past. She liked his look. The woman also noticed the button on his lapel. An Honorable Service pin given to discharged veterans, just like the one her brother wore, made Greye smile at the coincidence. The stranger's size appeared a good fit as well. She remembered her soft spot for big men in uniform and briefly wondered what the drifter looked like without his stubble.

"He's a bum," a gruff voice brought her out of her thoughts.

"Maybe so, but he could have prospects for the future," she said, holding on to a spark of an idea.

"You don't need no more boyfriends," Quincannon growled.

"I wasn't considering that," she told him flatly, although his suggestion intrigued her. Quincannon stared at her through the rearview mirror. She gazed back. "He's an ex-serviceman,
~~~

like my brother, just needing some help. You didn't need to strangle him."

"Your brother," the driver scoffed. "Nothing but a two-bit gunsel. Anyway, I do the thinking around here in this racket."

"Hugh is not that way!" she raised her voice. "You need to remember you're a handyman around here. Henry would fire you if he saw you beating up tramps on the street."

"Your husband might stomp around some, but he wouldn't do anything. We both know that. He's just another puppet on the strings controlled by what's prim and proper in this city." Quincannon continued glancing into the rearview mirror. "What'd ya give the bum?"

"You're the chauffeur. Keep your attention on the road," she reminded him.

"I asked, what did you hand him?" The chauffeur's voice boomed.

Greye took a deep breath.

"Don't talk to me that way. I swear to God that I'll go to Henry and get rid of you."

"Sweetie, you ain't doing any such thing. We both know it, so get off your high horse. Remember, this is Quincannon. Now, what did you give him?" His tone turned to a snarl.

She stared at the back of his head, contemplating her options. They were not good.

"All right, if you must know, I gave him a card for the mission. Just like Henry asked us, remember?"

The chauffeur snorted.

"Best that you remember as well. Don't make things any more complicated. We're too close to the end of this, and I'm not losing out on a fortune here. You're walking on a tight line along with the rest of us, and don't you forget it. You were supposed to keep that damn bishop happy, and now he's suspicious about Guy Young getting his meat hooks into you."

"That was your stinking fault," she replied hotly. "You and your bright ideas got me into this, damn you!"

Quincannon grunted his chuckle.

"Yeah, I didn't hear you complain at the time, sister. You jumped on this whole setup like a dog goes for a bone. Just remember that any slip up now could spoil that pot at the end of the rainbow. If this falls through, them butches running the state pen will trade cigarettes to play with that pretty little body of yours."

Greye La Spina went silent; her face turned angry as she stuffed the compact back in her purse. The guy driving the car held the cards, and that made it worse. She retreated to stare at the gray, wintry morning outside while Quincannon glared in the mirror.

~~~

Late in the afternoon, Irish walked along Bridge Street, leaving the dock area. Making his way back to the Salvation Mission House, Ray felt tired and frustrated. His feet hurt, and his stomach grumbled for nourishment. The day made the drifter yearn for three squares and a rack somewhere, and it could be anywhere, including hanging with the do-gooders.

After leaving his encounter with Mrs. La Spina, Ray found the mission just in time to grab a lecture and a bowl of soup served with a slice of day-old bread. It was heaven for the moment. The ladies and men running the vagrant facility were efficient. The director running the show gave Irish a quick look over before sending him on his way after the meal, advising him against liquor's evils. Irish scowled at his host, saying he could find better attitudes at a bar. The director's insinuation left Ray with a foul taste in his mouth as he went to the docks. Sure, Irish played a drunk for a while, but that was the past. At this point, Irish hoped he might pull a job just long enough to get some cash before hopping the next train out of Oyster City. In time, he'd find his place to land somewhere.
~~~

However, Ray's initial optimism quickly waned after he stuck his head into one office door after another along the waterfront buildings. He realized he needed to shave and to get better clothes. However, the way managers and supervisors responded to him reminded Ray why he didn't like people who held even a little power over others.

Too many of the bosses turned into crumbs, nothing but petty losers, he thought bitterly.

Worse for him, without the right contacts, Ray was out of luck. A drifter without a union card meant there were no jobs in town. The competition remained tough since many folks got laid off when the bustling wartime economy slowed.

Twilight hovered over the buildings, as Ray felt his frustration build with each step on the cold sidewalk. He remembered a saying that a little suffering might be good for the soul, but it made him damn mad as well. He'd seen enough sorrow for a lifetime. His existence over the last few years consisted of cleaning up after human cruelty. Ray couldn't count the number of crappy, little islands where he cut open slit trenches for Graves Registration people to dump the bodies of the stinking dead. When he finished, his bulldozer covered the open wound, leaving the landscape flat and barren. Ray could handle all sorts of jobs, but want ads in the papers were not crying for men with his lousy attitude to do nasty work that nobody else wanted.

Engrossed in his thoughts, Ray almost didn't hear the scuffle coming from an alleyway. A familiar sound of knuckles striking flesh forced him to stop. Turning back to the alley, he looked around the corner. In the dim light of creeping night, Irish could make out the outlines of three men clustered together. One man in a dark fedora held a smaller person from behind while a big goon with a light-colored hat kept slamming his fist into the prisoner's belly, muttering words Irish couldn't hear. The thin captive, doubled over in pain, just shook his head. The scene swept across Ray like the rotting smell of a jungle. It reminded him of sadistic Shore Patrol goons beating up drunken sailors on leave. It made him angry.

Irish let the fury overwhelm him, and he charged full speed into the fray. He tackled the goon throwing punches at the prisoner. They fell back toward the building. Ray felt a satisfying, painful cry released by his opponent as they struck the brick wall. Stunned, the big thug fell away, slowly sliding down the rough surface. Springing off the man that he used as a tackling dummy, the drifter bounced to his feet. He went after the hoodlum in the dark hat, who threw his little prisoner out of the way. The criminal's hand went inside his coat, but Ray struck the guy before he could grab his weapon. A rock-hard fist hit the hood right between the eyes, sending the thug's dark fedora tumbling away. Another quick slam from Ray's right fist landed on the goon's temple, and the guy dropped to his knees. Ray finished him with a kick to the ribs. The big man lay on his side, curled up in a fetal position, coughing and retching.

"Come on," the prisoner's voice cried out.

Irish felt a tug on his jacket. Reluctantly, he followed the skinny man, who ran with a limp out of the alley. Ray glanced back to see the thugs pulling themselves from the ground when he turned the corner. Then, the man did a double-take. In the blink of an eye, the drifter swore he saw a clown mask watching them from a dark window across the alley. When he glanced back, the shadowy figure in the black robe no longer remained, only a gentle sway of curtains still moving. Irish sped up to catch the stranger running in front of him. The man jumped into a new, black Hudson car. Impatiently, the driver yelled for Irish to get inside. The vehicle sped away just as the goons exited the alley.

"Damn, that was close. Thanks for the assist, buddy." The thin man in glasses coughed and then gave a nervous laugh.

His face flush with excitement and terror, he kept glancing at Ray.

"That's okay; I don't like bullies. Just keep your eyes on the road," the drifter replied as his foot felt for the non-existent brake pedal.

The car crossed the center line each time the driver looked at him, caused Ray to press down hard on the floorboard.

"Well, mister, if that's the case, you're in the wrong town," the man smirked before taking another glance at his passenger. "The criminals fill this place with them. Anyway, I owe you."

"Forget it. It looks like you lost your hat," Irish said. "Did those hoods get your money?"

Another chuckle came out.

"Nah, they weren't after that. They're some of Young's toughs, trying to give me a warning." The driver rubbed his abdomen. "I can replace the hat."

"Heading to the police station?" Ray asked.

The driver grunted.

"It's a waste of time; those hoodlums already have an alibi. Even if I knew their names, which I don't, they'd have a whole bunch of witnesses saying they were nowhere around that alley."

"So, that's how it works around here!"

Ray went quiet when the other man nodded. Instinctively, the drifter felt curious, but then again, he didn't need any trouble.

The driver turned the Hudson into another alley by the street sign that told Ray they had just left Broadway. The car came to a stop next to a white door with splotches of dark rust. With full darkness covering the city, only a yellow bulb lit the area around the door.

"It's safe here. Come inside and let's talk," the man in glasses told Ray as he got out of the car.

Suspicion filled Irish as he watched the driver exit the vehicle. He watched him walk around the front of the car, pulling keys from his trousers. Ray slid out, carefully inspecting the area while his driver fumbled at the door's lock.

"Damn thing needs some oil," he complained before the door finally yielded.

Inside, his host flipped on another switch, filling the room with light while Ray slowly followed.

"No need to be so nervous," the man said, extending his right hand. "J. Allan Dunn is the name, and this old place is an office and storage building. The building was a gift to the city a few years back, and we rented it out to some companies who took most of it over for storage."

"Ray Irish." The drifter shook his hand. The firm grip of Dunn's hand remained wet with sweat.

J. Allan Dunn took a seat behind the cluttered desk, his green eyes darting between the window and the drifter. Overall, J. Allan carried the appearance of a skinny owl. The guy had a touch of gray to the remaining hair that still clung around the edges of his sizeable, balding head. His narrow face and hook nose, along with the balding, suggested he could have been anywhere from thirty to fifty years old, Ray guessed. Dunn wore a tailored, dark gray suit with a colorful, red tie, nearly pulled off during the fight. His intense eyes appeared extra large behind the black-framed glasses he wore.

"I take it you are someone who knows how things work around this city," Irish noted as he looked around the room. Dusty shelves on one wall behind the desk held black binders, while various blue charts covered the walls on either side.

"I'm the Director of Public Works for Oyster City." J. Allan leaned back; his wooden chair gave a tired squeak. His face beamed proudly. "I have a direct line to the mayor."

"Then why is a city director getting beaten up in an alley?" Ray looked down at him. "And why bring me here to tell me?"

"Grab a seat, and I'll explain." Dunn pointed to two wood chairs, each filled with binders. He waited until Irish removed the files from one chair and pulled it closer to the desk.

"You see, the city is a pretty quiet place, or at least it used to be. People got along just fine, knew their places, and didn't make trouble. Since the war ended, there have been a few rotten eggs pushing in with their money and influence. It's kind of tug of war, if you will, between the good and bad sides. One of the bad ones is a racketeer named Guy Young, who's not even a local person. You just met with some of his hired hands."

The balding director leaned forward in his chair while readjusting his tie.

"On the other side, you have Mayor Hopley and his people trying to do good things for this city. They always have since their family has been here since the founding of the town. I'm local as well. My sister is married to a Hopley. Right in between, you have honest folk like me who are getting squeezed."

"Not a pleasant situation for you," Ray conceded. "Now, what's this got to do with me?"

Dunn pulled his chair close to the oak desk.

"Well, let me ask you a question. I noticed the ruptured duck on your lapel. I couldn't go myself, but I respect those who did. Are you a bindlestiff, or are you looking for a job?"

The drifter's eyes grew dark. "I'm not a bum, just got into town. I've been looking for a job. Nothing available without a union card, so they tell me."

"That's what I thought, probably down to your last dime at this point." J. Allan absently nodded while adjusting his glasses.

Irish hesitated.

"This morning, I came in with the overnight train." He passed on explaining his accommodations.

"Yeah, I understand. The problem is you got here about six months too late. They shut down the munitions plant outside of town. Mayor's trying to fix the problem, working with people to bring in jobs. Still, he's getting a lot of heat from the dockworkers and their union boss who can't see reality. Add to that mix is this Guy Young and his illegal operations; this city is at a crossroads. It grew up too fast during the war, quicker than the District Attorney or the police can handle. And they need help. You saw that yourself." The director smiled, apparently happy in his description of his fair city.

Irish listened patiently, waiting for the other shoe to drop. He instinctively liked the little guy, but he didn't trust him. Ray did not trust most people.

"Yeah, I'm sure there are lots of places like that. Lots of people come into a place and that upsets the apple cart," he agreed carefully.

Dunn's pale face looked over Irish again.

"Obviously, you can handle yourself in tough situations. But you'll need to clean up and get some clothes," he continued. "Then, get you in front of Cat."

"What are you talking about?" Ray's tone changed to suspicion.

J. Allan smiled again.

"I'm offering you one hundred and fifty a week to come work for me!"

Irish went silent. The offer seemed too much for a regular job, and something was wrong with how the man presented it to him.

"That's a lot of salad for an honest city director to pay a guy," Ray thought aloud. "What's the job?"

Dunn's eyes hardened at the comment.

"Some of us in the city help fix the problems I just laid out for you. I need someone who can keep in the shadows and figure out what is happening, particularly with this Young and his goons. You know, help get the dope on dirty laundry that doesn't get into the papers, kind of snoop, if you will," he said. "Plus, if things get tough, I want a guy who can get in and out without losing his head."

Ray stared at the Director of Public Works; for a moment, he was speechless. "Let's slow down, so I understand. Are you talking about a guy who sticks his nose in the wrong places? What makes you think I'm this guy? You've only known me a couple of minutes," he replied.

"Well, you're a stranger, yet you jumped in to help me, so I think I owe you a chance. Plus, you're a veteran, which means you can take an order when it needs to happen. And you are working on our side for a good cause," Dunn told him as he stood from his chair, leaning over the desk with his thin arms propping him up. "As I said, I go all the way up to the mayor. I've been thinking about this idea for a while. When the thugs are threatening businesses and those with money, some of us must step up. You know, help get the right people so they can fix the problems. What's your answer? Are you in or not?"

Ray kept looking at Dunn's face, searching for a clue about his sanity. Crazy plan or not, the drifter quickly mulled over his options.

"I stay on the right side of the law at all times," Irish finally replied.

"Not a problem. You just get information and relay it back to me. Occasionally, you take care of a few odds and ends that might come up," Dunn explained. "You know, help keep people in line who forget who they work for, and I'll make sure you aren't crossing the line. I have the ear of the mayor, and that means the police. Good enough?"

"Listen; despite the way I reacted back there, I'm not a heavy." Ray Irish tried to resist the offer. "You're not looking for some thug to go around knocking heads just for your entertainment? I don't think the mayor would go along with that idea."

"No, no, nothing like that," J. Allan assured him. "I'm talking about entirely legal work here. You're a troubleshooter, so to speak, trying to sniff out where the bad guys are heading. That means you can help head them off. Also, you'll be hanging out with them as you need to." He gave Ray a half-smile. "That means some of the fancy places they visit. There will be benefits in it for you beyond the pay that way."

"You know you could just pay a local snitch to keep you in the know? It would be a lot cheaper for you," Irish said with a nod as he rose from his chair.

J. Allan frowned. "Yeah, I know all about that. Cops can't trust them, so what makes you think I can? Besides, Young has more money than God right now. He owns the snitches," the director said. "Now, can you get me reliable information to weed out these folks?"

"I'm broke, so I can't look a gift horse in the mouth," Ray said, then took a deep breath before reaching out his hand to seal the offer with a handshake. "As long as what you tell me stays legit, then I guess I'm your man. How does this go now? Am I working for the city?"

"Not exactly," Dunn replied, pausing when he saw Ray's expression while he dropped his extended hand.

"It's not what you think. I can't put you on the payroll. There would be too many questions. The wrong people might notice. Besides, you would stand out like a sore thumb," the man explained to Ray.

"One of my trash men doesn't make enough money to go around some of these places to ask the questions and get answers."

He glanced away, and the director retook his seat.

"My idea is you will work as an independent agent for the paper here. The *Morning Beacon* would use you as kind of a legman for them. That way, you're working for the 4th estate with eyes and ears on reporters inside the building who can help get you the latest news. Plus, we can get the information before the paper prints it. You know, keep ahead of the muckrakers. I need someone to keep their mouth shut and their eyes and ears open. The last man couldn't handle the job."

"How's the paper involved with this scheme? I don't see their benefit," Ray said as his suspicions remained. He was suddenly curious about the last guy.

"That's not your affair," the director told him as he pulled his wallet from his jacket. "I'll get you lawfully tied into them with a small paycheck, which keeps everything on the up and up. But you can't forget who brought you to the dance. Is that understood?"

A few minutes later, the former drifter left his new office with three sawbucks in his coat pocket and a key to the office door. Ray made his way down to Cherry Street, following Dunn's directions to a hotel while he racked his brain to soothe his doubts. Irish knew that he should have asked more questions. Ray's insides told him to remain suspicious of Allan, but he convinced himself that it was better to take the cash that the director waved in front of him.

Several blocks later, the drifter found the Hotel Alexander. After the clerk behind the desk cast him a suspicious glance, insisting they had a full hotel, Irish pulled a ten spot. He told the clerk to book him into the place for a couple of nights. Suddenly, as Ray expected, a room became available.

The next morning, an oppressive fog covered the city's larger buildings' tops, leaving the air cold and damp. Ray walked along Chandler Avenue, sporting a new blue suit, along with a new black fedora. Before he stepped into the office, Irish took a quick walk around the outside of the rundown building. As he strolled along, inspecting the front facing the street, only boarded-up windows and a locked door greeted him. The old sign above the door spelled out *Swede's Fine Clothes*. Making his way back to the alley, he thought about his change in luck. A few bucks in his pocket and a hot meal for breakfast gave Irish a renewed sense of identity. He even wondered if a steady job like this might help him bury some demons he carried. For the first time in a while, Ray could almost believe in the future. He didn't realize he was smiling as he entered the dusty office.

Waiting around for his boss, Ray inspected every inch of the room, first out of curiosity and then from genuine interest. Nearly everything he found related to the municipal codes and legal documents needed for construction. Most of the material contained plans and contracts about the new buildings and key public works within the city. However, he discovered several items of interest. Ray might not be a private dick, but it didn't take a genius to figure out his new boss. Irish decided if J. Allan Dunn was an honest city official, then he was the pope. A couple of documents revealed his boss took money off the top of several lucrative city contracts. Also, he confirmed Dunn's name on several blueprints as the owner of the land before construction. Then, he remembered Mayor Hopley's name, which he noticed on some of the other plots and charts he looked through. Digging deeper, it became apparent that his boss, and probably the Mayor, owned several parcels of land where major construction happened. He would bet that they bought the land cheap, long before the construction began.

"My, my, my new benefactor is a busy man trying to get wealthy on the back of John Q. Public," Ray whistled as he leaned back in the squeaking chair. "No wonder he needs information." Then he heard a car pull down the alley. After the vehicle stopped, Irish listened to a car door open, then slam shut, followed by footsteps.

J. Allan entered the office a few minutes before eleven in the morning. At first, the Oyster City Director of Public Works didn't recognize the person sitting behind the desk, causing his owl-like eyes to widen in fear.

Irish slid his feet off the desk. "You didn't say what time, so I got here a while ago."

Dunn gave a quick, sheepish grin. "Well, you'll stay busy from now on." He closed the door, glancing outside before he turned back to the desk.

"Worried about Young's men?" Ray asked.

"No, it's just a habit. You'll pick it up quick enough if you plan on staying in this city." J. Allan's thin face grew hard. "Now, let's get to your work. You will go over to the *Beacon* and meet with Catherine Bennett. Just remember that she likes to be called Cat."

"Why her, and what am I talking about?" Ray rose from the seat and picked up his fedora from the desk.

"She's a photographer down at the paper and a pretty darn good one," Dunn stated with an air of pride. "Cat gets paid for special events photos when she's not trying to become a reporter. That means she gets paid only for the pictures. The good news is that she knows a lot of the town gossip and hangs out with the lady that handles the society pages." The boss nervously began pacing the floor as he laid out his thoughts.

"It may give you a headache listening to the girl, but find the latest news on Guy Young and any of his associates. You can learn more by hanging around the reporters there. Keep an eye open for anything that involves Young and another bad guy called Johnny Jacobi."

"Who is this Jacobi?" Ray interrupted.

"He's some Jew hoodlum from the capital upstate. It seems he's got some business down here, but nobody knows if he's tied in with Guy or not. It's probably nothing, so keep your focus on Young. Your job is to find out his rackets along the dock and any other places he's been muscling in. You can't fight a battle without knowing who the soldiers are."

Ray didn't like the reference to action from some damn civilian, but he held his tongue.

"All right, I just show up to the paper asking for this woman and go from there. How do I get paid?"

"I'll leave cash here each week. The first drawer on your right, the key is on the top of the shelf there." Dunn pointed at the spot.

"There's no phone here. What if I need to get in touch with you?" Ray asked.

"You won't," J. Allan told him flatly. "We aren't socializing. And don't come looking for me. Our meeting place will be here. Only a few know about this office, since the businesses use the rest of the building upstairs as a storage area for their records and other junk. I'll leave a message at your hotel when we meet again."

Ray nodded.

"You're telling me I'm strictly a guy working for the paper who's not associated with you."

"You got it. I don't know you from Adam. Now, get your ass over to 4th and Broadway. Cat knows you'll be looking for her. I'll be in touch in a day or two. I want to see progress. There's a lot on the line here." Dunn went to the entrance, checking carefully outside when he opened the door before he walked to his car.

Irish left the building a few minutes later. He exited the alley and found a taxi near the corner. Fifteen minutes later, Ray climbed out of the cab stopped in front of a gray, squat building flashing the Morning Beacon's name on the rooftop. Inside the lobby, he took the marble steps to the first office he found. Opening a door marked *Press*, Irish passed several cluttered desks. He came to a counter stacked with paper next to a water cooler, where several men stood. They were gabbing about a poker game from the night before.

"Hey, can any of you tell me where a girl called Cat hangs out?" Ray interrupted.

"Yeah, I might," a red-haired man with a kid's face told Irish as the stranger gave him the once over. His brown coat looked new and expensive, but the remains of breakfast showed on his black tie. "Who wants to know?"

"A guy she's expecting," Ray told him emphatically.

"Cat didn't say anything to me," the young man replied while moving closer. "What did you say your name was?"

Ray scowled at the person trying to intimidate him.

"I didn't know you were her secretary." Snickering broke out among the group as Irish continued. "Now, do you have any idea where she is, or do I have to find her boss?"

The red-haired kid blinked at the threat.

"She's up on the second floor, photography," he said before sullenly turning away. Ray listened to the men around the counter, making wisecracks about the exchange.

Ray Irish found Catherine Bennett standing by a messy desk, contemplating a line of photographs hanging by clips. The black and white images covered a portion of the wall between a file cabinet and the desk. The young woman with short, strawberry-blond hair wore a blue sweater and gray trousers. Ray took a double-take at the woman's nicely compact figure.

"Are you Cat?"

He moved to get a better view after closing the door. She wasn't a stunner, but darn cute.

Nodding, she remained focused on the photos in front of her. Finally, she pulled a single black-and-white picture from the clip.

"You must be Irish," she replied, not bothering to look up.

Ray remained quiet, looking around the empty room. A long table ran along the back wall. He could smell the chemical stench coming from containers running along the shelves above the table. A black curtain covered the entrance to another room near the chemicals.

Laying the photo on the desk, she turned her attention to Ray. She gave him a smug grin, her slight freckles showing beneath thin makeup.

"From the description of the encounter last night, I expected some big, rough-looking guy with a broken nose."

Irish smiled.

"I mend pretty quickly."

They heard the door open, and Ray looked around as the young man he left in the office downstairs was standing at the entrance. An uncomfortable pause filled the air while the red-haired man looked like he wanted to hide. The photographer saved him.

"George, come on in; I want you to meet someone." Cat waved him inside.

"Irish, this is George Hopley. He's a legman here, chasing down whatever stories he hears about on the streets."

Ray stared. Aside from George's deliberate intrusion, he didn't like the extra company.

"Yeah, we met. I thought he was your clerk."

The kid scowled, but he didn't take the bait.

"Listen, sorry about the third degree, but you're a stranger around here. How long have you been in town?"

"Hopley, eh," Irish changed the subject. "Same as the last name of the mayor. I'm betting you're local."

"Yeah, the mayor's my uncle." George's attention followed Cat as she picked up a brown camera in its case. She stepped next to Ray.

"You guys can catch up when we get back. I've got an assignment with Irish." She slid her arm inside his, pulling them toward the door. Ray couldn't help but give George a satisfied wink as they left the room.

"Well, sister, where are we heading?" Irish tried to keep up as the girl trotted down the stairs while she slipped the homemade leather camera strap over her arm.

"Keep up," she ordered. "Sam's Cafe is just around the corner."

They crossed the busy street, avoiding a couple of angry drivers who honked and blasted a few curses through closed car windows. Turning the corner, Ray glanced back. Shaking his head, he scolded himself for acting like his new boss. The couple went another block before entering a small diner holding a pair of customers at either end of the counter. They didn't bother to look up. Still taking the lead, Cat pulled into a booth, giving herself a view of the outside street through the large front window.

Ray slid in across from her, suddenly noticing how young she looked. Barely out of high school, if he had to guess. Her blue eyes twinkled with amusement as she watched him.

"I've been out of college for a couple of years," she told him, grinning at his expression. "Everyone thinks I'm younger than I am."

"You read minds as well?" Ray replied, and she laughed.

"Won't your boyfriend track us down here?" he asked lightly.

"He's not my boyfriend, just a bit too protective at times. Besides, the food here is too expensive for a reporter," Cat told him as the waitress came to the booth.

"Two coffees," she ordered.

She watched the server step back to the lunch counter.

"Yeah, it's the Ritz, with their prices. It must be a penny more," he told her, but his mocking comment went past the girl. "Anyway, George acted more than curious when I asked about you."

"George is a good egg, but he's not for me. Besides, I didn't bring you here to talk about him. Dunn says you're the new guy working for him." A determined look replaced the grin on her face.

"So I hear. I spoke with Dunn this morning, and he said to meet with you since you had the lay of the land."

Cat cocked her head.

"Funny, I never heard of him going into work before noon. You must be high on his list of to-dos since Young's men tried to pound on him. The crooks down at City Hall must be getting nervous if they grab a stranger for help. Do you have any idea of what you're up against?"

"Okay, how did you know about the thugs working over Dunn? Are you a reporter as well?" Irish noticed the cynical comments from those used to the city.

"No, but I will be," she told him enthusiastically. "Dunn called me last night to give me the scoop about you. He wanted me to size you up and give you the layout of things. Right now, I'm a photographer for the paper, mostly taking pictures of the women's club events or the political things going on in town." She patted the camera case next to her.

"Then what's the dope on Dunn and you? He tells me he's just an honest city official." Ray noticed Cat glance away before answering.

"Do you believe him?"

"Let's just say I have ideas against that. But I work for this director now, so I'm not sure how much I care," Irish told her.

"Good," she replied, seeming relieved at his statement. "Nobody is honest inside City Hall. Heck, there's no one honest in Oyster City. J. Allan Dunn pays me to do things for him, like keeping my ears open to news about the mayor and such. I let him in on things that the newspaper knows. He talks big, but he's only a minor cog in the political machine who owes his position to his wife's relations. But he knows who runs things, so he's good at getting things for the mayor. From what I've heard, he's the old boy's handyman."

"Then, who's the big guy in town, the mayor?" he asked. Ray believed the first hour in a town told you a lot about its character.

She stared at him for a moment. "Horace Hopley acts the part, that's for sure." Cat leaned forward. "But I wouldn't put my money on that, if you know what I mean."

"Kind of a puppet on the strings of someone else, is that it?" Irish raised an eyebrow at the comment.

She nodded.

"Yeah, Dunn likes to tell me he's part of the right side, keeping Oyster City good for all of us. But that's just Mayor Hopley's speech. I mean, I grew up here, and there's always someone either trying to knock off another person or some type of graft that people are involved in." She gave a slight frown at the thought, pausing to take a sip of her coffee. "First thing you have to know is to watch your back. You never know who you're dealing with, and people can get real mean."

Ray thought about J. Allan's edgy looks out the window.

"I'll keep your warning in mind. Any ideas on who pulls strings in this city?"

Cat glanced away briefly before she shook her head. Irish took a drink.

"What about you? Dunn acts like you are working on their side. Taking pics of events for the mayor and staying up on things."

Cat nodded. "Nearly every time a shovel hits the ground, I'm there. I never understood why the public works department thinks they need pictures before they build something. I mean, the paper never runs the photos. Then again, I get paid either way."

"Yeah, I get it." Ray nodded, wondering at Dunn's interest in keeping her employed. "What about this Young character?"

"Guy Young is unknown. He is a good-looking devil who came into the city right before the end of the war. Pretty soon after that, he brought in that large gambling boat. It's out in the bay, so the city can't shut it down. Otherwise, he's got his thugs running around making sure business owners pay him for fire insurance, so their places don't go up in smoke. All it took was a couple of warehouses burned out, and now people pay his thugs and keep quiet. District Attorney can't prove anything, of course."

"That makes him another textbook racketeer. Why don't the state cops take down gambling on the ship?" Ray wondered aloud.

Cat looked at him oddly.

"Why would they? Guy has paid off a bunch of people in the capital, so they don't bother him. I've seen some of the crooked politicians who bring down their lovers for parties out on the *Stanley Rose*. I even got some pictures of a couple of local bigwigs with their whores." Her voice conveyed proud satisfaction in her work.

Ray thought about the five-dollar token in his pocket, but he returned his focus to Cat.

"You have pictures of these corrupt politicians? You said you wanted to be a reporter. Don't you news hawks want to spill the beans on that type of stuff?"

"Are you kidding me? I ought to be a reporter, but I like the money these shysters will pay for the pics a lot more. The big newspapers won't spend money on those pics. And they don't care about political crooks running Oyster City. Those local newspapers that might have an interest would have an accidental fire, so they don't bother," she told him, giving a knowing nod. "Anyway, I have George contact the guy and see if the dope wants the negatives, which they do, of course. You see, George makes sure they know the guy's wife might take them to court with the pictures. Most of the time, they come through. Then we split the money." The smug look she gave him caused Ray to remain quiet for a moment.

Irish took a sip of coffee, suddenly wishing it had a shot of whiskey in it. The cute young kid across the table had the corrupt soul of a grifter. She acted like a person who would happily kick you into your grave if convenient, and the action brought her some cash.

"I get it. No wonder you work part time."

"It pays the bills," she said with a grin, while Ray's face remained unmoved.

"Get back to Young. He's got a racket going along with gambling and extortion. If nobody is pestering him, what does he want? Beating up Dunn doesn't accomplish much. It seems like this Young character already has it pretty good."

She shrugged her shoulders, looking down at her cup.

"Word is he'd like to become the owner of Oyster City. Maybe he's trying to build an empire. Either way, he's been going after some of those on the city payroll who can help him. Those related to the mayor like Dunn can't pay off when he threatens. Some coppers are taking his money, so it's not clear who those in City Hall can trust anymore. It's obvious that Dunn wants you to find out."

"Really? You seem to know a lot about what J. Allan wants," Ray observed.

Cat's face hardened.

"I'm smarter than you might think. I can figure things out. You are unknown, so if you ask questions, nobody gets wise to who pays you. I don't know how he does it, but getting attached to the paper means you can check things out. I'm guessing people will assume you're just another reporter sticking his nose in the wrong place. It's not like some reporters are taking sides depending on who's paying them. You're just like the last guy Dunn hired."

"Okay, you're smart," he told her. "Now, what about Jacobi?"

Her eyes widened at the name, but she quickly replied she knew little about the gang leader. The lie was obvious, but Ray let it go, sure that Cat wouldn't tell him anything useful. Already, Irish had difficulty figuring out the right pieces in this puzzle.

She looked at him when Ray grew quiet, wondering what he thought. She noticed how much his demeanor toward her changed during the conversation.

"Listen, I've got to get back to work. I'll check around and keep my eyes open."

Ray took a sip of coffee and frowned.

"Damn, coffee's cold." He looked at her, confident he could not trust his new partner. "Tell me something. Are you paid to keep an eye on me or just feed information?"

She smiled brightly.

"I'm not paid to be a private dick. From what you've told me, it seems you're on your own around here. I'm just the messenger."

Nodding, Ray stood and pulled a couple of dimes from his pocket.

"Well, you're honest about that. I'll see you around." He quickly turned and left the café, not bothering to wait for her. Irish paid no attention to her stunned gaze as he walked past the front diner window.

A few blocks away, Irish came to the newsstand on Main Street, where Pappy ran his business. Unexpectedly, the older man recognized Ray in his new clothes. Irish purchased the morning paper and started jawing with a wiry man sitting on a stool. It didn't take long to get him warmed up, and Pappy eventually spilled the news about the rough and tumble world inside Oyster City. The newsy's version also connected with Cat's understanding of the world. However, Pappy also explained more about the constant turmoil over the years.

"Been here most of my life," Pappy told Ray as he took a nickel from a passing customer. "Can't say it's changed in how things get done. Oh, there are new buildings and roads, and all those at the top seem to have their fingers in everybody's pie. Those that say too much against the progress appear to end up missing. I noticed you aren't leaving."

"Yeah, got a job," Ray told him before he asked Pappy about what he meant about missing people, but his new contact shook his head.

"You'll see it soon enough," Pappy told him stubbornly.

Irish changed the subject and asked about the Jacobi gang. The newsstand owner explained that Johnny Jacobi owned most pawnshops around the state. The gangster had his sights set on moving his game into Oyster City before the war broke out. Then, Guy Young showed up to put his stamp on the town. According to Pappy, recently, a couple of Young's thugs went missing after Jacobi's men spotted them. Irish tipped him a buck for the information, causing the old newsy's brown eyes to light up.

"Say, what side are you working for?" Pappy asked with a hint of suspicion.

"Just for me, keep your ears open, and some more of the green can come your way," Irish told him.

Pappy gave a friendly smile as Ray walked away.

The rest of the afternoon found Irish in the library. His attempts at flirting with the stiff blonde behind the book counter went nowhere, but he found a book about the local history. The man was curious about the suspicion he had witnessed in his short time there. Reading about the founders who established the city, Irish combed through a large stack of old newspapers. Stories from the *Beacon* and their rival newspaper, the *Star*, made him him feel like he was back in school. Still, he went through news clips from the last year, bypassing the war articles and concentrating on the police reports and political events.

When Irish finished, he believed he understood the city and its people. On its own, Oyster City carried a tragic history with floods and fires that nearly destroyed the early settlement in the 18th century. An early immigrant pioneer named Henry Andras founded the town, setting up his shipping and fishing company along the bay. Growing wealthy on the backs of slaves and Far East trade before the Civil War, the family ran the town like their fiefdom. According to one book, only in the last century had other wealthy families, like the Hopley's and La Spina's, earned powerful positions over the city.

Irish spotted something unusual in all of his reading. For such a small city, the number of murders, disappearances, and other violent crimes appeared to make Chicago look like a citadel of virtue. There was also a string of corruption stories that seemed to go nowhere. It appeared his employers were just as crooked as those trying to push into the town. At least Young and Jacobi were upfront about their corruption. The disappointing confirmation made Irish seriously reconsider his new line of work.

Not long after six, Ray stepped into the lobby tavern at the Alexander hotel. He watched the few patrons with casual glances at the large mirror across the bar counter. A salesman pitched his line of wares to a bald gentleman at one end of the room. The bored businessman kept his attention on a cute redhead across the room. After a couple of shots of Irish whiskey, the new troubleshooter ordered a grinder sandwich. Observing those in the bar again, he noticed the redhead was waiting for someone.

A few moments later, Ray got his food and glanced at a young married blonde lady passing behind him to join the redhead woman. Recognizing their forced discreteness as he covertly observed them, he knew a deeper relationship was going on between the two ladies.

At times, the world is pretty damn screwy!

He smiled to himself. Spending several months in bed with little to do, but watching people and their interactions gave him insight. Ray noticed the small things that showed something deeper in a person's expressions and mannerisms. Deducing the reasons behind the clues he viewed became a game to kill the time.

Irish reached into his pocket to pay the check, finding the five-spot token that Mrs. Greye La Spina gave him. He flipped the golden-colored coin in his hand. It came up heads in his palm.

"Say, how does a guy get out to the *Stanley Rose*?" he asked the bartender named Frank.

"There's an exclusive water taxi down at the docks, over on the last piers. Signs should show you." The burly man smiled, lifting his pencil mustache. "Say, if you're looking to lose your money, I can put you into a great Acey Deucey game that's closer."

Ray shook his head.

"Nah, I'm thinking of a gal with hazel eyes!"

His first view of the *Stanley Rose* gave Ray a quick flashback. A former cargo ship that sat low in the water had a passing similarity to the thousands of Liberty ships he saw filling the seas around Japan a few years before. However, the *Rose* carried a white paint coat and strings of flashing lights, making sure people knew its location. While the ship was not exceptionally large, Ray quickly noticed the loud music coming from a live band on board. It came to him over the sound of his taxi boat's motor and props churning through the water.

On the *Stanley Rose*, Irish milled around the deck after handing his hat to a young girl wearing too much makeup. The main deck held a dance floor with a small band playing some of the latest tunes. Several gaming tables in the corners of the sizeable area kept the focus of the small crowds. The deck below his floor had more tables placed inside smaller rooms. He assumed the quieter places held the poker cheats who played their loaded games against their marks. Ray saw enough crooked card games over the years in the Pacific.

I wish I had half of all the dough I lost!

It appeared half those hanging around the dance floor were drunken women in their best dresses while men, young and old, kept buying more of the cheap booze. Curious, Ray watched a staggering couple heading up and began following them as they took a flight of stairs above the main level. Trailing discreetly behind, he reached a passageway and then waited as they snuggled near a partially open door. Before they entered the room, he saw the woman expertly slip her hand into her client's suit pocket, quickly retrieving his wallet.

Passing by the now-closed door, Ray shook his head at the stupidity of the drunken sap inside. At least the prostitutes were nice looking around here, he thought cynically. Irish walked to the other end of the passageway, where he came to another stairway leading back to the main deck. Pushing his way through the crowd, Ray found the bar and got a whiskey on the rocks. Leaning against the counter, he noticed a closed door with a sign spelling out *Management* in stenciled letters on the other end of the room. He thought nothing of it until the door opened and he saw her.

Greye La Spina walked into the room wearing a tight, pale yellow dress, which accented her knockout figure. Just behind her walked a tall, sophisticated man wearing a tuxedo. Ray noticed her escort's self-possessed features, his blue eyes, sharp nose over thin lips, and jet black hair slicked back.

Guy Young made quite an entrance as well. Irish grinned when he saw the large goons in matching brown suits trailing behind Young. The only difference between the two bald men was one thug had a scar across his nose. Tweedledee and Tweedledum's cartoon picture immediately came to mind as he watched them follow their boss.

When Greye walked by Irish, and he got a close-up view. Her pale face carried the emotion of a porcelain doll. Her smudged lipstick and her hair were slightly out-of-place. The hallmarks of her fun behind closed doors. Guy guided her to the stairs leading to the deck below. Her racketeer escort beamed a ludicrous smile of satisfaction at her public humiliation.

"It looks like the bishop's wife is still coming up short on the tables."

The contemptuous whispered comment came from a half-drunk woman standing behind Ray. Short and overweight, the lady looked close to middle age. Wearing a tight pink dress made for a younger woman, the caustic lady kept trying to get her husband to dance. The gray-haired man obviously wanted to be elsewhere. Slugging back the last of his whiskey, Ray stepped in front of the woman, holding out an arm.

"Come on, I need a partner," Ray told the cheerful lady. As he led her to the dance floor, Irish noticed the gray-haired man wander away. Unspoken thanks appeared from the released prisoner's eyes.

Dance moves slowly came back to Ray as he tried to make his best impression of Fred Astaire, which needed a lot of work. Luckily, she remained happily unconcerned, sloshing her words during their conversation.

"So, young lady, what's your name?" he asked.

The woman giggled. "Just call me Pearl. You dance well."

"As do you," he smiled gamely. "I'm a stranger here. Have you been to this place before?"

"Yes, dear, we…I mean, I come here quite often. It's such a blast. You stick with me, and I'll show you around." Pearl stepped in closer as the tempo slowed during the next song. The overabundance of her perfume reminded Irish of the sickly sweet smell of flowers on the Solomon Islands.

"What about your husband? I don't want to make enemies."

Pearl smiled, giving him a wink. "He'll wear himself out at the poker tables downstairs. We have plenty of time."

After several drinks, the chubby woman became more talkative. She and her husband, a banker, knew the social circles of the city. Most of what she knew was second hand or idle gossip. However, he gathered some details about Greye La Spina.

"You know the bishop comes from a long line of La Spina's in this city." The married woman pushed in close to him. "But that thing he married, nobody's ever heard of her. I understand his wife hangs around this boat most of the time."

Pearl made it clear that Greye carried a low reputation as the wife of a respected bishop. The drunk woman considered Henry La Spina for sainthood for dealing with such a situation.

"What about Guy Young? Why does he let her hang around? From some women looking at him, he has plenty of opportunities," Ray mused.

Pearl shook her head, nearly stumbling as he helped her recover.

"He's a collector of things. I hear he likes to use her to show off he can do anything he wants. Now, let's get another drink." She batted her eyes; the thick mascara left little lines around her eyelids. "I want to show you some of the cozy hideaway places they have here."

Ray decided he wasn't drunk enough for a turn with Pearl, so he took her to the bar before breaking away to find the restroom. The information gave him the idea for a quick exit from the ship with hat in hand. Irish made his way back to the small dock where the water taxis dropped off the passengers.

Intrigued by Greye La Spina's relationship with Guy Young, he decided she could be a way into the racketeer's inner circle.

Stepping down a metal stairway, Irish went over the stories he heard as he exited the ship. Then Ray saw Greye standing alone on the dock; her attention focused on the dark water just a few steps away.

"Ma'am, you forgot something," Ray told her, coming up behind her while holding out his closed hand.

She jumped at his words before turning to him and instinctively holding out her hand. Ray placed the five-dollar token in her palm, and Greye looked at the item. Confusion filled her face.

"You gave it to me yesterday morning after I knocked you down," he explained with a grin.

Her hazel eyes lit up, the porcelain mask gone. "My, you clean up well." Greye glanced him over. "And a new suit. You must have hit the jackpot here."

"No, just got a job," Ray told her with a bemused smile. "You look fantastic."

He meant every word.

"Thank you. And you look better without the beard." Her smile appeared relaxed and genuine.

"Yeah, I know. A bath helps as well." He intentionally looked her over. "Mmm, there's something else about you." He paused again, then snapped his fingers. "I know! I don't see a great ape hanging around."

Greye chuckled at the comment.

"Well, that can happen with the right people."

"That's good to know. Perhaps you can get a drink with me to finish out the evening?"

Her nose gave that cute twitch again, and her smile fell away.

"Unlikely. You read the card that came with the chip I gave you. I'm unavailable."

Ray went for broke when he saw two boats approaching. One boat looked to be a private one for the bishop's wife since he saw Quincannon in his gray suit driving it.

"I remember every second, along with the smell of your perfume. You're not the type that a guy forgets. I figured I could repay you with a drink. It's a shame you're not into fun."

"Then you give a call to Oscar 2525. You can ask for Bishop La Spina. He's known to take in strays." Her snicker caused Ray to smile at her jab.

"Ray Irish is the name. Now you know me, so I'm not a stray to you. When I call, it'll be for that lovely lady who likes more entertainment than just throwing down tokens on a table. Anyway, there's good Irish whiskey at the Alexander Hotel." Ray tipped his hat, and he jumped on the water taxi, which arrived first at the dock.

He smiled at the ape-man when his taxi pulled away, allowing the chauffeur to guide his smaller boat next to the ramp. Ray nodded to Greye as his craft left the dock.

~~~

A wheelchair's wooden wheels gave off a hideous squeaking noise as a tall man in black pushed the mechanism along the hallway. The attendant's face remained impassive, drawn, and wrinkled tightly like dry leather. The man's suit carried the lost style from generations before. At a distance, he could have passed for an eerie copy of Abraham Lincoln with the tall hat he wore. In the wheelchair, an elderly lady stared ahead at the open door where a rotund man nervously stood. The old woman's eyes were dark, unlike the colorful gypsy outfit she wore. An incredible display of bright yellow and red flowers covered her dress. A golden headscarf, wrapped tight around her skull, covered much of the woman's white and gray hair.
~~~

When the wheelchair reached the nervous man standing at the door marked with the title of mayor. Mayor Hopley hastily stepped aside while he nodded his welcome.

"You are looking well. It's been such a long time since you have come to my office."

"Bah, don't bother with the platitudes, Horace. I'm here because the spirits are restless. You've been weak." The gypsy directed her companion to stop the wheelchair next to a large oak desk. She shoved aside a small stack of papers that were in her way, sending several files to the floor. Mayor Hopley kneeled to retrieve them. He was visibly upset, but he said nothing.

She pulled a pack of cards from her lap and quickly placed several of them face-up on his desk while the mayor of Oyster City sat in his chair. Carefully, watching the tarot cards she laid out, the potbelly man's blue eyes glanced back and forth between the woman and her companion.

"There, the cards tell me everything," the gypsy said as she leaned back. "The Knight of Swords enters this world; he is a foolish one. Carried in by The Card with No Name." The woman tapped her finger on the card.

"Look well at the card, Horace. The spirits came to me, and they know. The outsiders will seek your overthrow."

Horace stared at the depiction of a corpse wielding a sickle. His eyes widened at the rest of the cards he recognized.

"Your vision cannot be correct. Over many years since the last cycle, nothing puts the elders at risk. Many came here during the war, but they leave with the munitions plant gone. What does this mean?"

The gypsy gave a nearly toothless grin as she pointed to the ancient, cursed symbol closest to him. The thick paper held a picture of a demon. It rested on top of the Emperor's card.

"You see the cloven one," the woman's finger tapped on the image. "He stands in judgment of people who cannot stop the outsiders who come close to the throne. The strangers grew strong from the war years, leaving our rule at risk. Horace, you have been weak!"

"It will be up to the Shadows to fix this. With the coming blood moon, the great one's spirit must arise and bring order to the chaos. Like times of old, the Shadows will bring forth a new cycle, so justice against these outsiders comes."

Two nights later, a bored and frustrated Irish stared at the banana leaf wallpaper in his room. He decided it was ugly, which went along with his mood. He still knew little about the operations of Young and his band of merry thugs. Despite the money laid out around town, everyone seemed to clam up when Ray asked for details. Also, he had scant information about any connections with Jacobi. Cat gave him nothing from her contacts when Ray looked her up. However, he considered the possibility she might go directly to Dunn to get some extra green. Irish wouldn't put it past the cute little picture taker. Worse, J. Allan Dunn already expected miracles, upset that Ray gave him nothing to show for his money so far. His initial confidence changed, and Irish strongly considered taking the next week's pay and skipping town. Such thoughts made him even angrier, since he hated the idea of quitting. Like a dog with a bone, once he got started working on something, he finished it.

The phone rang, and Ray picked it up, about to bark at the caller. However, the soft voice asking for him changed his mind.

"The Irish whiskey is better at the Six Jolly Squires. There's a dark booth in the back," Greye's voice purred.

"I'll be there," he replied without a second thought. He heard the phone click, and Ray put the receiver down while he scanned his room for pants.

Taking a taxi to the city's outskirts, Irish found the tavern just off Route 67, which led to the state capital. The Six Jolly Squires stood like the last building on the way out of town, its squat adobe-style architecture out of place among the surrounding farmland. Pulling into a nearly empty parking lot, Ray got out and noticed a rundown motel with most of the lights missing on the flashing sign across the street. Otherwise, the area around the highway remained undeveloped woodland. Walking to the front door, he noticed a new red Packard convertible parked on the dark side of the building. The flashy vehicle had difficulty trying to hide between two older black cars parked on either side.

Inside, Ray found a quaint bar with a row of red cloth-covered booths running along the front windows. A young couple ate dinner while two men sat at the bar, working types, judging by their overalls. Both men stared at their mugs of beer, quietly listening to a song by the King Cole Trio coming from the radio behind the bar. In the back, off to his right, Ray noticed another booth, partially concealed by a thick, dark curtain. The red glow of a cigarette appeared to float inside the dark and secluded spot. As he walked closer, he noticed a definite feminine figure nearly hidden in the shadows. He slid into the booth.

"Nice and quiet." Ray looked Greye over; he wasn't disappointed. The seductive woman wore a low-cut, dark red dress, with a mink stool lying across her shoulders. A stylish black hat sat on the table beside her. She held a whiskey tumbler in her hand.

"Give me an Irish straight and another drink for the woman," Ray ordered after a bored-looking waitress arrived. He kept his eyes on the quiet woman, who finished her cigarette and took another drink.

"Do you always take charge when you arrive?" Her words sloshed a bit.

He smiled and replied, "Bad habit, I guess. I'll try to fix it."

"I don't like wimps," she said simply, her eyes watched him like a cat staring at a mouse.

"Then we'll get along famously," he said, sliding closer as the waitress brought their drinks. Ray raised his glass. "So, what do we toast to?"

Greye smiled.

"To our health, of course, and to no men in gray suits following us." She lifted her glass before taking another sip. "I noticed the pin on your lapel. You must be ex-army, like my brother."

"Seabee," he corrected her as he took a drink, "one of the thousands."

"But you walk stiff, were you wounded?" Greye didn't appear to hear him.

His face turned dark.

"Yeah, you could say that. But my parts still work just fine."

She smiled.

"I'm sorry. I was just trying to know your background. You come into this city like a tramp, now you're wearing new clothes, and you say you have a job. It appears you move fast."

"I get it, looking for the flaws." Irish took a sip of his whiskey. "Good luck to you with that idea; I'm just an average Joe."

The cheap fake whiskey made him frown. In Greye's expression, he observed a vulnerable and caring quality. But he was cynical enough to believe that she knew all the tricks to keep his attention.

"Everyone has secrets. You're not quite the lady that you project, are you?"

"I'm not sure what you mean?" Her hazel eyes lit up with a quick flare.

"Mrs. Henry La Spina, age twenty-nine, married to an older man for about two years. Before that, you were unknown in Oyster City, which helps fill the streets with many rumors about you. Now, you frequent the home of an infamous man named Guy Young, the *Stanley Rose* owner, and other assorted rackets. Not quite the demure preacher's wife that many in your social class expect." He leaned back in the seat, taking a sip of his drink while observing her. Her reaction slightly surprised him.

"You act like a private detective. I'm flattered that you've been checking up on me." Her tone was even, not hostile like he expected.

"I like the package, and curiosity just got the best of me," he told her. "Plus, I had time to think. Most pretty ladies don't hand their card to a bum to get acquainted. That makes you a smart woman."

Greye beamed.

"I'm glad because few men can figure out the clues they receive." She set her tumbler down, staring at it. "Tell me the truth. With all the rumors and innuendo, why are you here?"

"I guessed you must be lonely living among those who resent your presence. Why else would you give me the card?" Her nod confirmed his thoughts.

"It's not what you think about the *Stanley Rose*," she told him, her eyes remained fixed on the nearly empty glass. "I like to gamble. Henry doesn't think it proper for the bishop's wife to be there. But he tolerates it because he loves me."

"Yeah, I saw how proper you were the other night as you came out of his office. Anyway, it's none of my business what you do with your spare time."

She didn't look at him.

"I know what people say. I'm a gold digger who married Henry because his family has money. They don't realize he's not that wealthy. Then, some say I enjoy being a whore outsider who shacks up with Young to rub my husband's face in my misery. Is that why you're here? You need another notch in your belt with a lonely wife?"

"I told you why I'm here. I've got a lot of faults, but lying ain't one of them. People make all sorts of accusations when a person doesn't fit the mold, been there myself. I know what it's like to be an outsider."

"Do you?" Her eyes widened, disbelief cascaded down her face as she looked up. "Have you attended social functions where you stand alone the entire night while the people mock you? They're oh so silent, but the glances are there. Life among those with money isn't what people dream about."

"No," Ray told her, finishing the drink. "I can't say I've been there or that I understand."

"Stay around long enough, and you'll see the evil this place tries to hide." She shook her head bitterly, taking another drink. "They hate anybody who wasn't born here."

"Well, then we have something in common; I'm not from here either," he told her. "Maybe we will find out more."

"Are you married?" she asked suddenly.

"No, and it's probably best," he told her with a shrug. "Some say I have a chip on my shoulder, but mostly, I haven't found a place I like enough to stay around."

"Don't get married," Greye warned him. "You learn all sorts of things you don't want to find out."

"What's your story?" He glanced over at the bar, but no one appeared to pay them any attention.

"I needed stability. Henry gave that to me." Her reply seemed rehearsed, but he let it go.

Ray remained quiet for a moment, knowing she wasn't telling him the whole story. "I guess I can see that. Doesn't make for a pleasant thought about the future." He changed the direction of the conversation.

"Why don't we go for a drive?" he suggested. "I'm a stranger, and you can show me around,"

Greye smiled at the thought and nodded, moving closer to him. And he liked the smell of her perfume when she leaned on his arm.

"I don't have to be back for a while," she whispered in his ear. "Let's find a nice, quiet spot."

They walked out to her red car. Greye climbed into the driver's side. When Irish was about to get into the Packard, he noticed a dark car parked behind them with someone inside in the driver's seat. Something in the way the person sat, leaning against the door, bothered him.

"Just a second." He glanced inside at Greye, leaving his door open.

"What is it?" La Spina turned to look out of the rear window.

Ray did not reply as he wandered toward the dark vehicle. The pale light coming from a sign hanging on the back of the tavern made it difficult for him to see. He heard Greye open her car door, and Irish glanced back. When he reached the front of the car, he thought the person inside the vehicle must have passed out.

"Hey there, are you okay?" He paused.

The figure inside did not move, and silence filled the air. Irish stepped along the driver's side; the crunch of his footsteps sounded loud in the still night. He stopped and heard Greye's footsteps coming closer. Shadows filled the inside of the car, making it difficult to see.

"Hey there, wake up!"

A car turned out of the motel parking lot across the street. Its bright lights outlined the scene for Irish. In the brief flash, he saw a large man's head lulling eerily to the side. A long line ran across the guy's throat with dark red blood covering the upper half of the body. While he stood momentarily frozen by the ghastly sight, Ray Irish heard a woman's muffled scream. By the time he turned around, Greye had reached her car and was frantically climbing inside. As he shuffled after her, her Packard spun around the parking lot, the passenger side door swinging wildly as the vehicle reached the highway. Watching the red taillight disappear down the lonely road, Ray Irish stood in the dark lot as the dust settled around him.

~~~

Catherine Bennett confidently strode through the hallway to Room 402. She knocked on the varnished door, but no response came from inside. Scowling, Cat pounded on the wood forcefully. Finally, a gruff voice told her to hang on, and she heard the heavy footsteps come to the thick, wooden door. As soon as the door opened, Cat pushed her way past the surprised man.

"What the hell are you doing? I don't need no hotel peeper knocking down my door," Irish growled, taking a quick scan around the hallway before shutting the door.

She laughed at him, going to the unmade bed where she sat, picking up his blue suit jacket from the brass footboard. "Don't worry; I know my way around here. By the way, Dunn is looking for you. You realize it's nearly noon. Most of us begin work in the morning." She looked at Ray in his underwear, his legs showing jagged, thick scars along his thighs and calves. Her smile faded momentarily. "You might want to put on your pants around a lady."

"And you might want to get the hell out of my room," he replied crossly, pulling his pants off the back.

"Don't be like that. I'm a friend, remember?" Her eyes danced at his discomfort. "I came up with George, and he's already talked to the hotel cop. The newspaper got George a room on the third floor. We're keeping a watch on the restaurant across the street."

"Should I care?" he inquired as he finished buttoning his pants.

"You might; it's got something to do with Guy Young."
~~~

Ray stared at her.

"All right, give!"

"They say Guy is coming off his boat to meet with someone at the restaurant. That's mighty rare since City Hall has the word out to arrest Young if he ever comes into town. But, since some cops take his money, that's not happening. George brought along some binoculars, and he's going to be heading down when he spots Young. He wants to find out who shows up to meet with Guy. I'm here for any pictures I can get."

"Thanks for the news. Now, you can beat it," Irish told her as he pulled a white shirt from the dresser.

Cat frowned.

"I thought you liked me."

Ray took a deep breath before glancing at her.

"Sure, I like you. You've got spunk, that's for sure." He refused to say more while he went back to buttoning his shirt.

"Who's the girl?"

"What do you mean?" Ray continued his work.

"I told you I was smart. I can smell expensive lady's perfume on this jacket, and the doorman told me he saw you pull up in a taxi late last night." Cat smiled smugly at him.

"Then you can figure out that it's none of your business," Irish told her point-blank. "Besides, I don't need you checking on me. I had a long night, and I'm tired."

The girl slid off the end of the bed, handing him his jacket before stepping to the door.

"I bet so," she cooed. "If I had to guess, you're barking up the wrong tree. Gold diggers don't like coming down from their society perches."

"What a minute. You said Dunn wanted me." Ray took a seat to put on his shoes. "I didn't get any message."

"You just did. Get to that office nobody knows about," she told him, her voice dripping with sarcasm as she closed the door.

As Cat walked down the hall, she felt her annoyance still growing. Ray Irish was a chump, she decided. She knew he had been with Greye La Spina; the scent coming from his jacket gave him away. The one time Cat met Greye, and she remembered the same expensive and exclusive smell from Paris. That meant the haughty bitch played the newcomer for a fool. The woman was walking trouble, according to everything she knew. She heard about the wife of the bishop acting like Guy Young's hot little mole. And she hated how Greye rubbed her husband's face in her escapades with other men out on the gambling boat. Henry La Spina deserved better. It wasn't fair how the Greye woman grabbed a good guy like the bishop. Cat knew from personal experience the decent things Henry La Spina did for the poor families of Oyster City. The kind, big man who ran the large Episcopal Church set up the foundation that helped her family many times. The young woman understood only too well that her single mom would have given up had it not been for Henry's help. It was one of the few positive memories growing up in the tenements along the docks. Catherine Bennett never trusted men, but Bishop Henry La Spina always came through for her family.

Coming to a stop at the end of the stairs, the would-be reporter looked across the lobby. Despite her annoyance with the guy, she liked Irish. Not particularly handsome, he still had a rugged, honest, square face and penetrating brown eyes. She saw through the gruff way he spoke. Ray carried a chip on his shoulder, but she noticed something else in his demeanor that he kept well hidden. She guessed it had something to do with his injuries and his distinctive walk. Curiosity got the best of her as Cat went to a line of phone booths to make a call.

~~~

Ray walked to the dingy little office, his mind still on the events from the night before. He'd seen enough death that the thought of the body failed to bother him that much. After his
~~~

experience in the Pacific, another corpse would be a minor annoyance, just another grisly image to recall in his nightmares. However, he remained upset at being left behind by Greye. Irish briefly considered calling the police about his discovery after she left. However, the headlines would not help his plans to keep quiet and remain in the background. Ray decided to walk across the highway and phone for a taxi from the motel. With reservations screaming inside his head, Irish left the body for others to discover.

As Ray rounded the corner into the alley, he noticed the black car by the door. Dunn was unhappy, sitting behind the desk and tapping with the gold ring on his left hand as Irish walked into the room. When Irish spoke, the director interrupted.

"I expect results. You haven't shown me anything, and the word is coming back to me about you hanging around Henry La Spina's wife. You can play with floozies on your dime."

Irish held his gaze on Dunn for a long moment.

"Well, if you have a better idea of how to get closer to Young, you let me know. It's not like I can walk up to Guy and ask him questions about his latest racket. So far, I've learned that big-shot wrapped some people like Greye La Spina around his finger. I noticed several city bigshots hanging out at that gambling boat, so it's clear everything ties back to there." Ray tried to remain calm despite his rising fury.

"Everyone knows about Greye La Spina and Young. What makes you think she'll tell you anything?" J. Allan remained unimpressed.

"Well, if she's a girlfriend, they are not a happy couple. From what I heard last night, this Young character has something on her. Enough to get a woman to act like the racketeer's moll in public. I watched Young, and I could tell he liked her humiliation." Ray sat down on the chair, tipping back his fedora as he leaned against the chair back.

"Add to that fact, your little girl photographer told me she and George Hopley are hanging out at the hotel. They're checking on something about Young," Irish continued. "It might be something, or it might not, but I'll keep looking into that meeting. Either way, Greye seems to be a path into Guy Young's motives, or at least into his world."

Dunn leaned back in the squeaking chair, putting his foot on the desk.

"All right, maybe I get what you're telling me. Who says she can get you that?"

"Listen, I never claimed to be an expert here," Ray refused to back off. "You told me to get information; I'm doing that. It's still your call; you want me to get more dope on the racket or not?"

J. Allan slapped at his pants, knocking off the dust from leaning against the desk. "Do you think your angle will work?"

"Your guess is as good as mine, but I'm telling you, that bishop's wife is the way to get inside. I'm willing to bet my money on that. So, unless you get someone talking or you have some way to shut down that boat out there, you can bet Guy Young keeps making trouble for your boss."

The city director looked at Irish for a moment.

"All right, keep it going. I guess I'm asking for a lot, and you're making sense. By the way, you heard that Henry La Spina's chauffeur got knocked off last night?" Dunn misread the surprised expression on Ray's face. "Yeah, state police found him in a car by a tavern out on 67. It was a bloody mess; somebody slit the guy's throat."

"Christ, what is the name of the bar?" Ray asked, putting on his best poker face. J. Allan replied with the name Irish already knew, *The Six Jolly Squires*.

"Any ideas on who did it?" Irish shifted in his chair, thinking of Greye, who left him at the tavern.

"Hell, do I look like a newspaper? For all I know, it could be Greye La Spina. Unless this murder gets that rat Guy Young out of this town, I don't care. I have enough pressure coming to me about other things." J. Allan suddenly stopped. "That's an idea. Maybe you can find something that might tie in Guy Young with the murder. Get something like that, and the police could ride him out-of-town right into the big house. See what you can find out."

Dunn walked to the door, putting on his hat. Ray's voice grew tense.

"All right, I'll see what happened. If it smells like Young is involved, I'll let you know. Just need my pay soon, or else I'm back on the street. These people don't play cheap, and I'm nearly busted."

Dunn opened the door and turned back.

"Just don't bring Cat into this conversation." He paused at the look on Irish's face. "She might decide to run with it in the paper, just to become a big-shot reporter. We don't need too many people involved. You can leave a message on that desk. The money will be there tomorrow."

~~~

When he heard the first two shots, Irish instantaneously reacted by sprinting to the closest building corner. He peered around the corner of Cherry and 8th, watching people scatter while two men pumped several more rounds into a man lying on the sidewalk across the street. Ray recognized the familiar sound of gunfire. The killer ran toward a nearby car. Ray was close enough to see that one assassin looked about his size.

The killer wore a blue suit and black hat while his face beamed a smile from under a pencil mustache. As he ran, the assassin tried to shove a semi-automatic pistol into his jacket as he ran. The other killer looked like an ex-boxer, overweight, with heavy jowls, his brown suit shaking with his fat. The two
~~~

assassins jumped into a black DeSoto coupe before they sped away.

Irish noted the numbers on the automobile's plate as he followed the crowd over to the person lying on the pavement. Slowly, the victim rolled over, his hands trying to stop the bleeding. It was a useless endeavor. By the time Ray pushed through the thin line of people who stood in his way, the man in the tweed coat had died. The dead man's one good eye stared helplessly while a dark socket remained open on the other side of the face where a glass eye once resided. Irish noticed an older lady bent over to retrieve the fake eyeball and then pocketed the macabre item in her handbag. No one moved to stop her.

As the thickening blood pool drifted from beneath the corpse, Ray overheard someone's voice identify the dead man as One-Eye Cornell. Just then, he felt a presence next to him. Catherine stared at the body for a few seconds before quickly bringing her Watson camera into operation. She pulled the film holder out of the bulky box with experienced ease and promptly placed a new holder inside. After a couple of pictures of the scene, the photographer moved away for another angle. Irish observed her as she pushed through some bystanders, yelling at them to move for the press.

A few feet away, George already had a distinguished older gentleman in his clutches, trying to get the white-haired man's view of the killing. Something in the way the interviewer kept talking bothered him. The reporter attempted to lead the witness into confirming details about the men. George appeared to know more about the appearance of the killers than the witness.

Curious, Irish looked back at the Hotel Alexander, trying to understand how someone could have observed such a minute detail. The third room overlooked the scene from half a block away.

As he stepped away from the crowd, something gave under the leather sole of his shoe, and he looked down to find a shell casing left on the sidewalk. Crouching down, he carefully picked up a half-crushed shell casing using his fingernails. The troubleshooter looked closely to verify the engraving.

Wow, a .38 Super Auto.

Now he understood why the gun looked familiar to him. It was an unusual caliber explicitly designed for a model 1911 semi-automatic pistol. Irish carried a different caliber version of the gun during the war. Dropping the casing back on the sidewalk, Ray stood and slid his way out of the crowd just as the police arrived. The black, four-door car with a single, flashing, red light mounted on the driver's side window came to a stop along the curb. Two uniformed policemen got out and pushed through the crowd. Ray worked his way across the street to the hotel, trying to confirm his suspicions. Reaching the entrance, he looked back at the group of people. Irish looked at the *Beacon*'s legman, now talking with another witness. He could make out George's face, but he could not make out enough details to say for sure if the killer had a mustache or not.

While Ray watched the scene, the meat wagon arrived, parking behind the police car. The crowd was now being moved away from the body by another policeman, who hurried over on foot. The troubleshooter observed Cat take more pictures of the scene, including the ambulance drivers loading the body onto a stretcher. When a plainclothes detective, wearing an old-fashioned derby hat, arrived in another squad car, Irish waited for a few cars to pass, then he drew closer. He watched the events unfold as he kept glancing at George Hopley. Cat joined the silent man.

"You'll never guess who that is," she whispered to Ray, bringing him out of his trance.

"They called him One-Eyed Cornell," Irish replied. "I overheard your pal talking to a witness."

"Yeah, but did you know he's Young's number two man?" she asked.

Irish glanced at her.

"That's right," she said with a smile. "And guess who I saw leaving like a bat out of hell down the alley?"

"Are you going to tell me or spill it to your boyfriend over there?" He took a deep breath, expecting he already knew the answer.

Cat gave him a frown.

"Well, I noticed Guy Young's car leaving down an alley. I guessed you might care."

Irish nodded absently. "Thanks. I guess that means George had the information on Young all right. Your boyfriend seems to know a lot for a legman."

"Quit saying that. George is not my boyfriend," she insisted. "He's a talented reporter."

Ray stared at her. "You told me he is normally chasing down crime news after it happened. As I understand it, a legman finds the story at the time, then heads to a payphone to unload his notes to rewrite men back at your paper. So how did he get the tip ahead of time? Who'd spill the news like that unless it cost money?"

Cat went silent, looking at George while her partner nodded to his last interview and started toward them.

"Tell me this, were you waiting in the hotel room when the murder happened?" Ray kept his voice to a near whisper.

"Sure, I got bored, but George wouldn't leave the window. Suddenly he gets excited, and he looked back at me, waving me to the window. Then we heard the shots," she explained.

"Did you see either of the guys who killed Cornell?" Irish whispered to Cat.

She shook her head as George came up to them.

"Cat, I've got a great story here. How were the camera shots? Do you think you got enough?" The reporter beamed at the girl, who gave him a hesitant smile back. "We need to get back and get them developed. This story is page one stuff." George took her by the arm, and they hurried away. Cat glanced back at Ray several times before the partners walked out of sight.

Irish noticed the thinning crowd and walked over to the detective, who stood by his police car. The large man looked bored as he listened to the conversation between a uniformed officer and a witness.

"Officer, did anyone give you the license number from the killer's car?" Ray looked at the detective.

The detective's icy blue eyes widened, and he stopped chewing on an unlit cigar.

"You have that? Where the hell have you been?"

Irish pointed to the curb where he stood with Cat.

"Watching you guys work. I figured you might want to look over the area where they parked their getaway car."

The cop clamped his cigar back into his mouth, then pulled off his bowler hat, running his hand through his sandy hair.

"Let me guess; you're a damn private dick going to tell me how to do my job. What's your name?"

Ray just smiled.

"Hell no, I ain't no shamus. I just was standing on the corner as they ran to their car." Irish then gave the cop the information on the car and the tag numbers.

The lieutenant turned, interrupting the uniformed policeman.

"Willy, take this gentleman's information. Then get word back to headquarters immediately from his description. I want the information out to state patrol as well. You can bet they will head upstate."

As Irish stepped near the policemen, the big, sandy-haired man stopped him. "You didn't say your name."

"Ray Irish. I work for the *Morning Beacon*."

"Like hell," the detective told him. "Since when do reporters give us something before it's in your damn paper?"

"I didn't say I was a reporter," Ray told him. "Just don't like seeing folks murdered as they walk down the street."

The cop held out his right hand; his smile revealed yellow, stained teeth. "Lieutenant Campbell is the name. Irish, if your information is solid, I think we'll get along just fine."

Ray accepted the handshake and recounted the events he had witnessed earlier.

~~~

That evening, Irish got a message at the lobby desk with a number and the initials he recognized. He made the call from his room, and a couple of rings later, the sultry voice of Greye La Spina answered.

"I have some time this evening and an unopened bottle of Macphail's if you're still interested."

Suspicious but intrigued, Ray took up the offer.

"Where at?" he asked.

"Meet me at the corner of Peach and 8th; I'll pick you up," she told him before hanging up.

The red car carrying the quiet couple came to a stop on a bluff overlooking Oyster City. The moonlit night gave them a splendid view of the bay from the secluded parking area. Greye turned off the car and looked at the moon low on the horizon.

"You left me holding the bag," he told her flatly when they came to a stop. He noticed she was wearing a black dress and wondered how much was a put-on show about her driver's death.

"I'm sorry, but I couldn't get involved in that. You know that." She sniffed, pulling a handkerchief from her purse. She
~~~

dabbed at her nose. "Quincannon worked for my husband for years. They were close."

"Yeah, it's terrible. Any ideas on who might have killed your driver?" Irish kept watching her.

Greye shook her head.

"No, he didn't have an enemy."

"Remember, I met the guy," he reminded her, trying not to laugh. "The loud gorilla had plenty of people who would have hated him. The question is, how many people fought for a spot to bump him off? But that's not why we're here, is it?"

Greye said nothing for a moment, then she shook her head and pulled a bottle from next to the seat.

"I saw nothing so horrible like last night. I was up all night, thinking about the blood," she said while slowly turning the bottle in her hands. "This is my way of making up for leaving you. I stole it from the liquor cabinet. There are two tumblers in the glove box."

Her vulnerability came through with a tired sigh, and Ray reached into the compartment for the glasses.

"You can pour," he told her as he held out a glass.

While it wasn't Irish whiskey, the drink went down smooth, and the warmth did Ray some good. It also brought Mrs. La Spina sliding her body close to him.

"It'll get pretty cold soon." She settled in next to him. After another drink, Greye placed his arm over her shoulder.

"Well, I think we can work on warming things up." He smiled before pulling her close and planting a kiss on her full lips.

She reached for him, instantly reacting to the kiss by pressing closer. Then she pushed away from the kiss, telling him, "I'm not like this with other men."

"I understand."

However, his mind sarcastically wondered how many times she'd told such a lie as he pulled her close again, his lips pressed to hers. His hand quickly slid behind her back, his rough hands feeling the goosebumps on her delicate skin. A quick move with his fingers unhooked the lace bra while his other hand smoothly slid up to cradle her left breast. Her response, along with a nearly silent moan, told him they would be there for a while.

Yeah, she's not like this! His inner voice smirked at the thought.

~~~

It was late afternoon two days later when Cat left Irish a message at his hotel's front desk. Using one of the several payphones lined up in the lobby, Ray dialed the unknown number. Several rings later, Cat's deadpan voice answered. It took a slight pause for him to recognize the voice.

"What's up?"

"George is dead." The lifeless answer came from Cat. He heard a sniffle before she continued. "They found him behind Levine Pawn Shop on 8th. I'm in the shop right now."

"Sorry kid, I'll be right down," Ray replied before hanging up.

It took about twenty minutes for Irish to get to the alley, and the taxi stopped behind a police cruiser blocking the alleyway. Catherine stood halfway down the narrow and isolated lane behind the row of buildings. When he walked up, he noticed how her camera still hung from her shoulder, uncased. A *Beacon* reporter, with notes in hand, walked past Ray, looking at him strangely. Irish stood next to Cat, noticing her vacant stare at several trash cans and a pool of blood on the ground.

"Shot in the back last night," she told him, after coming out of her thoughts. "I overheard the police say it was two shots from a .38. One bullet while he ran away, and the other finished him. They just carried his body away."
~~~

"When did you hear about it?" he asked while he watched as the police finished their investigation. He guessed the hit came from a professional by the way the men were talking. There were few clues and no witnesses.

"Dice, one of our other legmen, called me. A garbage man found the body." The girl leaned against the dark red brick wall. "Why would someone do that to George?"

Irish expected tears, but she refused to cry. He guessed that would come later, in private.

"Come on, let's go. No reason to hang around here."

Ray led them away, taking Peach Avenue toward the Alexander. Irish remained quiet, remembering his suspicions about George. A couple of blocks later, Cat finally began to talk.

"You didn't trust George, did you?"

Irish paused before telling her the truth. "Not since the Cornell killing. At first, I thought he was just an eager beaver, like you."

"You were trying to tell me something that day," she said, glancing at him. "You asked a lot of questions about where George and I were when One-Eye got shot."

"No, not really; I was trying to work it out in my mind. Something about the way he interviewed the first witness bothered me," Ray explained. "He had a description of the two assassins down like he watched the whole thing, more detail than the witness remembered."

"That doesn't mean anything. I told you George had binoculars," Cat objected.

"All right, but explain how he would know what they looked like unless he tracked them going to Cornell and watched the whole thing? You told me he called you to the window. That must mean that he had to spot the two men closing on Cornell. But you told me you were looking for Guy Young. Isn't that right?"

She stopped, thinking back to that day. "Well, maybe he saw the killers when he got downstairs. He ran to the sidewalk when I was just getting to the lobby. He must have got a look when they drove away."

Ray shook his head.

"Even if George left the room just after the first two shots, like you said, he couldn't have made it down to the street soon enough to see the men getting into the car. Remember, I stood near where they parked the getaway car. It drove away from the hotel. Now I stood close enough to see the killers. But there's no way he could have spotted a small mustache from that distance. That means he could have only seen him with the binoculars, or he knew the guy."

"But why?" she stated, mostly to herself.

"He took a payoff. Somebody doesn't want anyone to know the reason," Irish finished the sentence with a curse.

Another block of silence followed before Ray asked another question. "Are you sure the cops said it was a .38 that killed George?"

"Yeah, they found two cases in the alley. They don't expect prints," the woman nodded. "Why do you ask?"

"It means the weapon was a semi-automatic like the other day. Most people using a .38 have a revolver which won't leave the cases," he explained. "If George was too close to something after they paid him, it stands to reason that it's the same killers."

Cat visibility deflated at the thought, and he cursed himself for mentioning it. They continued along the street, taking a turn on Cherry Street to his hotel. Inside the lobby, they went to the bar. He ordered two drinks.

"If George took a payoff, I need to find out who set him up," Catherine spoke after staring into the mirror behind the bar.

"Why? It won't bring him back," Irish reminded her. "And it might get people coming after you."

Her blue eyes flashed as she glanced at him. "I'm not afraid."

"You should be," Ray told her. "Even if you find out, who's going to do something about it? The police might if you can get to one who isn't paid off by the same folks. Otherwise, you'd be risking your neck for nothing."

Cat gulped down the drink, slamming the glass down on the counter.

"I don't want to drink with a coward," she fumed. She slid off the stool and walked out of the bar. Irish watched her through the glass doors. He smelled trouble, and he guessed someone would need to keep an eye on her. Ray decided it would not be him.

~~~

After finishing several drinks, a very high Irish found a message waiting for him at the counter in the lobby. The familiar initials asked him to come to the *Stanley Rose*. Walking away from the large marble counter, Ray passed by LeRoy, the hotel dick, who eyed him suspiciously. Cat told him once that the retired cop distrusted almost everyone who came into the hotel. Ray gave him a grin, then went out of the lobby doors to the street.

As he rode in the water taxi across the bay, Ray kept thinking about Greye. Curious why she wanted to meet on the gambling ship, he reminisced about their last time together. Irish decided the wife must be getting lonely again. Not that he minded, since she reminded him of an Australian whore. He considered Greye to be a bit more refined and generous than the prostitute. Ray liked her company more than he would admit.

On the *Stanley Rose*, Ray checked in his fedora with the pretty little thing still wearing too much makeup when he heard a gruff voice next to him.

"The boss wants to talk with you."
~~~

Ray turned toward the thug, still wearing the same brown suit. As Irish considered making a smart comeback to Tweedledum, he felt someone walk up behind him. He glanced back at another goon, not liking where the conversation was going.

"Come with us," said the brawler.

"And if I don't?" Irish asked while knowing the answer.

"Then we get to hurt you," Tweedledum told him with a gleam in his eye.

Ray nodded.

"Then, I guess I'm coming with you." He didn't like the invite, but his other option was less appealing. He wasn't drunk enough to take on two thugs bigger than he was.

Following the first Twiddle in the brown suit, the trio walked across the nearly empty dance floor. Ray glanced around for any familiar faces, but he didn't recognize anyone. They went through a door by the bar, which led them into a small hallway. The lead thug knocked before opening another door.

The room they entered looked like a gilded bedroom with a large, circular bed in the middle. Several large mirrors hung over the bed and along the walls. Occasional chairs, overly ornate and painted in gilt, sat along one wall along with a couch with gold-colored fabric. However, in one corner of the room sat a large, blond colored desk facing them. Guy Young stood next to the desk, his blue eyes staring daggers at Irish.

"I'm glad you accepted my invitation," Young said. Dressed in most of a black tux, he picked up a white bow tie from his desk and expertly began putting it on.

"I didn't have much choice with Tweedledee and Tweedledum here. So, what do you want?" Ray felt a growing distaste for the black-haired man.

Suddenly, Irish took a powerful punch to the lower back, and he dropped to his knees. Ray wondered if he still had kidneys as he tried to recover from the blow.

"You need to learn manners. A stranger who comes into Oyster City with a terrible habit of asking questions about me and my business." Ray's host stepped to a large mirror on the wall, where he adjusted his bow tie.

Before Ray replied, he took a vicious punch to the side of the head. The blow sent him over to his side, the thick carpet doing little to protect his head when he hit the steel deck. He tried to shake his head to stop the multiple images of Young he saw as he looked up. One thug yanked Irish from the floor. Ray swung his fist, but it glanced off Tweedledee's broad shoulder. The air escaped from his lungs as a fist buried itself in his abdomen. Irish folded over, and Tweedledum pinned Ray's arms behind his back. The other goon lifted their victim's head, slapping him several times across the face. Blood flowed from his swollen lip while Ray tried to get his wind back.

"My men are impatient to get back to their work." Young stepped away from the mirror. "Now that I have your attention, why are you so interested in my affairs?"

Ray hesitated, his muddled brain trying to think of a story. "I'm not sure what you mean." The next sentence didn't make it out of his mouth as he caught another strike in his mid-section.

Pulling up one of the gilt chairs, Guy sat down.

"You will tell me the truth, or you will continue to suffer a beating which will probably kill you. In the end, I will get what I want." There was nothing in Young's cold voice that hinted at compassion. "The way the tide runs, your body will wash up on Mile Cove Beach. There will be no link back to this ship. What's your choice?"

"Okay, okay, I get it. I work for the *Beacon*," Ray confessed, desperately trying to think of a cover story.

"That's better, but I don't believe you. You're an unknown in this town. Now you're suddenly working for the local rag and asking about me. Next, you're making all dizzy with one of my girls. It doesn't make sense." The thug leader nodded, and his men used Ray's face and body as a punching bag for several more minutes. The battered prisoner's left eye quickly swelled shut, and his nose leaked blood like a sieve. Crumpling to his knees, he felt Young's hoodlum lift him to a standing position.

"I swear that's the god's honest truth. You can check," Irish insisted, trying to think of anything to survive. Tweedledee pressed the prisoner's arms behind his back while his partner pulled Ray's head up.

"All right, prove it to me," Guy demanded.

"I worked with that legman that got killed last night." Ray went cold at his mistaken cover story since George was spying on Guy Young. He tensed, expecting more punches. Instead, the racketeer put his hand to his chin.

"Yeah, I heard about that reporter getting gunned down. I would have liked a chat with him, considering all the lies the punk put into the paper about me. What about Greye La Spina? You were with her the other night, the same night that Quincannon got knocked off. Did you bump him off for her?"

"No. I didn't know that her driver was dead until the next day. I first met Greye downtown after I got off the train in Oyster City, and she gave me a five-dollar token from your ship, so I came to thank her," Irish told him.

Laughter exploded in the room from the two thugs, and the gangster smiled. "Yeah, she likes it when men thank her, the epitome of virtue that share crop is. Quincannon used to keep her occupied before she got too greedy and needed my help." Guy's face grew dark again. "What else did she want?"

Ray shook his head.

"I swear I only met her a couple of times. We never talked about you. She was upset over their driver's death. I didn't even know she was with you until I saw her on this ship the other night."

"You're telling me you were working with that dead reporter, and you just happened to meet one of my girls on my ship? That's mighty thin."

The prisoner turned his battered head to stare at Young.

"I know it sounds crazy, but I've got no reason to take anything to the grave. I'm on the level. Even the police can verify I was working for the paper. I even told them what I saw the day Cornell died."

The statement struck a chord with the gangster.

"Hmmm, that's interesting. I heard a reporter talked to the cops, giving them the dope on One-Eye's killers. But that might mean you were hanging around there, and you're involved with this scheme. Since I was late getting there, they only took out my friend," Young observed icily. Ray instantly understood more than a few policemen were on Guy's payroll.

"No, I swear I was just coming up the street when I heard the first shots. I got there when they put a couple of more bullets into your guy, then watched them run across the street to their car," the prisoner on the floor explained. "I gave the cops all I know."

The black-haired man appeared to be considering Ray's words before he replied.

"Then you're not worth anything to me. Why should I let you live?"

Irish jumped at a desperate gamble.

"Because I am the one that got the best look at the men who killed your number one guy. The police have the description, but you know they aren't going to turn over this city to look for them, are they? Like you, I'm putting my money that someone is gunning for you. Since I saw the killers, I can be the one to help you find the guys. Knocking me off won't help you."

The boss's blue eyes stared at Ray for a long minute, the longest minute of his life since the Pacific.

"Why would you want to help me?"

"It beats a watery grave," Irish told him honestly. "The way I see it, you can run the town. I don't owe this city anything."

"You have my attention," Young nodded. "Tell me what you told the cops."

As the battered man described the scene he witnessed, Guy suddenly rose from his chair. He put on his tux jacket, smiling.

"Tonight, fortune smiles on you, Irish. Your bet is right that I didn't kill my friend. One-Eye and I went way back, and I want those sons of bitches that put lead into him." The racketeer stared down at the prisoner. "You've got a job now, legman. You're going to find the killers and let me know where they are so I can take care of them. Is that understood?"

Ray nodded slowly.

"Yeah, I get it. What about Jacobi's gang? Do you think they are in the middle of this hit?"

Moving back to the mirror, Young picked at his jacket, finding invisible lint on the black cloth.

"You've been checking up already. Good for you." He paused, considering the idea.

"Johnny, putting a hit out on me? We have an arrangement, but I don't trust him," he told Ray.

"You have your work cut out for you, shamus. I expect something soon from you, or the next conversation will not end well."

As Young left the room, he nodded to his two men. Tweedledee dragged the beaten man out of a side door while Tweedledum followed his boss.

~~~
~~~

Irish finally reached the Hotel Alexander as the light of the morning sun broke over the horizon. Tied by his wrists from a pipe inside a makeshift cell on the ship for several hours, Ray finally heard someone enter the room to release him. Most patrons had left the vessel, so Young's men dragged Ray to the main deck before dropping him into a skiff with a small outboard motor. The thugs took their beaten guest to the city dock, where they kicked him a couple of times with a reminder to find Cornell's assassins. From there, Ray staggered to his feet and walked to the hotel, determining that taxis were nearly impossible to find that early in the morning in Oyster City.

Battered and exhausted, Irish refused to acknowledge the horrified look he got from the hotel clerk while he walked to the elevator. The operator inside, who leaned dozing against the wall, suddenly jerked awake when Ray closed the elevator doors. A blonde teen with acne, dressed in a red uniform, started apologizing.

"Jeez, mister." The kid scrambled from his stool. "Are you all right? I can get a doc if you need it."

"Never mind, just get this thing to the 4th floor," he told him gruffly. Ray could only think of sleep.

After he got to his room, Ray removed his coat and went into the bathroom. He stood in front of the mirror, trying to clean off the blood while inspecting the damage. Irish heard his hotel door suddenly open. A man in a dark brown suit walked in as Irish looked out the bathroom door.

"You're in the wrong damn room. Beat it," Ray growled as he held a wet washcloth on his injured eye.

"Lieutenant Howard." The cop didn't bother to pull out his badge. Instead, the stone face flatfoot pointed to his chest pocket as he closed the door and sat in the chair by the entrance.

"Looks like you made some friends," the detective told him snidely.

"Yeah, maybe you coppers should be on the streets taking care of those friends instead of hanging around my room," Irish replied.

He instantly disliked Howard, who glared at him.

"From the way you look, you have enough problems with Guy Young and his group," the cop continued. "I wouldn't make it worse by pissing me off. We have a witness who states you were down at the *Six Jolly Squires* a couple of nights back. The same night that a chauffeur for Bishop La Spina got bumped off."

"I heard about it, but don't know anything," Ray told him, dabbing at his fat lip to clean up the dried blood. "I went in for a drink and left."

"Did you leave alone?" The way the detective asked, Irish knew better than to lie.

"No, I left with someone. But your witness saw that."

The cop nodded as he got up from the chair. He walked over to a bureau and opened the drawer. As he rummaged through the clothes, he asked what Ray did for a living.

"I work for the *Beacon,*" Irish was already tired of telling people the lie.

Howard grunted. "Who was the dish you left with?"

"Not your type," Ray told him, taking the chair. The sidelong glance from Howard caused Irish to realize he was close to heading to the police station. He changed tactics as the cop went through another drawer.

"Listen, she's a married woman, so there's no need to get her involved. We had a drink and left together. Drove around the city, and I didn't get back to the hotel until late. I have witnesses for that if you need it."

"All right, then save me some time and give me your knife," Howard told him.

"I don't have one, not even a penknife. Reporters don't need to carry them." Irish carefully leaned against the chair back. His head still hurt from the beating, and now he felt dizzy with the exhaustion.

"Yeah, you're a reporter like I'm the Duke of Wellington," Howard's reply came as he searched the last drawer. The grimace on the cop's face revealed a couple of missing teeth. Ray also noticed he had several scars along the temple line of his brown hair. Irish would have made a bet the mark came from a bottle breaking across the flatfoot's head. No wonder the guy carried a lousy attitude.

"Satisfied I don't have a knife? Say, what gives? You don't think I cut the guy's throat?" Ray's curiosity started to get to him.

The cop finished his search, stepping closer to Irish; his brown eyes showed a growing irritation with Irish. "How did you know about his throat? That wasn't in the papers.

"I'm with the *Beacon*, remember? I hear things." Irish dabbed at his face with the towel.

"Alright, wise guy, since you know. Some crazy nearly decapitated the victim. Nobody heard anything, or so they say," Howard growled out the words.

"Well, as I said, I don't know anything beyond what the papers say. And I don't have a knife. It seems like you are fishing in the wrong hole, lieutenant. I'm new to this city and have no reason to knock off some chauffeur." Ray tried to keep his smugness out of his tone. He failed.

The cop stepped closer, nearly hovering over Irish.

"You might if the married dame was Greye La Spina. She's known to be keeping Quincannon wrapped around her finger. Could be you might have done her a favor."

"I'd laugh, but my ribs hurt too much. Listen, I'm not dumb enough to kill someone over a dame. Are you going to book me or something? Your net has sizeable holes in it, I mean with no weapon and no real motive. Since the bishop's name is bound to come up, do you want the heat from City Hall accusing his wife of involvement in this murder?" Ray slowly stood, his ribs aching. He walked by the cop, going to the bathroom again. "You can let yourself out."

The detective followed Irish, forcing him to turn around.

"Listen, smart man; you better watch your step around me. Young's men are weak sisters compared to the grilling I'll do on you."

"Thanks, I'll remember that. But you just told me something already. Since nobody knew about Guy's thugs using me for a punching bag, I take it your inside information came along with a little cabbage from his side."

Ray couldn't say more when his breath left him again. The wicked punch coming from the cop struck him square in the belly, sending Ray into the bathroom doorframe. He slid to the floor, his arms folded around his abdomen.

"Your smart mouth will get you a tomb. Don't leave town, wise guy, unless you want a cell as a material witness. I'll put the screws to you and have you singing like a bird about you and that La Spina dame." The cop stood up and straightened his tie before he left the room, slamming the door on the way out.

When Irish finally recovered his breath, he crawled to the bed.

Damn rough night, he thought as he sank into unconsciousness.

<center>~~~</center>

A harsh ring kept going and going, finally pulling Irish out of his dreamless sleep. His hand fumbled around in the general direction of the sound, finding the phone handset.

"Yeah, what do you want?"

"Ray, it's Cat. I've got something, but I'm not coming to your hotel. Where can we meet?" Her tone was a mix of fear and excitement. It forced him awake.

"Your coffee shop," he told her, trying to shake the fog. "Give me twenty minutes."

"I'll be there. And make sure you're not getting tailed. I caught sight of one of Young's paid off coppers watching the Alexander." She hung up, and Ray winced as he tried to get out of bed.

Irish made it to Sam's nearly thirty minutes later, avoiding the front lobby and taking a couple of alleys to his destination. He loosened up some seriously stiff muscles during his walk. The man groaned at his efforts while he wondered about what Cat might have. He also carried suspicions about the little woman. When the troubleshooter sat down at the booth, Ray felt someone step from the back of the room.

"You look like hell. Who did that to you?" Cat quickly slid into the booth across from him, her eyes betraying the concern about his battered face. The pair waited to talk after a gray-haired waitress brought them a cup of coffee.

"Guy Young and his friends asked me some questions," he told her, pulling his handkerchief to wipe his sweating face carefully. The long walk took a lot out of him. "So, why did you call in a coward?"

She was about to say something, then halted. Her face betrayed a mix of emotions.

"I'm sorry for what I said. George's murder got to me. I mean, it wasn't like I loved him or anything, but he was always there."

She looked at him, but his face remained emotionless. "You probably can't understand," she finally said.

"No, I probably can't understand a friend dying," he replied sarcastically. "What a crock. If you're looking for sympathy about George, I'm plum out. He got killed because he was a crook, on the take, or both. Just like everyone else I know in this damn city."

Her face darkened.

"Like me, that's what you're saying."

Ray nodded.

"Listen carefully. When I say crooked, I'm talking about everyone, including myself. Since I took this damn job, I'm as dirty as the next guy. But I'm not taking beatings for lies and deceit."

"What do you mean? Are you leaving?" Cat's eyes flared.

"No!" Ray growled at her, then looked around and lowering his voice. "It means if you come to me for help, then I have to trust you. What's more, you need to trust me. It's as simple as that."

Ray paused, rubbing his sore left side.

"I'll start first and lay it on the line with you. As of last night, I'm stuck in between that favorite racketeer, Guy Young, and our mutual friend, J. Allan Dunn. No man can have two masters and survive, especially not in this damn town. Now, if I'm rough on you as we go along, that's the reason. There can be no ulterior motives between us. I know you're smart and ambitious. However, I can't trust you any more than I trust Dunn. You've been putting your hand in a dirty cookie jar too many times. In my mind, all the filth in this place is rubbing off on you. Prove me wrong if you want my help."

Irish waited for her to think about what he said. He saw her blue eyes searching his face, looking for a sign. Ray tried not to think about how attractive he found her at the moment.

Cat sighed.

"All right, I guess I deserve that. I called you for help. But I also realized I was wrong about what happened at the bar. I know you aren't a coward, even when I said it." She gave a glance around, leaning forward. "I know a little bit about you. I had a friend check on you."

"Was that your idea?" Ray's mocking smile hurt his face as he stuffed his handkerchief back in his coat pocket.

"Dunn asked me to check up, since nobody knows you. But I didn't give him everything," Cat pointed out. "Your war record is only so-so with all the time you spent in the brig for things like striking an officer and insubordination. I decided not to pass that stuff on."

"Yeah, I have a problem with people ordering me around. I'm not sure I should thank you for that. Might have been a favor had he fired me the next day." The irony of what she told him forced a smirk.

"Are you working for only Dunn?"

"He's been good to me since I can remember," she told him. "Even though he was just a clerk working for the city, he helped my mom and me out. I owe him a lot."

"Then you're not taking a little cabbage from anyone else? Something you might just kind of forget about?" Ray wanted to see her reaction. Cat passed his test when her eyes flashed at him.

"I swear, I'm not. Whatever else you think about me, my word is good, damn it," the woman boiled.

Irish held up his hand. "Okay, I'll accept your word."

Ray finished his coffee and waved over the waitress for more. When the older lady arrived, he told her to bring him a sandwich.

Cat waited until the waitress left.

"I have a lead on one of the assassins, the guy with the mustache. But I can't take him and his partner alone. I need your help."

"Keep it down and explain," Irish cautioned her.

She leaned in close.

"Jack Ripley had a hot tip today down at the *Beacon*. He told me the police believe one of the Cornhill's killers is a known convict. The guy's name is Hugh Pendexter, and he did time in the pen after a couple of holdups. He's been lucky since they can't pin any killings on him. Jack says the kid is crazy as a loon. Even Johnny Jacobi's gang doesn't want him."

"The last time we met, you didn't know much about Jacobi." Irish raised an eyebrow.

"Yeah, well, that was Dunn's idea." Her face reddened. "He only cares about Guy Young and his gang, so he told me to keep anything I learned between him and me."

"From now on, you tell me when Dunn wants to filter things," Ray told her. "You and I can figure out what's useful, not him."

Cat nodded.

"All right, I'll accept that, but what about my information on this Pendexter hood?"

Irish shrugged.

"I'm not sure. Do you know if someone tipped off the police?" She shook her head.

"Alright, let's start with the idea that your lead is probably correct. But I think there's more to it. Call it a gut feeling," Ray told her.

"Then you think Ripley's working for Young?" Cat's face turned angry. "Not everyone is on the take!"

"Calm down," he warned her as the waitress brought his sandwich. He gulped down a couple of bites while she waited impatiently.

"It could be legit, but I'm careful now! Somebody tried to put a hit on Young. He did not know who killed his friend. I could tell when I gave him the full rundown of what happened."

Irish wondered if at least one cop wasn't on Young's payroll, but he kept that thought in the back of his mind.

"Now Young wants me to track down the assassin," he explained.

"But why would you tell him?" Cat insisted and then stopped when Ray cocked his head, food still in his open mouth.

Cat quickly went on, her face reddened again, "Sorry, I forgot you didn't have much choice. What I mean is, why you? He's got a bunch of thugs who take orders from him."

"Hell, I can only guess. If the police know something, that means Young knows this as well. All I understand at this point is that I'm a useful stooge for him since I'm a witness to the killers. If the cops grab the murderers first, then the case will take weeks. Young might just wait for the right opportunity; have prisoners knock the killers off in jail. Hell, around here, he'll probably have a cop do it."

Ray told her before finishing off his sandwich.

"Something else just came to me. Young can't be sure about everyone in this city. He's probably covering all his bases to make sure he gets the killers. And if I were him, I would try to finger what person put the hit on me. Who else could have known that the mobster left the *Stanley Rose*? When I asked the guy about Johnny Jacobi, he said they had some arrangement, but he indicated he was going to be more cautious." He shrugged his shoulders. "Your guess is as good as mine on where this leads to."

"It'll be back to Greye La Spina; I'm willing to lay my last buck on that," Cat told him emphatically.

Irish noticed the flash of dislike in her eyes.

"Why? Young chases her around the bed. Hell, everyone in town knows that. The mobster even told me a little about her and Quincannon, her driver. She's probably been in bed with half the city, if the rumors are right. Greye may be no saint, but how does this hit on a racketeer involve her?"

Cat shook her head.

"As you said, call it a gut feeling! I found out that Quincannon spent time at the state penitentiary. He was the strong arm for grifters before becoming a driver for La Spina. Seems like a pretty strange pairing, if you ask me."

Ray Irish let out a low whistle as he carefully leaned back on the bench seat. His mind raced with thoughts, and none of them was good about Greye. Deep inside, she seemed to play a game, and he wasn't sure of the rules. After a moment, Irish pulled himself out of his thoughts. He did not like the self-satisfied expression on her face.

He gave Cat a sour look.

"Well, we have another twist in this puzzle. I guess I need to talk with J. Allan Dunn. Arrange some time with your boss as soon as you can and give me a call. I'll be around."

The morning air had the same chilly dampness that went through the coat and right into the bones. Irish came to expect the clammy atmosphere in Oyster City. It seemed as natural to the town as the stink coming off the wastewater, spilling into the bay. However, Irish had other thoughts on his mind as he walked to the dingy office in the alley behind Chandler Avenue.

"You're late. Cat says you have something important." The boss scowled at Ray, in an unhappy mood as usual.

"Good to see you again as well," Irish told him, the handle of the still opened door in his hand. He swung the door shut and pulled a chair next to the desk. Ray glanced at Cat as he leaned his large frame on the back of the chair. "Did she give you the latest?"

"Yeah, I know all about your run-in with Young," Dunn told him, drumming his fingers on the desk.

"Then, first things first," Ray told him. "I stopped by the *Morning Beacon* and found out something fascinating. When I spoke with Max Brand, he said he had never heard of me. Nearly had me thrown out when I asked about my employment with his paper. Since he's the publisher and editor, I suspect he knows what he's talking about." Ray observed J. Allan, expecting a reaction.

"So, boss, what am I missing?" he asked.

Dunn blinked his eyes quickly.

"Yeah, you're not with them. The *Beacon* knows nothing about you."

"Really? That's all you can say." He paused. "Well, it got me to thinking. You screwed up, and you made me a marked man, just like the first so-called troubleshooter you hired."

Irish noticed Cat's surprise at the news, but he centered his attention on Dunn.

"I've already told that damn lie to the cops and Guy Young. That means the word is out on the street. They aren't going to take too kindly to me when they find out. And I can guarantee you. Somebody will check on me, just like you had Cat look into my past."

Dunn's fingers paused their drumbeat on the desk, and his face twisted into a grimace, looking like he needed to find the bathroom.

"Okay, what do you want? If it's an apology, it's not going to happen. You're a drifter, and you're getting paid well. Besides, I haven't seen much for all of the money I've spent."

"I don't want a damn apology, you son of a bitch," Ray growled as he leaned over the desk above the balding man. "I want the damn truth. Your lie has me exposed to the wrong people. Cat pegged you; you're nobody in this town. I say you're full of shit. I want honest answers quick, or, by God, I'm going to throw your ass out of that window behind me."

His owl eyes widened at the thought, but J. Allan quickly regained his composure in front of Ray. Slowly, he nodded.

"All right, all right, I guess I owe you an explanation."

The boss glanced at Cat.

"I don't have the pull over at the paper by myself. I swear that a little pressure from the right people would have it worked out before it came to this. It's a good idea, but they wouldn't go for it."

"Who are they? If you don't have the pull, then tell me who you think does," Irish told him as he hovered over the desk.

"People I know," Dunn replied. "You won't know them, but I'm telling you they run the show. They run around like fools, but they don't understand the danger this Young and his gang represent. But they do now, by God."

"I don't care about that crap. You've been filling my head with all sorts of malarkey. But the buck stops here, tonight. I have a cop who's making it clear I can't leave town, and he's probably working for Young and his hoodlums. And that damn racketeer is telling me I'm hunting down Cornwall's killers like some cursed shamus." Irish pushed away from the desk.

"You've gotten paid well." Dunn gave a grim smile.

"To hell with you and the dirty money." Irish glared at him. "You can delude yourself all you want about your honesty. Hell, you don't even cover your tracks. Look around this office. It's filled with the documents about your game, so don't give me the business. You son of a bitch, you saw how Young worked when his men went after you the other night. Do you think your friends will do anything about that? They'll let you hang."

Ray noticed how Dunn's expression changed. His boss finally recognized his whole corrupt lifestyle was at risk.

"I'm standing out like a sore thumb now. According to Young, if he doesn't like my answers, you'll find my body out at Mile Cove Beach." Irish turned from the desk, disgust on his face.

"Remember that you can wind up there just as well."

"Just like the last guy," Cat spoke up with a stunned expression on her face. "That's why the last guy Dunn hired is missing."

"What do you mean?" Ray asked, seeing a grimace in the director's expression.

She stood up, stepping closer to the desk.

"What you just said reminded me of someone. A guy named Pulaski started poking around just like you."

She turned her stare to the fidgeting, thin man behind the desk.

"You probably did the same thing to Irish, didn't you? You promised Pulaski this cover that didn't come through. But he didn't leave the job suddenly. What really happened?"

"Listen, I don't know where Pulaski went." J. Allan stood up, his eyes darting back and forth between Cat and Irish. "He just didn't show up one day after I paid him." Their boss started pacing behind the desk. "He told me about some cop he was following around; then he just quit showing up. I checked at the hotel. But he never checked out and his room was empty."

"And you never assumed something went wrong with your scheme?" The sarcasm dripped while Ray walked back to the desk.

"I followed up," Dunn glared back. "Everything pointed to Pulaski taking off. Damn fool acted like a bull in the china closet. Someone might have paid him to leave town. Who says the guy didn't just leave?"

"I say so," Cat snapped. "You know as well as I do that the state police found several bodies on that beach across the bay over the last year. Everybody knows people come up missing when they go to that gambling ship. The local cops would not bother with something out of their jurisdiction."

"And maybe you're reaching, assuming Pulaski got knocked off. Each time the state folks found those bodies, they could not identify them since they were in the water for so long. You have no proof," J. Allan told them defiantly.

Ray Irish slammed his fist into a pile of papers sitting on the desk.

"Enough! Dunn, you wanted someone to do your dirty work with no ties back to your office. Well, unless you find me some cover, I'll make sure you get the heat. Just remember, the police won't need to use some rubber hoses on me to get me to talk, and Young's thugs will be happy to beat it out of me."

Irish paused, seeing his words sink in.

"I'll put money that your cronies will leave you to the wolves if word spreads that the Oyster City Director of Public Works is spying on racketeers. Plus, he's acting like the District Attorney. You think you will last very long?"

J. Allan Dunn grimaced at the thought. The director fully understood his idea might backfire. He did not want a scandal to upset his applecart. Then his eyes lit up.

"I just figured out how I can make this happen. Those cronies, as you call them, will now see the light."

"What do you mean?" Ray's curiosity got the best of him.

"It's another angle I should have thought of before. With Fordham stepping into the ring to go against our mayor, nobody will argue with me." The boss leaned back as the chair squeaked in protest.

"What are you talking about?" Cat asked. "What's that low life got to do with it?"

"You haven't heard that Mark Henry Fordham is getting in the upcoming election?" J. Allan looked at both, surprised at their blank stares. "It just came out today that he's holding a rally down at the union hall tomorrow." He gazed at Cat. "And you know that means he's running to take over. He could win the damn thing with so many workers down on the unemployment lines."

"Remember, there's a stranger in this office. Who the hell is this guy, and what does this have to do with me?" Exasperation flowed with Ray's words.

Cat smiled sympathetically.

"Fordham is a union boss who controls a lot of what happens along the docks. He's got a squeaky-clean reputation with the public. But I've heard that he has a lot of dirty ties with Jacobi and Young. Rumor is Fordham makes Mayor Hopley and City Hall look like cheap chisels with their graft."

J. Allan frowned at her description of him and his cronies. Irish couldn't help but give a smug grin at the reaction.

"Anyway," Dunn interrupted, "I have a way to get you the cover you need. It'll be entirely legal, and you won't have to act the part. Even better, Oyster City is your employer. I'll have the backing of the mayor for you. Just give me a day since I have to get the right paperwork in place. I'll call you when I've got everything ready."

Ray stared at Dunn for a long while, then glanced at Cat. She gave him a shrug. Ray picked up his fedora from the floor, where he dropped it.

"I don't like it, but I guess I don't have much choice. You let me know what you got, and I'll keep my head low. Don't let me down on this, or I might just walk over to Fordham and see what he can do to help me out." Irish walked out of the office, walked out of the alley, and turned onto Chandler Avenue. He heard running footsteps.

"Hey, slow down." Catherine pulled next to him, trying to catch her breath. "Where are you going now?"

"I have an appointment with a hazel-eyed bitch who set me up," he replied severely. "And you're not welcome to join me."

"I wasn't planning on coming along," Cat huffed. "I just wanted to tell you I'm sorry about all the lies. You know Dunn lied to me as well."

The sound of their footsteps was the only noise for a block as Ray remained silent. The chill of the night air blanketed them while a few cars passed them.

"Cat, I'm not blaming you for Dunn. I'm a big boy, and I should have told him to jump in the bay when he offered me this mess." Ray shoved his icy hands into his pockets.

"That's all right. Like I told you before, J. Allan has been good to me, and I never paid much attention to some of his double-dealings. It comes with the territory; you know what I mean?" She tried to sound confident. "By the way, you mentioned something about a cop who might be on Young's payroll. What did you mean by that?"

As they walked along, Irish explained his run-in with Detective Howard and his hotel room search. She listened without interruption. When he finished, Cat waved down a taxi.

"You go find your girlfriend," she told him when the cab stopped at the curb beside them. "I've got a couple of errands of my own."

Ray stood with the taxi door open, his face wearing a puzzled expression while watching Cat walk away.

In front of the *Six Jolly Squires*, his taxi stopped, and Ray climbed out while feeling a sense of déjà vu. The nearly empty parking lot looked the same as he remembered. The only difference was that the traffic on the highway was busier on this night. Ray made his way to the bar inside, sitting at the end after a glance at the empty booth where he met Greye a week before. The bartender, he recognized, but there was no waitress that evening.

Ray ordered an Irish on the rocks and thought about his situation and his options. He couldn't leave town without cops sending out flyers about him, and he was not sure when Guy Young's thugs might suddenly come up looking for answers. Tired of playing defense, Irish decided he would play offense now.

The second round came, and he asked the bartender if he recalled seeing Greye La Spina in the booth the other night. The bartender looked him over carefully before shaking his head. Irish pulled a Lincoln from his wallet and laid it on the bar with his hand remaining on the bill.

"Stunner with hazel eyes, wearing a tight, red dress along with a mink stool and black hat last week," Irish told him. "She drinks whiskey straight and comes here with a big guy occasionally. Now, do you remember?"

The beefy man smiled, his teeth showing noticeable dentures. "Yeah, you two were drinking over in the corner there. You had a drink and left; you're a good tipper."

Irish inched the five spot closer to him. "What's your name?"

"They call me Ralphie?" Misgivings filled the bartender's features.

"Don't worry; I'm only looking for information. Do you know the woman's name?"

The bartender looked at Ray. "Why are you asking? Don't you know her name?"

He pulled back his hand with the money. "That wasn't the question."

"Oh, I get you," the bartender said. "No, mister, she's never said but a couple of words the times I've seen her. At first, I thought she was just a lonely wife type, ya know, with the ring and all. Just comes in for a drink, and then a man will show up. She acts all prim and proper, but the way she acts after the joe shows, I'd guess she's a high-class whore. Boy, she's hanging in the wrong place. We don't get high-class guys in here much."

"So, who are the guys coming to see her? Can you describe them?" Greye's real motives for coming to the bar grabbed his attention.

"Most of the time, a big brute of a guy dressed as a chauffeur came for her. That's why I thought she pulled the tricks at the place across the street. Occasionally, other joes pulled into the bar looking for her."

"The driver, you mean the one killed outside?" Ray watched Ralphie staring at the bill on the counter. "Do you know where they went?"

"Nah, I don't know. You know I found the chauffeur guy in his car after I closed up the place. Like I told the cops, I never saw him come inside that night. I thought the guy just fell asleep, but then I saw the guy's throat. It was gruesome."

"Yeah, I bet." Ray took another drink. "Give me more about the people who meet her. What do they look like?"

From the bartender's description, it was clear Guy Young came by the tavern on one occasion. While that wasn't a surprise, the last description forced Ray to ask another question.

"You're sure the young guy who met with her had a pencil mustache? Did he keep glancing around a lot, like a guy not wanting to be seen in public?"

The tavern keeper grinned as he watched Ray remove his hand from the bill from the counter. "You described him to a tee. He's about your size and acted like he didn't want to see no cops hanging around."

~~~

After one more drink and a long drive from the bar, Irish got out of a taxi stopped in front of a large, stone mansion of Henry and Greye La Spina. With its sizable front façade and large windows appearing like two eyes on either side of the front entrance, the bishop's home gave the creepy impression of a haunted house. However, the dwelling looked minuscule next to its neighboring building—a massive stone church. A bell tower, soaring into the night sky, rang out the final peal of notes from the hour chime. Before he left the tavern, Ray called the house asking for Greye, but the butler told him Mrs. La Spina was not home. He did not believe it. Irish took the marble steps two at a time to the twin doors of the house. A weathered-looking, thin man in a black suit opened it.

The butler again told Irish that Mrs. La Spina was not available. When Ray asked for the bishop, the thin man let out
~~~

a resigned sigh, informing him that the La Spina would return soon from a benefit.

"Then, I suggest you tell the lady of the house that she will meet with me right now, or I might need to speak with her husband instead. That will light a fire under her." Irish growled out.

He noticed the gentleman raise an eyebrow at the implied threat and asked Ray to wait. A few moments later, the butler returned to escort Irish into a large room, which Ray guessed was the study. Antiques filled the room while rows of books covered the walls. A large oak desk sat on one side, near the windows covered in red curtains. Behind the desk was a large shield with the family coat of arms, the elaborate display surrounded by rows of ancient, ceremonial daggers. On the other side of the massive fireplace, an ornate couch sat with several baroque tables and chairs clustered around.

In a few minutes, Greye walked into the room, her eyes betraying her surprised shock. Ray nearly forgot that his bruised and swollen face would make most people do a double-take. However, her expression turned frosty.

"Why are you here?" Greye asked, smoothing her one-piece jumper nervously.

"I got a message to meet you on the *Stanley Rose* two nights ago. You didn't show up. I'm trying to figure out why you set me up for my beating?" he told her gruffly as he came closer, catching a whiff of her perfume. It didn't soothe him.

Greye stared at him for a moment.

"I don't know what you're talking about, Ray. My husband and I attended a concert that night."

"Really, and who else was there?" he asked snidely.

"Well, Mayor Hopley and the rest of the town's upper crust were at the concert. Trust me; you wouldn't have fit in." Her eyes flashed before she turned away.

"Yeah, like you fit in with the upper crust. But as you noticed, your boyfriend, Guy Young, entertained me for a while, before his men took me home after their fists got sore. Now you're telling me they were using your name to get me out to the Rose." He drew close to her. "Can you explain why they would decide to use that rouse?"

"I have no idea. You must have upset someone." Greye continued, staring at the bookcase.

Ray noticed the titles were mostly in Latin, and it reminded him of the woman's husband. He kept his focus on her reflection coming from the gold wall mirror.

"Yeah, they told me more about you. You have quite a partner there with Guy Young. He thinks so highly of you he said you were one of his girls. Quite the romantic guy. I guess you don't mind that as much as me showing up here." His words dripped with scorn. Greye La Spina remained quiet, her face emotionless.

"It got even better when I got to my hotel; a cop named Howard came by my room. He was very interested in the death of your chauffeur. He gave me some powerful hints that I was a suspect." Ray saw a sudden flash of concern on the porcelain face.

"Did he ask about me?"

Irish gave her a grim smile.

"No, fortunately for you, he didn't ask me for an alibi, at least not yet. But you'll be there for me when I need you, won't you, sweetie?"

Greye glanced at him.

"I don't know what you're talking about."

"Yeah, I'm sure of that." His frustration with her came out with a growl. "But, so that you know, I gave a fiver to the tavern owner, and it jogged his memory. Lady, I'm not sure of your game here, but should I send the copper over to the bar for information?"

Her eyes widened.

"What do you want? You know where things stand. Are you looking for money? I don't have much."

"Yeah, when I look around the room, I see how poor you and your husband are. It's amusing to see how well the charities do." He came around to face her, and their eyes met. "Unlike you and the rest of the people in this city, I'm not here to shake you down. All I want is the truth, and I'm not leaving without it."

Her face went a shade paler at his demand. She shook her head. "I can't right now, especially not here," she told him. "I'll meet you somewhere tomorrow."

Irish scowled at her. "I'm not dumb enough to fall for another one of your games. If not here, we can leave now, and you can tell me."

Fear filled her face.

"I swear I can't. My husband's due to arrive anytime. He can't see you with me."

Ray stopped, deciding he had pushed his luck enough.

"All right, I'll call you tomorrow at noon, and we'll meet. You'll have plenty of time to explain what's going on. And I mean to know the truth about this."

Irish turned to leave when Greye stopped him.

Muffled voices came from outside the door.

"That's my husband," Greye told him as she tugged on his arm. "Come with me. Hurry!"

Irish pulled free of Greye and opened the door. Inside the foyer, a large, older man dressed in a black suit was just taking off his wool topcoat. As Ray entered the lobby, the weathered Jeeves quietly exited with the bishop's hat and coat. The fat face of Bishop Henry La Spina showed his shock at the stranger in his home. Henry's eyes narrowed, darting back and forth between Ray and Greye, who came in behind Irish. Her face betrayed the growing anger at Ray.

"Sorry to bother you, bishop, but my name is Ray Irish, and I'm trying to follow up on some leads for the *Beacon* concerning the death of your driver. Would you have a moment to talk?" Ray extended his right while giving the gentlemen his cheesiest smile.

Momentarily stunned at the display, the gray-haired man slowly shook Ray's hand. The bishop's hand was large and cold. Irish noticed La Spina's brown eyes scrutinizing him.

"At this time of night? I say this is most irregular." Henry suddenly turned firm as Irish continued smiling. He stood taller than Ray, but his hefty form showed soft and overweight from the years of quiet living. Henry appeared quite a bit older than his wife, despite knowing that he was in his mid-forties.

"Well, you're a tough person to get a hold of." Irish glanced back at Greye, who stood like a marble statue. Ray wondered if she was holding her breath. "Your wife was gracious enough to chat with me while I waited. I promise I won't take up but a couple of minutes."

Henry walked past his horrified wife, going toward the study.

"Oh, very well, please come inside. I don't know what more I can tell you."

As Ray walked past the frozen statue, he gave her a wink, amused at the panic he saw in her. Irish made sure he closed the doors to the room. Taking a chair across from the bishop, who sat on the couch, he tried to imitate a reporter.

"I understand it's a difficult time for you and those in your household right now. I'll only bother you with a couple of questions. How long did you employ Quincannon?"

The fake reporter noticed the bishop's calculating attitude. The change surprise Ray; he expected a meek cleric.

"Your people have already asked this question," Henry told him. "Judging by your battered condition, I don't believe you are a reporter. Why are you here, Mr. Irish?"

Undaunted, Ray continued.

"Well, the reality is that I'm more of a troubleshooter for them. I'm focused on the reporter that got bumped off the other day. It's bad for the newspaper business."

"What's that got to do with my chauffeur?" La Spina asked.

"Well, similar crimes with both men killed in an isolated location and no witnesses. We're trying to determine if there might be any connection," Irish replied.

The bishop's expression turned friendlier to Ray. "Really? How interesting. I understood the murders occurred in two different ways. Well, Quincannon had been with me for...let me see now, at least five years."

"Before you married?" Ray asked, wondering if Greye was discretely listening from a nearby room.

"Yes, a few years before, he came to work for me as a handyman while I was the parish priest. You see, he had some trouble with the law and made every sign of trying to reform. He made good on that and took on additional duties as my responsibilities increased." Henry leaned back on the couch, pulling a cigar from an Asian style box. The bishop failed to offer Ray one of the cigars.

"Do you know why he might need to be at that particular tavern? Can you think of someone he might have been waiting for?"

La Spina froze, his hand half-extended toward his silver lighter.

"Absolutely not," Henry said too quickly before he paused. "What I mean to say is there was no reason for him to be there. I certainly did not order him to go there. I had gone to my room early that evening to finish some of the diocese paperwork. He had the evening off, so his time was his own."

"What about Mrs. La Spina?" Irish decided to do a test of the water. The instant harsh reaction didn't surprise him.

The large man's eyes narrowed, and his face soured.

"What has my wife to do with this? You were discussing my servant."

Smiling again, Irish forced himself away from a sarcastic comment about his wife.

"I'm not saying anything, bishop. I was just wondering if you or your wife might have asked him to go there for some reason. By the way, did you happen to know George Hopley, the reporter? I'm sure you know he was a distant relation to the mayor."

"Neither of us knew this person. Now, I'm a busy man." The bishop rose from the couch; the cigar remained unlit in his hand.

Ray rose from the chair.

"Yeah, I get the hint. I appreciate your time, and I'll see myself out."

When the large wooden door closed behind him, Irish stopped at the bottom of the steps, tightening up his coat as the chill enveloped him. He felt a pair of eyes, glanced up at the light coming from an upstairs window, and caught the outline of Greye as she stepped away from the curtains. Irish didn't notice the other pair of eyes watching him from a dark window on the first floor.

~~~

The sun slowly sank as Cat tried to stay warm inside her frigid car. She wondered if she was a fool. Ray's story about
~~~

Lieutenant Howard gave her an idea. At the corner of the street and alley, Cat watched Howard while shivering from the cold outside the abandoned warehouse.

After leaving Ray, Cat followed the cop from the police station based on her hunch. She recognized Howard's name, remembering rumors of the cop on the take. She wanted proof about who was paying the cop. An excellent photograph might be a scoop for the paper or a quick way for some cash. Either idea was good with her.

However, she didn't enjoy waiting for something to happen, her hand resting on her camera case. She looked down at the box. In her hurry to track down Howard, Cat forgot to bring a smaller camera. Oh well, she would improvise, she decided, as she glanced at Howard. Covered by the smog of his cigarette, the cop showed his impatience as he paced around in a circle. Then he recognized the long, black Cadillac coming closer. Cat noticed his change and began rolling down her window.

Quietly cursing at the poor angle of her shot, she took the picture anyway before sliding in a new negative. Sliding across the front seat, she silently exited her gray vehicle on the passenger side. Trying to appear as casual as someone could while holding a large reporter's camera, she worked her way over to the side of a nearby building. She lined up another shot. Then she caught her breath.

His large head leaning out of the window, Mark J. Fordham barked orders at the detective. From the anger in his tone and the few words she could make out, the union boss was upset with the policeman. The growled response from Howard was unclear. He flicked away his cigarette, and the smoke around Howard cleared, and she got her photograph. Just after that, she saw Fordham disappear from the window, tossing a package out. As the vehicle drove away, the policeman kneeled to pick up the small bag.

I guess City Hall doesn't pay enough!

Moving quickly, Cat walked to her car, glancing to ensure Howard was not looking in her direction. When she got to the vehicle, she noticed the cop heading to his old Ford. Hurrying, she threw the camera into the seat next to her and started the car. Cat drove up next to the detective as he was about to get into his vehicle. She stopped and opened her door, standing on the running board to see over the top of the car.

"Lieutenant Plug Howard, you remember me, don't you? Cat Bennett, do you have any updates about the murder of George Hopley?"

The detective turned, recognizing her. He glanced inside her car while pulling a cigarette from his coat pocket. "I've got a couple of leads I'm following up on," he told her gruffly. "You're off the beaten path. Why are you down here?"

Cat frowned. "I want someone to catch the bastard that killed George. When I saw you, I was hoping you might have some news."

The cop stared at her for a long moment, glancing at the large truck driving up behind the girl's car.

"Is that right? Well, maybe your friend poked his nose into someone's business, and it came back to bite him." His scarred face remained impassive as she slid back inside her vehicle.

As Cat drove away, she didn't like how the corrupt cop stared at her.

~~~

Late afternoon of the next day, Irish paced his room, still unable to meet with Greye. Despite his threats about exposing her, every time he called the house, Greye was not there. He left a message, but over four hours later, he remained in his
~~~

room, trying to figure out his next move. When the phone did ring, it was J. Allan Dunn at the other end of the line.

"Get your butt over to the second floor of the Mayflower Building. Go to the office past the District Attorney and ask for Hobart. Just sign the forms and get your license; everything is in order. You're a private detective working for my office. You're looking into graft with some of our contracts." Dunn hung up before Ray responded.

Fifteen minutes later, Irish entered an odd-looking, dark gray structure that resembled a small castle with Grecian columns on the front. Above the fortress-like doors, *Oyster City Courthouse* showed him he was at the correct building. Ray remained uneasy as he climbed the white marble steps to the second floor. He debated the wisdom of trusting Dunn. The troubleshooter walked past the open double doors of the Oyster City District Attorney's office. A glance inside showed him a mix of people in suits and police uniforms. When he arrived at the end of the hall, a door marked *Records* greeted him. Inside, Ray found a small vestibule with a gray-haired clerk sitting behind a caged window.

"J. Allan Dunn told me to ask for Hobart about signing some forms," Irish explained to the old employee standing behind the counter.

"That'd be me. You must be Ray Irish. Let me see some identification." Hobart squinted as he looked out of his cage, his spectacles dangling at the end of his long nose.

Ray pulled out his wallet and showed the clerk his old military ID card. Since he left the service, Irish never bothered to get a driver's license. Drifters seldom had the opportunity to drive a car. The old man behind the counter hardly glanced at the trifold document before he pushed two pieces of paper under the bars.

"That's the paid-up surety bond, so you sign both copies and give me back one of them," the clerk told him.

He quickly began pecking on a typewriter, which looked like it came from the 19th century. Irish skimmed through the document, still debating the idea of becoming a private detective. Becoming a shamus was the last job Ray might have thought about when he drifted into town. He shrugged his shoulders.

"Why not?" he said aloud.

"Huh, something wrong, mister?" the ancient man asked as he pulled a wallet-sized card from the typewriter.

"No, I guess not. Just wonder how that little piece of paper will stop bullets," Ray joked with the baffled clerk.

Irish stepped into the lobby with an official license in his breast pocket when he noticed Lieutenant Campbell leaning against the wall, apparently waiting on him.

"I thought I recognized you when you passed the DA's office," the policeman observed. Ray noticed his unfriendly tone. "I thought you were working for the *Beacon*? Were you lying to me?"

"Somebody lied to me about my employer. I'm getting it cleared up," Irish told him.

Campbell nodded. His eyes were like a vulture looking at a dying animal.

"I can guess," he said. "Being a working shamus gives you an out if someone like me or the District Attorney asks too many questions, is that it?"

"More like it might help prolong my time here with some rats who messed up my face. You got time for coffee or do you have something against a new private flatfoot?"

Campbell's face brightened at the offer.

"As long as you're buying, I can risk it."

The two men took the detective's car to *Sam's*. They conversed long enough for Ray to find out his driver's full name.

"Lieutenant Arizona Charlie Campbell." Irish grinned as he spoke the name aloud. "Your parents must have hated you."

The driver gave him a sidelong glance.

"Nah, they liked me well enough, but Mom loved the cowboys in the Wild West show that came through town. Arizona Charlie was the major attraction. According to her, he did some amazing trick shots while riding his horse."

"Let me guess, like your namesake; you're a hell of a shot as well," Irish inquired as he watched the people walking by on the sidewalk.

"I hit what I aim at," Arizona told him lightly. "Army did their share of training to help. What about you? I saw the ruptured duck; what service?"

"Seabees," Ray replied. "Three years on God knows how many crappy little islands."

The detective nodded approvingly. "Yeah, European theater myself, following around some bastard who kept trying to get us killed. Got back early in '45."

Irish remained quiet as his thoughts went back to the Pacific. He scraped a lot of sand and dirt while working a bulldozer while he toasted brown under the tropical sun. Ray remembered the stench of destruction and mayhem. That came after the mind-numbing terror when the shells flew in close.

"Yeah, well, at least now we're getting paid better when they try to kill us," Ray finally said as they pulled up to the curb in front of the café.

"Speak for yourself, Shamus. You aren't a cop," Arizona replied as he got out of the automobile. "By the way, how'd you get your face busted up? You get sideways with a girl?"

Ray's expression grew serious.

"Young and his two mugs didn't like the look, so they helped me understand things."

Arizona slowed by the front door of the building. "Did that have anything to do with Cornwall's killing?"

"Not really," Irish told him. "They had a beef about my interest in things about this city. I was asking too many questions since I'm unknown around here."

"Yeah, that probably put you between them and the deep blue sea," the cop told him, his expression turning grave. "Watch out for that group. People end up missing after they get around Guy Young."

"Yeah, so I hear. That's part of the reason we're here." Ray opened the door to the café with a smirk on his face.

After getting their coffee served, Irish asked the cop about the recent murders. "I'm curious about the .38 slugs that killed George Hopley and One-Eye Cornwall. Do you know if the bullets match? The papers never revealed that information."

The cop gave him a funny look.

"You have been reading those magazines on becoming a detective."

"Yeah, page forty-three, under how to find the murderer. Listen, I don't want to get under the skin of a local copper," Irish told him before burning his tongue on the scalding coffee. "If it's sensitive information, I'm only curious."

Arizona shrugged.

"I guess it's fair to discuss since nobody but you and I see the possibility," he said. "I asked Ron Howard about getting it checked, but that never happened."

"Are you talking about Detective Howard, the big guy with a scar on his face?" Ray asked.

"Yeah, he's one of the other lieutenants on the force," he told him. "Do you know him?" Arizona glanced at Ray as they turned the corner.

"Just met him recently," Irish replied. "He stopped by to rearrange my furniture at the hotel, looking for that knife which killed Quincannon, the La Spina's chauffeur." Campbell's right eyebrow rose slightly at the news.

"Why you?" the cop asked.

Ray blasted himself for digging a hole, but he gave him a quick rundown of his stop at the *Six Jolly Squires*, making sure not to bring in Greye La Spina's name. "Apparently, going to a tavern for a drink gets you on his bad side."

Arizona remained noncommittal.

"Yeah, that can happen when a guy gets bumped off in the parking lot, and nobody saw it," he said thoughtfully. "It's funny how he tracked you down if you only had a drink there. Did you have an alibi for Howard?

"His sucker punch over my attitude must have caused it to slip his mind." Irish dodged the question, noticing the detective gave a slight umm sound as he took another sip of coffee. "So, what's the motive behind Quincannon's death? I mean, coming after a stranger in town doesn't make a lot of sense. It's not like he owed me money or anything."

The cop shrugged his shoulders. "Howard's just checking all the leads. I doubt there's much to go on since nobody heard anything or saw anything. Now, why did you ask about the slugs on those other killings?" Curiosity mixed with suspicion in Arizona's tone.

"No particular reason. I thought it was odd that both guns were semi-automatics of the same caliber. The shell casing I saw on the sidewalk near One-Eyed Cornell was a .38 Super. Since the war, many guys came back with their 1911s, but those are .45 caliber. I figured there wouldn't be too many of those .38 autos. But what do I know? I'm not a cop."

"Well, there's some sense in your thinking. The .38 Super out guns most cop weapons, so the gang types like it," Arizona told him as he glanced at the waitress. He turned back to Ray. "But you're thinking like me. That's why I went to the coroner and had the bullets sent out to the state lab to see if there's a match. I'm waiting on word from them," the policeman told him.

"I wonder why Howard didn't think about doing this." Ray waved over the waitress for a refill.

"Some of us flatfoots are better than others. If Howard found just a penknife on you, then you'd be sitting in the slammer." Arizona watched Ray nod in agreement while they waited until the lady pouring the scalding sludge left them.

"You can bet Howard hasn't forgotten about you," Campbell continued. "Now, tell me something. Why are you sniffing around these murders and hanging out with Guy Young?"

Irish went silent for a moment.

"Well, let me put it this way: a client thinks it's Guy Young who committed the killings. But I'm not biting on that. When I met Young, I was pretty convinced that he wanted One-Eye's killer. Something makes me think there's a link, but I'm not sure where. I guess you cops would call it a gut feeling."

Campbell laughed.

"Yeah, you could call it that. Guy Young knocking off his right-hand hoodlum." The cop mulled over the idea for a moment before he shook his head.

"No, I'm not buying it either. The description of the two guys you gave isn't any of his people; I know that. Plus, I haven't heard of any hired guns in town. Young is a son of a bitch, but I don't think he'll be going to such trouble to take out one of his own. He'd just make them disappear."

Ray looked out the window at the nearly empty street outside.

"Yeah, that's my thinking as well. Heard anything about Jacobi pushing into this city? It seems pretty obvious that knocking off number one and number two in Young's gang would make it easier."

The cop gave a grim smile.

"Yeah, and the Jacobi group would be the type to set up a hit. But I haven't heard anything like that. Before you get involved with Jacobi, you might want to rethink your career. Being a lion tamer is safer than snooping around Jacobi."

"Luck of the Irish," Ray said lightly. "Are they in the city?"

"Yeah, his mob controls a couple of pawnshops in town. Nothing major we know about since they like to stay upstate in the capital. Johnny is an ex-booze runner who stays quiet. You know, keep out of the limelight. There's supposed to be a truce going on with Johnny Jacobi and Guy Young."

"Yeah, Guy mentioned that when he left." Ray finished his cup.

Arizona stared at him.

"You know you're damn fortunate that Guy let you walk away from that boat of his."

"I know, but it was only because my great charm persuaded him I can identify the guys who killed his man. Guy says he wants the assassins for himself."

"You better find them before we do." Arizona pushed back his cup. "And a free piece of advice. You better have an alibi for Howard when he comes back looking for it. He's known to work people over until he gets the confession he wants." The tone of the cop's voice made Irish look at him.

"Good thing I don't own a knife, especially one with blood on it," Ray made a thin joke.

Campbell slid out of the booth, standing as he put on his hat.

"That won't make any difference if the weapon somehow shows up in your room or inside your coat after you take a beating. Just something to consider when dealing with Howard, especially since you're a stranger in town." Arizona threw a dime down on the table. "Anyway, we're square."

"Yeah, thanks for the advice," Irish told him. "Let me know if those bullets match, and I'll owe you another coffee."

Arizona replied with a mocking half-laugh, nodding at the waitress when he left.

~~~

Irish stopped by Pappy's newsstand on his way back to the hotel. The energetic newsy was just closing up the wooden shack as Ray approached.

"Been a few days since I heard from the Irish," the black man told him, giving a self-satisfied grin. "The Young boys did a pretty good job on you."

"So, you heard," Ray replied, mildly surprised the newsy already knew his name. He helped Pappy lift down the thick, wood panel which covered the front of the stand.

"Word gets around here pretty quick when people want it to." Pappy pulled a few copies of the late paper and tucked them under his arm. "My wife uses them to wrap things at the meat market each week. There's an advantage to having these stands," he explained.

"Any other items about me I should know," Ray tried to make a joke about it, but he wasn't surprised when the newsy continued.

"Aside from that missing Bird girl, not much news is coming out right now. However, I heard one of the detectives seems interested in you. You might be at the top of the list with some killings." Pappy gave Ray a curious look at the idea.

"Yeah, I can bet who that is," Irish replied with a curse. "That son of a bitch Howard acts like the shore patrol goons I
~~~

remember a few years back. Tell me about this mayor race I just heard about. Anything unusual?"

"Nah, Mark Fordham has wanted to get control of the city for a while now. Lost the last election by a landslide against Hopley, but times are tough now for some folks. I guess Fordham likes his chances." The newsy gave Ray a toothy smile before lowering his voice. "But I wouldn't take his odds."

"What do you mean? Are you saying they already fixed the election?" It did not surprise Irish, but he was curious.

"Well, some would say that's impossible. Then again, accidents have been known to happen. A few years back, Bob Marlow, a shoo-in for the local council seat, shot himself in the head the day before the election." There was an air of conspiracy in his voice as the streetlights turned on down the street. Pappy lit himself a cigarette as he leaned against the building.

Ray looked around the clearing streets, watching the cars slowly make their way home. He noticed the night was coming fast as the air took on a chill. "People do strange things when they feel the pressure."

His companion smiled thoughtfully.

"That's what I hear. Still, it's hard to explain how such things happen in a locked room, and no gun found at the scene. Reporters never could square up that angle. Oyster City seems to have strange cases like that."

Irish guessed Pappy was hinting at something.

"What do you mean?"

"Well, I'm a bit like you," he explained. "I grew up here but left with my parents until coming back in '29 with my new bride, Emma. We both waited a while before we took the plunge. The first job I found when I got back into the city was over at the *Beacon*, delivering the bundles all over the city's black district and out to some of the rural areas. Long-time residents were not happy with changes made by outsiders."

Not seeing any links to his problems, Ray changed the subject as the two men started walking along Main Street.

"What did you think of George Hopley?"

The gray-haired man shrugged his shoulders as he lit another cigarette. "Just like most of the legmen I've dealt with, had some good traits and some not so good."

Ray's attention perked up.

"What is not so good?"

"I don't want to speak ill of the dead, but he lived pretty high on the hog, if you know what I mean?" Pappy replied as the two men turned the corner, heading along 13th Street.

Irish nodded as he remembered the reporter's expensive suit. "Yeah, I see what you mean. Do you have any ideas where a guy like that pulls extra cabbage?"

"Oh, there's tons of ways. It depends on what team you play for," the old man said stoically. "Either tip-off folks about the crooks or help keep things buried when people ask. There's no end of larceny in some folk's hearts."

"Yeah, it goes with this city," Irish told him sarcastically.

There was a snort from his new friend, who remained quiet for a while.

"Any feel for what team George might have been playing for?" Ray asked.

"Nah, but if I were a gambling man, I would lay my bets on his uncle, the mayor," Pappy told him as he flicked his finished butt away into the street. "Those folks have been here forever. The families have a lot of money, and they stay real tight. Those in charge don't like outsiders mixing close to them from what I hear, almost as bad as the Andras family treated newcomers."

"Wait, you mean like Henry Andras?" The name of the original town founder surprised Irish.

Pappy gave him a surprised look.

"You have been reading your history. Me too; I like to hang out at the library, reading all about the past. Yeah, Andras is the same family who has been living up on the hill since the founding. The old lady runs the place. I've only seen her once. She looked old as the hills and wearing some gypsy clothing when I saw her. I guess the rich folk get pretty eccentric at times."

Ray chuckled at the comment before fishing for additional information about the La Spinas. Giving him five bucks, Ray listened to Pappy and his views about the La Spina family. The newsy believed the bishop was a decent person with a lousy wife. He pointed out that a lot of the gossip came from the gray-haired ladies' club who disapproved of the younger woman. Pappy even recalled a previous encounter with Quincannon, the driver and handyman, who threatened the newsy early one morning. It seemed the chauffeur walked away with one of his papers without paying. As Pappy told Irish, a lot of folks hated the giant thug.

Pappy stopped as they arrived in front of the building on the corner of 13th and Federal.

"Say, my wife told me to bring you over for dinner sometime. Why don't you come on up? I can show you some of my books."

Ray hesitated. "I don't want to intrude on your wife at the last minute."

The black man eyed him skeptically. "You sure that's the reason, Irish?"

Irish understood.

"Well, if you insist. It's not like my dinner card is full, so all right by me. I tell you what, let me grab a bottle of wine from that liquor store down the street. I'll come over in a few minutes."

"Wine, eh? That's a first." Pappy rubbed his chin. "Make it snappy. We have smothered pork chops, and I'm hungry. Our apartment is 3A."

"Sounds great. Just give me a few minutes." Ray turned toward the liquor store they had passed a half a block away. It was a quick walk back to the building, where he found Pappy waiting on him in the lobby.

"I went to the manager's apartment to drop off a paper, and we got to talking. He's been a loyal friend to my wife and me," the newsy explained as he led them to the small elevator.

Ray found a spotless living room inside the apartment with a comfortable couch and sitting chair, both with a matching green and yellow floral pattern on the cloth. Along one wall was a set of bookshelves filled with books and various knickknacks on the shelves' top. A telephone chair sat next to the radio.

"Hello, Emma," the older man called out. "I brought Ray Irish over like you asked." Pappy turned back to Ray after closing the door. "I'll take the wine, and you find a seat. The pork chops will just need some warming."

Pappy walked past the radio, stopping to turn it on as he went into the kitchen. Ray went over to the bookshelves and browsed through his host's reading material. The scope and breadth of the books on history impressed him. He picked up *Caesar's Conquest of Gaul* and decided his Latin remained too rusty to read the book.

Irish heard the sounds of pots clanging inside the kitchen. "Say, Pappy, where did you go to college?" he asked.

The wiry man stuck his head out of the doorway, smiling when he recognized the substantial book Ray held. "I didn't, but my momma was a teaching assistant at a private school.

Since it was a white school, they couldn't let her be a full teacher, being colored and all, so she made darn sure her boys could read Latin. It helped whenever we ran into the headmaster. He didn't like us colored folk that much."

"Sounds like your momma was a hell of a woman," Irish told him.

"That she was," he told Ray as Pappy walked out of the kitchen carrying plates, which he placed on the table. A couple of trips back to the kitchen and the table had three plates with silverware and glasses. Ray offered to help, but Pappy told Irish he would handle it.

"Go listen to the radio, and I'll call you when everything is ready," his host insisted. "Jack Benny should be on pretty soon."

As Irish half-listened to the radio, he wondered about his host's wife. He had heard no one but Pappy moving around inside the apartment. When he was about to ask, the newsy stepped from the kitchen with the plates holding the main course.

"Find yourself a seat while I get the potatoes and okra," he told Ray.

Taking a seat, he waited as Pappy placed the fine china bowls on the table and took a seat. Unexpectedly, Ray's host grew uncomfortable, glancing at the empty chair across from him.

"You're probably wondering where Emma's at," he said sadly. "So you understand, she's here with us. You see, most people think that my wife died a couple of years ago." He continued staring at the empty chair next to him. "But my Emma's still with me. We talk every night once I come home. And every morning, she's there telling me to have a great day. That's why I'm always happy at my work, knowing my Emma is waiting for me."

Stunned, Irish could not think of anything to say at first.

"Well, can you tell me what happened?" he finally asked.

Pappy frowned, then nodded.

"A young punk stole a car and ran over my wife as she crossed the street downstairs," he explained. "She was going to the butcher for pork chops. When I got there, the policeman told me she never knew what hit her. It's funny because I know what he said was true. Emma said she just woke up in our bed when I saw her the next day. It's kind of comforting to know that's she still here, watching over things. Helps get me through the days, if you see what I mean?"

Irish stared at the wine on the table, then he looked at the empty chair, almost seeing the image of a woman in his mind. Ray recalled a Marine corporal who survived a mortar round striking his foxhole in Guadalcanal. The red-haired kid swore his dead father warned him to get out of the trench just moments before the explosion.

If it happened there, then it could be the same here, Ray reminded himself. He reached over and picked up the wine bottle.

"Do you have a corkscrew?" He asked. "I would like to try this wine with those pork chops. I'm hungry, and I can't wait to hear more about Emma."

~~~

Deep in thought as he walked back from Pappy's apartment, Ray stepped off the curb when he heard his name called. Looking over, he recognized the red Packard and the lady inside. He walked to the driver's side window, which was open.

"I'm sorry for the delay, but it took a while for me to work my way free of my husband. He's getting suspicious of me recently. I can't get a moment's peace."
~~~

"I can't imagine why," Irish said evenly. Greye's eyes flashed with anger.

"Do you still want to talk or not? If so, get in," Greye told him, her manner cold. "I know someplace quiet."

Irish looked around, then went to the other side of the vehicle and got in. As Greye pulled into the street, he looked her over, noticing her black dress and hat.

"Where are we going?" He turned around to make sure no one was tailing them on the nearly deserted street.

"There's a place just outside the city where no one will bother us." Greye's expression changed, and she gave him a sultry   glance. "That's what you wanted. I even got some whiskey to make the evening a little more pleasant."

Ray leaned back in the seat. "You think of everything."

~~~

Catherine spent most of the day searching for answers about George Hopley and receiving only more questions. Much of what she learned agreed with Ray Irish about her friend. George was heavily on the take, at least by inference. Worse, she could find nothing to pin down which single person her friend might have done favors for in return for cash. The legman worked all over the city, searching for the latest story, which made her work difficult.

One lead sent her to a tavern along the waterfront, a place called Anthony's. She did not have a handle on who owned the joint. When she walked in, Cat immediately did not like the place. Several tables held men who looked like they recently escaped from prison. They eyed her suspiciously. After taking a deep breath, she walked to the back of the room, where she spoke with the bartender despite her initial disgust. The man was an ex-fighter named Joe Knapp. He wore black pants and a white undershirt that could not cover his hairy back or
~~~

enormous belly. It was hard to tell the primary color of his shirt from all the food and sweat stains.

When Cat stepped up to the tall wooden bar, the slob behind the counter leered at her. He smiled, listening to her questions while his eyes remained transfixed on her breasts. Despite the unpleasant experience, the photographer discovered George came to the place often, and he arrived at the bar on the day of his murder. It took a five-dollar bill to get the information out of him, but she only discovered that George left with a fat guy wearing a brown suit and gray hat.

"I don't know who the guy was," Knapp told her. "Maybe my memory is failing. You come back to my office, and maybe I'll remember. It won't cost you any more cash. I'll have you work it off."

Cat forced herself not to punch the leering man's face, but she made sure to knock an empty bar glass from the counter when she turned away and left the bar. She dealt with such treatment her entire life while living around the docks with a single mom. Pigs like Knapp were one reason Cat did not trust men.

After getting in her car, she drove to the *Beacon* to finish her pictures from the morning. A couple of times, she felt like a black sedan was following her. After taking a couple of quick turns around corners, Cat decided it was her nerves getting the best of her. When she arrived at the home of the paper, Cat was already mulling over the information she had got. Taking the steps two at a time, the photographer nearly ran into Tom Brand, son of the editors and one reporter she trusted.

"Hey, next time, look up as you come up the stairs," the thin man scolded her with a grin.

"Sorry, Tom, I was thinking about something." Cat stopped with a sudden thought. "Would you know anything about some characters hanging out at Anthony's?"

The reporter gave her a frown. "You mean that dive along Waterfront Drive?" His face remained grave when she nodded. "I wouldn't hang around that place, especially if I was a woman."

"I was checking out a lead," she confessed lightly. "Who owns the tavern?"

Tom shook his head. "Nobody knows, so I would guess it's a front. My suspicion is Fordham has his money in there. I hear that's where his people recruit their heavies to keep some of his business partners in line. What are you checking out?"

Cat gave Brand the description of the person seen leaving with George Hopley.

"I'm trying to figure out who might have killed George. This guy left that bar with him on the day of his murder. The bartender claimed he didn't know the guy, but I'm suspicious."

"Yeah, I would be as well," the reporter paused. "Your description seems to match up with a new guy in the city. Nobody knows much about him, but he's been showing up all over the place recently."

She looked at him. "Are you sure? Any idea what his racket is?"

He shrugged. "No, I'm just telling you what I've heard."

"Okay, thanks for the tip." Cat walked away.

"You still have a bee in your bonnet about Greye La Spina?" Brand asked.

Cat nearly tripped over the step in her haste to find out more.

"Sure, what do you have?"

"Well, I overheard part of a telephone conversation that Gladys was having. From what I can tell, someone thinks they need money to reveal something in Mrs. La Spina's past. You need to speak with Gladys for more of the scoop. I know the paper will print nothing about the bishop's wife, but it sounded kind of interesting. I figured you'd want to know."

Thanking him for the information, Cat immediately jockeyed past a couple of men who were jawing in front of the building entrance. She made her way to the office where Gladys sat, working on her latest Mrs. Purvey article.

"All right, spill it," Cat told her as she slid into an uncomfortable chair next to the desk.

The woman behind the typewriter looked up, her dainty glasses perched precariously at the end of her bulbous nose. Her green eyes twinkled as she gave a mischievous grin.

"Mrs. Purvey is unsure of what you are talking about, my little reader." Gladys returned to her typing. Cat sighed impatiently. Mrs. Purvey was the pen name of Gladys Peer, who wrote the weekly society column. While the work was famous throughout the northeast part of the U.S., it came from the entire persona Gladys took on when she worked. She was successful, but more than a few of those in the building considered Miss Peer a leading candidate for the nuthouse.

"Enough, it's been a long day, Gladys. You know, I only come in for the juicy tidbits. I hear you have something on Greye La Spina." Cat moved around in her seat, trying to find a comfortable position.

Mrs. Purvey stopped typing again.

"Dearie, you shouldn't be eavesdropping on my conversations." The social reporter saw the stare from Cat and changed her persona again. "It's an innuendo to a dead end," Gladys told her. "I got a letter from a gentleman named John Robertson a couple of months back."

Gladys informed her that John Robertson claimed that Greye La Spina had a relative who was a criminal out of Boston.

"The person who wrote the letter wanted money from the paper for the proof. I called out to a friend at a Boston paper to check on the guy, and they called me back today. They told me this Robertson chap died during a bank robbery in Brockton a couple of months back. He was a clerk in the bank."

~~~

Late that evening, as Ray Irish drove away with Greye La Spina, Catherine Bennett sat alone at her small table inside her apartment. She half-heard the song by the Ink Spots on her radio. In her hand, there was a small glass of Irish whiskey and ice. She paid little attention to the hazy smoke from the charred remains of a cigarette drifting up from the ashtray. Instead, Cat was trying to put the pieces into place from her long day of snooping around the city.

Like her friend, Gladys, Cat believed the information about Greye La Spina meant nothing. The description of the fat man who left with George was too vague for her to go much further. The only real traction she had for the day was her photos of Fordham stretched across the table. She picked up one picture showing Detective Howard taking something from the union boss. She smiled, wondering how much the photo and negative might be worth to the mayoral candidate and the crooked cop.

Stretching her arms above her head, she yawned, thinking about her next steps. Cat's lips turned to a frown at the realization that she would have to find out more about Fordham and his goons. She didn't want to step in with the sharks without some backup on her side. With another yawn, she got up and dropped the photo as she set the tumbler down. The photographer turned off the light as she went to her bedroom.

The distant chime of a mantle clock struck its third note, which went unheard as Cat slept. Suddenly, she woke to the pressure of a rough hand over her mouth. The dark figure pulled
~~~

his legs over the top half of her body, pinning her arms inside the blanket as she futilely tried to struggle. Then, cold steel pressed against her cheek, and she froze.

"Don't scream, bitch, or I'll start slicing you," the ominous male voice told her as the figure leaned on her. "Now, nod your head if you understand."

The woman followed the instructions, trying to see who was above her in the pale moonlight that filled the room.

"Good, now I'm gonna let go of your mouth." She felt the blade slid from her cheek and press on her neck. "Try an' scream, and I'll cut your throat. Understand?"

Cat nodded again, and she felt the pressure over her mouth relax and move away.

"You were asking a lot of questions at Anthony's today. Why?" His foul breath crossed her face.

"Please, don't hurt me. I…I was trying to find out about who killed George Hopley." She felt the sting when he slapped her, then put his hand over her mouth. She did not cry out.

"Why were you at Anthony's?" The man pressed the side of his knife blade hard on her windpipe before he let her talk.

"George went there on the day someone murdered him." Cat prayed silently.

"All right, you little tomato. Who are you working for?" The threatening voice hovered near her ear.

"For me," she replied, but swiftly got another slap across her face for the effort. Then, the creep struck her with a backhand.

"Am I gonna have to cut the answer out of you? Who are you working for?"

Panic overwhelmed her as her voice grew shrill.

"I swear to God; I'm telling you the truth. He was a friend of mine. I just want the bastards that killed him."

The rough hand went over her mouth again. "Then why the camera?"

The intruder let her speak again. "I'm a photographer for the *Beacon*. It's my job," she said as he shifted his body. The goon slid over to the side of the bed. His hand remained over her mouth, and the knife still pressed on her throat.

"You're gonna get up and give me the negatives and pictures you took," he told her.

She tried to shake her head, wanting to say she did not have them, but the goon gave her several hard backhands across her face. Cat felt the taste of blood coming from a swollen lip.

"Don't lie to me, twit. I followed you to that fleabag building where you work, so I know you have the developed pictures. Plus, you didn't leave any negatives there. Now give them to me, and you have nothing to worry about."

He grabbed her hair, painfully pulling her from the bed. Cat gave a quiet cry from the pain.

"Keep quiet," the thug warned her, pulling in close behind her.

They plodded into the next room, the man only pausing to let her turn on the switch to light the room. Cat glanced back, but she could only see a black mask over the intruder's face. However, he caught her glimpse.

"If you want to stay alive, get the pictures, bitch," he growled as he pushed her across the small living room.

She led the intruder to the table. After forcing her to gather them into a small pile, the man quickly pocketed the articles inside his black jacket. After a quick scan around the room, he asked if that was all the pictures. She nodded.

"It better be. Now back to your bedroom." He forced his prisoner across the apartment.

When they arrived next to the nightstand, he forced her to turn around. Panic filled Catherine as she saw his dark brown eyes meet hers. He pushed her down to a sitting position on the edge of the bed. "Too bad. I have my orders, or we could have some fun."

The intruder dangled the long switchblade in her face. Holding the weapon in front of her eye, he placed his hand on her throat. Then, he pushed her to lie back on the bed. Slowly, the creep sliced through the silk cloth of her pajama top as he gave her another warning not to move. Reaching the top of her garment, her attacker pulled back the pajamas, exposing her breasts. She felt the tears welling up in her eyes as he roughly groped her breasts with a calloused hand. He leaned in close to her face, his intense breaths compelling her to expect the worse.

"Now that I have your attention, this is your only warning, bitch. Everybody knows your racket, taking pictures and getting men to pay off for them. If you go anywhere near Fordham, I'm coming back to enjoy you like a whore for the night. Then I'll cut you up into small pieces for the cops to find."

The creep suddenly slid off of her bed. Cat did not move as she watched his dark figure cross the room to her bedroom window, silently climbing out into the night. After the soft creaking sounds of his steps going down the fire escape receded. The only sound in the room was Cat's sobbing as she curled up under her sheets.

"Your face is healing up," Greye said, glancing at Ray. They passed through the open gate leading into the abandoned ammunition plant. The words sounded stiff and rehearsed.

"Well, my insides are mostly in the same place," Ray replied. He tried to remain aloof, doubting her motives. But he told himself that she might be a patsy as well.

Greye La Spina pulled her car between two silent buildings after passing through an open gate, which led into an abandoned ammunition plant. The yellow light of a single bulb coming from the corner of the wooden structure created a romantic atmosphere.

"This is the perfect place for us to talk," she told him as she turned off the engine. "I understand no one comes out to this place so that we will have it to ourselves. It's amazing how quiet this factory is since it closed down."

"That's not what you want to talk about, is it?" Ray asked.

Greye shook her head, her soft eyes appealing to him. "What did you tell my husband?"

His scowl darkened at her question. "You think I'm enough of a rat to tell your husband about you and me dancing in the back seat? I didn't say a damn thing about you. I asked why Quincannon was hanging around that tavern when you and I were there," he said. "But you figured it out already, or your husband told you. I don't think you realize this game you're playing could blow up in your face. That means it could do the same to me. You need to tell me what you're involved in," Irish told her.

"I don't have to tell you anything," she replied, her voice rising. "I'm tired of people telling me what to do."

"Really?" He raised an eyebrow. "Babe, you better explain and get me to believe you so that I can help both of us. That might keep your name away from the cops and the papers. If they get wise, we'll need each other as an alibi. Otherwise, you can play your little charade for them by yourself."

"You're a rat," she said, refusing to look at him.

"Lady, I'm getting squeezed from two sides here, so I'm not helping unless I know the rules." Irish tried to keep his voice calm.

She remained quiet for a moment, then nodded. "All right, if that's how it has to be." She reached into her purse and pulled out a silver flask. "You can have the truth." Greye took a swig from the small vessel, making a show of shivering before she handed it to Ray. He tipped it back.

"Not bad whiskey," Ray told her approvingly. "Well, since we have some time, start with your husband. How does he fit into this mess?"

"I met Henry in New York when he was out there for a conference with a bunch of religious leaders. I was working behind the cigarette counter, and he started talking to me. He was lonely. Anyway, it wasn't anything to me, but he was nice enough. I overheard one of the bishops there say he was a man on the rise…well, I got interested in him. Like I told you, I married Henry because he had prestige and I wanted something stable. I just didn't know he was a eunuch." Ray noticed her tears in the dim light. She pulled a handkerchief from her purse and dabbed her nose.

"Then, how does Quincannon come into this? You said he was acting like your husband. Did he come to your rescue at night when hubby is gone?"

"No." She paused, watching him take another drink. "Well, not a first. I'll admit I was lonely, but I had no interest in him.

He's crude and a slob; I mean, he was. Then, something happened, and he helped me find a temporary solution to the problem."

Ray glanced at her. "You're not saying what something is, but it sounds like his fix cost you more than you thought. How did he help you?

Greye shook her head. "Let's just say he came up with enough money to help me avoid legal issues," she told him. "After that, he acted like I was his property. He even treated Henry differently. My husband became furious."

"Quincannon must have decided you owed him enough to do as he pleased." Ray leaned back, tipping the flask.

"The jerk told me he was in love with me. He would get jealous if I went someplace without him. He complained about me going out to the ship." She gave a scoffing laugh. "Damn fool is the one who came up with the idea."

"Are you saying that you're not quite the gambling addict you pretend to be?" Irish sounded pleased with himself.

The lady in black shook her head.

"I seldom go to that place to gamble. Guy Young treats me all right as long as I do what he wants. Gambling is the cover story for my husband."

"I think I can figure it out," he said drolly.

The wife refused to give Ray the stern glare for his statement.

"Is that why Quincannon was hanging outside the tavern where we met?" He was interested in her story, but still skeptical about how much of it was true.

She looked at him, her face showing a range of emotions. "I'm not sure, but I guess he followed me that night. He was always trying to find out what I was doing. It was like he had me on a leash. You got a taste of it. You know how he reacted when you accidentally knocked me over, and I gave you that card."

"Yeah, that whole thing makes me a suspect to the cops if they figure out I was with you that night," he told her offhand. "I don't get it, a classy dame like you hanging with a racketeer. If it's about the money you owe Young, your husband could find a few wealthy friends and pay it off. You wouldn't have to be the guy's…" Ray stopped himself.

"His whore, that's what you meant to say." Her face grew dark. "It's not that simple, and I'm not explaining it to you."

"That's fine," he replied. "Just remember you, and I are the only alibi for each other the night that Quincannon got knocked off. Nothing good would come from going to the cops. We should keep it under wraps, but that doesn't mean they won't show up looking for answers. The police might find out your driver followed you around."

Greye stared at her hands and nodded.

"That's why nobody can know. Quincannon came to my room the night before and told me we would quit the charade soon. He said that he figured out a way to leave town, and we would have everything to ourselves. Nobody would be the wiser, and he had it all worked out. Difficult to believe, isn't it?"

Ray took another swig from the flask. He kept his voice even, although he was thinking of his first night with her.

"I don't know. A guy gets ideas about the woman he chases around the mattress." His thoughts drifted a bit before he came back to her dead chauffeur, and he shook his head again, suddenly feeling an unusual calm settle inside him.

"Yeah, he was a fool," she replied bitterly.

"I don't know. Either your chauffeur was lying to himself, or..." Ray slid down the seat, feeling the effects of the drink.

"Was your husband home the night Quincannon told you to stop?"

He slurred his words, and Greye looked at him strangely. "Yes, Henry was downstairs. Are you okay?"

Ray nodded sleepily.

"So, you and Quincannon were in deep into something. That might explain what happened. What's this charade and the favor you owe him?"

Irish saw the world spinning around him, and he caught a glint of disdain in Greye's eyes as she studied him. He lifted his arm to open the car door, and his hand fumbled with the handle, unable to grab it. Then the door opened, and he fell out of the vehicle. Landing hard on his shoulder, Ray found his face only a few inches away from a dark pair of leather shoes. He rolled over to look at two faces peering down. In his blurring vision, the vaguely familiar images of a fat guy and a thin man with a small pencil mustache leaned over him.

"Take him to your place, and I'll be there in the morning. Don't do anything until I get there." Greye's voice faded in and out. "We have to make this look perfect."

The stranger with the pencil mustache gave Ray a foul grin, then kicked him in the head. Ray Irish fell into the deep cavity of unconsciousness.

~~~

A small, circular room held a five-sided table with chairs for each person walking through the entrance's black door. The night sky, filled with stars, sent in a trickle of light through the glass cupola ceiling. As each masked person took their assigned seat, while an attendant, dressed in a flowing black robe, lit a small red candle. The servant placed the burning tallow on the table in front of each seat. The masks, which thoroughly covered each of the participants' faces, had large openings
~~~

looking like smiles while exposing the wearer's lips. A deck of ancient tarot cards lying near the head of the table revealed the cast of disguised characters. An empty gold cup with five sides, each engraved with symbols, sat on top of the cards.

The Magician, The High Priestess, The Empress, and The Emperor took their respective seats. Two other masked people moved to their positions by the entrance. Standing next to the door were two figures wearing the faces of Death and Judgment. All the characters wore black robes.

The last person slowly entered the room, the tiny figure using hands wrinkled by age to keep the horned mask from sliding down. The face bore the image of a demon-like creature, and the frail body underneath wore a flowing red robe. Taking the seat in front of the door, the person under the mask cursed at the sight of a drugged rabbit lying on the large plate.

"What is this? Animal blood has little power and only whets the appetites of our protectors," the frail voice complained.

The masks exchanged glances around the table. No one volunteered information.

"Must my servant find human victims for us each full moon?" She pounded the table. "Well, no more. It's time the Shadows brought their own. Empress, you'll work with the High Priest to give us our next sacrifice. Since he could not join us this evening, the task becomes his."

The woman across the table let out an audible huff, but she nodded.

The masked demon picked up a jewel-encrusted dagger that was lying on the plate.

"A human sacrifice when the blood moon rises, or we'll select a member of the Shadows to volunteer their blood. Is that understood?"

Sliding the blade from the sheath, a shaking hand brought the engraved knife above the sacrifice. With a quick strike, the blade cut the throat of the unfortunate animal. It lay there, silently dying, while the human creatures chanted a series of words over and over.

Death stepped forward, picking up the plate and carefully pouring the blood into the golden cup. The demon wiped the dagger clean with a cloth, reinserting it into the engraved gold-covered sheath. Death placed the half-filled cup in front of the devil, who took the first foul drink. Each creature around the table shared in the blood sacrifice. The High Priestess giggled nervously before tasting the blood, while the Empress told the person to remain quiet. Death took the last drink before returning to the entrance. Only Judgment stayed away from the table, carefully watching but remaining aloof from the proceedings.

The demon flipped over the cards, mumbling incoherent phrases. Following the exposure of seven cards from the deck, the old woman in the red robe spoke.

"The dreams you have troubled each of you. The nightmares tell you that the souls of our ancestors are distressed. Those around this table know this truth and the time to act is upon us. We will take action against the people who threaten our city."

The faces around the table turned their heads to glance at the others. Slowly, the group nodded in agreement. The Magician asked for guidance, and the demon held up a hand, now devoid of wrinkles and age spots. The frail voice grew more robust, while her tone remained grave.

"Nightmares will scare some of those against the Order, but some of our opponents are brutal remnants of philistines who value nothing but power. I've seen the spirit who will stop those people who work against our families. Death and Judgment will ensure that our Empress finds our next sacrifice for the master. When you receive the word, follow their instructions. If you fail, the master will have your blood."

The demon gazed around the table. "As a reminder, the laws of our society remain inviolable since our founding over two centuries ago. Death will come to rip your soul from its shell, and Judgment will cast you to Andras for your failure."

~~~

A dark and quiet world greeted Irish when he came out of his stupor. The rag stuffed inside his mouth threatened to choke him, and Ray panicked. Turning his cheek, he saw a thin line of light coming from underneath the door. The peek calmed him after a moment, and he tried to focus his thoughts. Discovering his feet remained unbound, Ray twisted and turned, his numb wrists behind him, unable to help his struggle.

Through his turns inside the confined space, he gradually determined he lay inside a small closet. Working his body around, Ray lifted his feet, trying to find the door handle; his movement's noise seemed loud. He stopped, intently listening, but silence remained outside the door. Unable to turn the round knob with his polished leather shoes, Ray twisted his body around, his legs causing him to groan as the muscles cramped. Finally, Irish turned over, and he got to his knees. A fog came over him again, but he shook it off as he stood. Ray's head struck a shelf, causing him to curse silently. Using his bound hands to feel around the door, he finally found the handle. He found the door latch and pushed with his back to open the door. However, the latch popped open, sending Irish falling to the floor when the door swung open. Landing hard on his shoulder, he shook his head while he rolled over.
~~~

Ray Irish stared into the open eyes of a dead man. The pencil mustache was dark against the pale skin, his face still showing the combined expression of horror and disbelief. Irish pulled his face away from the corpse, his dazed mind reeling at the pool of blood he fell into while his body twisted away. The throat of the dead man held the same extended red cut across, just like Quincannon. A horrified shriek began, then instantly cut off from the other side of the room.

Greye La Spina stood by the doorway, her fists clutched to her mouth while her wide eyes remained focused on the corpse. He watched her back into the opened door, her head shaking back and forth.

"No, no, no…" The words were a whisper, barely audible past her clutched hands.

Cat pushed past Greye before coming to a complete stop as the bloody scene came into full view. Her expression went from shock to relief. She came to him, kneeling beside Ray.

"Are you all right?" she asked, reaching around his head to unbind his gag.

The man nodded, trying to spit out the rag. He coughed out his thanks to her while his mind continued to shake off the effects of his spiked drink. Finally, he told her to help remove the bindings on his wrists.

Cat helped him over and saw the rope tightly cutting into his skin. She noticed the dagger lying in the blood, and she paused. Cat steeled herself to the uncomfortable dampness and picked up the weapon to cut through the rope.

Freed, Irish tried to get to his feet before he fell again. His head still swimming, Ray noticed Greye tearfully leave the room.

"I'll call the sheriff," Cat told him, dropping the dagger in front of Irish. He stared at the weapon briefly, trying to remember where he had seen it before.

Carefully, Ray stumbled while trying to get up, his legs refusing his attempts to walk. He finally made it to the door, leaning against the wall. He looked down the hall, but Greye was gone. Pushing away from the wall, his still numb hands clumsily closed the door.

"Put the phone down," Irish heard himself tell Cat. She looked at him, about to say something to the hotel operator. He gestured for her to hang up while he held her gaze. Cat put down the phone.

"Why don't you want the police?" she asked.

"I'm saving us from questions that we can't answer. Now wash your hands. We have to get out of here," Ray told her as his brain slowly pulled things together.

Glancing at the dagger on the floor again, he suddenly felt an icy chill fill him, along with a boost of adrenaline. He carefully picked up the murder weapon, taking it to the bathroom. After he washed the blood from the dagger and his hands, Ray dried both using a white hand towel hanging by the sink.

Cat stared at him as he left the small bathroom. Irish walked across the room while he wiped the weapon thoroughly clean of any fingerprints before throwing it down by the body. He noticed she remained standing by the bathroom door, watching him.

"Damn it, wash your hands. We have to get out of here. I think this might be a setup that went wrong." He went to the phone, wiped the receiver's black handle, then went to the closet and wiped off the closet handles. Ray glanced at Cat, who finished with her hands. He told her to wipe down the sink and faucets with the hand towel. Irish quickly scanned the room for any obvious clues.

"All right, I think I've got everything. Did you wipe everyplace you touched?"

Cat nodded as she stepped around the floor's bloodstained areas, and Ray cautiously opened the door. After he cleaned the door handle, Irish motioned for Cat to leave ahead of him. The troubleshooter took the hand towel she carried and stuffed it into one pocket of his coat. Then he used his towel to close the door. The pair rushed down the hallway while Ray used the wet cloth on the bloodstains on his coat.

"I'm a mess; let's find the back stairs out of here," he jammed the wet and bloody cloth into his other coat pocket.

The photographer led them along the passageway to a narrow door that opened to stairs. A minute later, the couple exited the building's back, stepping out onto a gravel path. An old rock fence with a large, open field on the other side informed Ray they were no longer in the city.

"My car's out front," she told him. "You go to the side of the building, and I'll meet you there." Before he could reply, Cat stepped back into the building. Irish looked over his clothes with a scowl, trying to wipe the worst of the blood away after pulling out one towel again. Then Ray cautiously followed the wall until he reached the corner of the structure. Soon, Cat drove up in her gray Olds coupe. He slid in on the bench seat, and the pair drove away. Not long after pulling out of the parking lot, they passed a black and white sedan blaring sirens as the county sheriff sped to the crime scene. Ray watched the car running through the parking lot and saw the sign to the Sleeping Acre Inn by the road.

"Well, you saved my hide. Thanks," Irish opened the window to ward off his drowsiness. "Now, the next question: how in the hell did you find me?"

Cat glanced at him.

"I followed your girlfriend." Irish waited for a moment. "Give me more than that."

"La Spina came out of her house this morning in a big hurry." His driver kept glancing in the rearview mirror. "I knew something was going on, so I tailed her to that hotel."

"Wait, are you saying you were staking out her place? I'm not complaining, but where the hell did you come up with that?" He looked behind again, breathing a sigh of relief that no one followed them.

"Yeah, I couldn't sleep," Cat replied. The clipped tone of her voice got Ray's attention. She changed the subject.

"Will that cleaning we did to the room work?" she asked.

Irish glanced back again.

"Yeah, any fingerprints they find will come out too smudged for the detectives to make anything out of," he replied. "As long as nobody saw us, I think we'll be fine. What happened at La Spina's house?"

"Greye made a beeline to this place. I thought she might have another boyfriend up here, so I figured I would check out what room and come back to take a private photo of her and this person." She glanced at Ray. "You know, to get her to talk. That's when I found you. What happened?"

"The bitch gave me a mickey, and when I fell out of the car, that dead guy decided to kick my face in for fun. That's the last thing I remember until I woke up in the closet."

Ray stuck his head partially out of the window. The breeze felt wonderful. Then he turned back to her.

"Next thing I know, I'm lying in the blood, staring at a dead man. I'm sure that's Pendexter. The other guy's face was hazy to me, but I'm betting the other killer was involved. I remember two of them staring down at me."

"You have any idea what they took you out there for?"

"I think that bitch and her hoodlum friends were trying damn hard to leave me for a big fall. But I have no idea what their plan was. You didn't see Greye's face, but that dead guy had to mean something to her. She was behind this, and now I have to figure it out. That's why I didn't want to explain to the cops. They will never believe my story; she's the bishop's wife."

"I was there, and I would have backed you," Cat told him empathically, then her voice softened as she thought about the situation. "But La Spina could have paid off someone, forcing them to go after you and me."

"Exactly my point." Ray looked at the drying blood stains covering his clothes. "I don't plan on waiting in jail to figure out the score. We need to find someplace where I can get cleaned up and ditch these clothes."

"I've got that covered; we'll go to my place," she told him.

It took a while before the pair could get into Cat's apartment after the drive. She ran into an elderly male neighbor at the front door of the building. The friend began telling her about his recent trip to California. Ray felt very exposed by the back corner of the building in the alleyway as he waited near foul-smelling trash cans. Irish could almost imagine a police car suddenly turning into the alley to find him.

Finally able to free herself from the gray-haired man, Cat let Ray into the building through the back door. They made their way up the staircase, each person expecting the worst.

Fortunately, their luck held, and the unlikely couple went inside.

"Remember to keep it down," she warned him. "I can't have any male visitors here."

Irish gave her a cheesy grin. "You weren't too worried about that back at my hotel."

Cat's face remained serious.

"Get that jacket and shirt off, and I'll dispose of them down the incinerator. The landlord has the boiler running all the time for the hot water."

A few minutes later, Cat threw the garments and towels into the incinerator on her way out of the building. With only his pants on, Ray waited for her to return. While she went to the Hotel Alexander for his clothes, the man helped himself to a cheese sandwich. Then he wandered around the apartment. The place's décor was stylish and straightforward, with a small couch and a matching chair in white, along with an art déco chrome end table. The kitchen was tidy; however, the tiny dining table had two nearly empty folders on the top, which looked out of place. On top of one folder sat a bottle of Irish whiskey and an almost full ashtray with ashes covering part of the tabletop. He moved around one folder and saw a picture underneath.

Irish recognized the dead detective in the photo. Ray guessed Cat was still working on some blackmail to bring in some extra cabbage. He frowned as he tossed the picture back on the table, taking the bottle of whiskey to the sink. The troubleshooter pulled a tumbler from the cabinet and poured himself half a glass. Irish took a sip as he went to the couch in the living room.

For some reason, the photo bothered him. Not the picture itself, but the larceny which seemed to fill Cat's heart.

Somehow, Ray liked to believe in the initial wholesome picture of her he created in his mind when they first met. He did not like the reality which came out the more he knew about her. She was playing a dangerous game that had already killed her partner, George Hopley. He questioned why he felt the need to protect her. There was something about Cat that he liked. She was strong, willing to help him, even though she knew little about him. He downed the whiskey in the tumbler.

I need another drink!

When Cat arrived back at her apartment, she found Irish sitting on the couch. She barely recognized him. Ray's usual calm changed into an embittered rage. Cat noticed the nearly empty bottle next to him. Silently, he took the clothes and disappeared into her bedroom. She talked through the door, happily explaining all the strange looks received when she smuggled the clothes out of the hotel. Cat heard no reply from Ray. He walked out of her bedroom wearing a clean blue suit. There was a slight wobble in his walk, and his eyes carried a murderous look that scared her.

"Where are you going?" Cat asked him, heading to the door as she cut him off.

"I have business with someone," Irish told her, his voice low, nearly inaudible.

"You can't kill her." Cat recognized his murderous intentions.

Ray stopped when she placed her hand on his chest. He looked at the small woman with a raised eyebrow.

"Why the hell not? The whore has it coming," he told her viciously. "Get out of my way!"

She remained in front of him. Cat knew drunken rage, and she hated it, considering such actions as pathetic. Still, she tried to reason with Ray.

"Listen to me. You're not a murderer; I know your record. If you kill her, you will die. Those who are friends of the bishop will be happy to send you to the electric chair. As far as the people that run this city are concerned, two more dead outsiders are a good thing."

"It doesn't matter as long as she gets it in the end," he fumed at her. Unexpectedly, she smacked him hard across the face. Fear crossed her eyes, then anger, but her action worked. His bruised face hurt from the strike.

"Don't be a stupid drunk. Some of us are on your side. Now, sit down and relax for a minute. I'll get us a drink. You can wallow in your anger, but just stay here." Cat took a step over to the end table and picked up the empty glass.

Shocked by the slap, Ray's eyes narrowed as he felt his nose bleed. Grudgingly, he pulled a handkerchief from his pocket and dabbed at his nose. His murderous glare subsiding, the man went to the couch, his expression remaining cold. He took a seat and watched her.

Cat went to the kitchen and pulled another tumbler from the shelf. She filled the glasses, making sure one glass had water only. The woman talked while she worked, trying to forge a plan.

"Greye La Spina isn't in a good position. You're still alive and her partner is dead. Let's use that to our advantage. She can't be sure what happens next."

Handing Ray a glass of water when she came to the couch, she sat next to him.

"You have a bad temper, and it gets worse when you drink," she told him as calmly as she could. However, there was an intensity in her eyes when she turned to him. "I don't like drunks, and I don't like self-pity. I've seen enough of that stuff in the past."

"Yeah, maybe so, but save the analyzing for someone else," he told her gruffly, staring at the glass. "Now you've got my attention. Do you have something like a plan, or do you just like hitting me?"

Cat gave an unexpected grin.

"Well, mostly the hitting part, but you know I'm right."

Irish grunted, still staring at the glass before he set it on the table, untouched.

"The way I see it, Greye wanted me out of the way. She worked me into her trap, but I can't figure out her angle. The bitch has two male partners who could have killed me at that old military base. That's where she gave me the mickey. Nobody would have found my body for days, so why drag me out to the motel?"

He leaned back in the chair.

"Maybe they didn't want to kill you, might have wanted to find out something from you," she suggested.

"It's possible," he agreed as he let out a deep breath. "I remember she told the guys not to do anything until she got there. After that, it's all black." Ray shook his head. "No, there's something else going on here. You don't take a guy out to a motel. There are too many people around to hear things if they planned on beating the information out of me."

"Then, what?" she asked.

Irish shrugged.

"It was a setup, but I guess I'm going to have to ask her."

Cat glared at him.

"Forget that idea. Do you think La Spina will leave that lovely mansion of hers now? If I'm standing in her shoes, I wait until you show up and have the cops haul you away. Greye could claim you raped her. In this state, you get the death penalty for that. Besides, we still have to worry about her accomplice." She leaned back, taking a large sip of her drink, and sighed.

"That's assuming the cops don't trace you and me back to the Camelot somehow. You know, it would only take an anonymous call from her partner to have the heat come down on us."

Ray nodded, remembering the scene at the motel room. "Yeah, that means we put the heat on Greye."

Cat remained silent, a sudden weariness creeping over her. She didn't like the implications of his idea. She yawned, and it reminded Irish of an unasked question.

"What's with the picture on your table?"

"What do you mean?" Her surprise showed when she asked. Cat looked at the table, getting up from the couch to see. Walking toward the table, she picked up the photo carefully.

"There's something you're not telling me." He wondered at her dramatic reaction to his question. There was a hint of dread in her eyes when she turned back to him.

"Where did you get this?" she asked, trying to keep the rising anxiety from overcoming her.

Irish went to her. "It was under the folder with the bottle sitting on it. Why, what's going on?"

Cat remained quiet as she stepped back to the couch and fell into the soft foam. Irish took a seat on the chair across from her. The room remained quiet, like a tomb. Finally, Cat told him what had happened after the intruder came into her room. She kept the story brief and avoided the part about the assailant groping her.

"I'm sorry it happened," he said. "You said Fordham played dirty. And now we know he has at least one cop on his payroll. I don't like it. Detective Howard must have tipped off Fordham, who sent that thug after you."

She nodded, then drank down the rest of her glass.

"Yeah, I'm not going to lie to you. I can be tough, but that bastard scared me. He followed me from Anthony's. It could have been that bartender who tipped him off. Knapp wasn't telling me something, even though he admitted some guy left with George." She explained what the bartender told her.

Irish got up from the seat and walked to the table in the kitchen. He looked at the picture again.

"That doesn't tell me why you decided to be a shamus and stake out the La Spina's house this morning."

Cat rose, going into the kitchen as well.

"I was too afraid to fall back asleep. I couldn't stop thinking about everything that was going on," the woman confessed. "The more I thought about it, the worse it seemed. Howard appears to be working for both Young and Fordham. Remember when I said that it all went back to Greye La Spina?"

Ray absently nodded as he held the picture.

"Well, maybe Fordham and Young are working together if they are using the same cop. I wondered how much your girlfriend might know. I can't ask questions about Hopley's death anymore, since Howard might have tipped off Fordham about me. Since I couldn't sleep, I followed Greye. I figure if I was lucky, I might confront her about Fordham and John Robertson."

Irish put the picture on the table.

"Who the hell is Robertson?"

Cat explained what she had discovered from Gladys at the *Beacon*.

"Someone needs to do some snooping into that bitch's mysterious background," she told him as she walked into the living room with a tired sigh. "I need some sleep," she confessed.

"No time for that; you need to pack," Ray told her.

"What are you talking about?" She turned to him, surprised.

"It sounds like you need to get away for a few days. You're going to Boston to track down that lead," Irish told her with a smile.

"Are you saying I should let that bastard scare me away? That's not going to happen." She crossed her arms defiantly.

"No, I'm not saying they are scaring you away. But let's be smart about this," Ray explained. "You have a substantial lead; I don't care what Gladys says. Nobody from Boston writes a letter to a small city paper about the illustrious bishop's wife unless they have something."

"I'm not running away," she said again.

"Damn it; it's your turn to listen! Let them think they ran you off. You're not a cop, and you've got a big target on you. There's no reason to get killed. I can't leave town, but I can follow up with that bartender who you said knows more. We'll just swap the assignments."

"What if nothing pans out?" she asked.

"Well, then we know. But let's see if we can get something on Greye that every big shot in this town will have trouble handling. If she has a secret, we can use it. It might explain something she mentioned about her debt to Quincannon. While you're gone, I'm checking out the bar. Plus, I'll go talk to a friendly cop about the match or not on the slugs that killed George and One-Eye Cornell." His mind raced with questions.

"You be careful," she warned. "That creep who came into my apartment had a knife."

Ray appreciated the concern in her eyes, but he remained stoic.

"I'll be okay. You just worry about yourself."

Cat frowned. "What about Dunn?"

"What about him?" Irish asked with a chuckle. "Just tell him you're looking up some background on Guy Young, and he'll pay for your trip. He can stew on it if he doesn't like what you come back with."

"You like to control things, don't you? I mean, you dislike people telling you what to do."

She grinned.

"You're the second person to say that since I got to this place," Ray replied as he took her arm and turned her to the bedroom.

"Now get yourself packed. You're heading to Boston on the next train. You can get some shuteye on the way."

~~~

Ray Irish pulled up to Anthony's in Cat's gray Olds about thirty minutes after dropping her off at the station. While he waited for Cat to pack, he called the station to get her ticket. After watching her enter the train station building, the man felt a slight sense of loss, which the shamus quickly buried. He knew he had to keep his focus on finding who attacked Cat. Ray looked around the busy street when he got out of the car, trying to steer clear of any potential trouble.

A simple tin sign identified the tavern among the line of weathered, two-story weather buildings along the street. Walking inside, a blast of stale beer and body odor greeted Irish as he pushed past the door. Most of the regular's attention followed the stranger as he walked past them, before going back to their whispered conversations. Ray stepped to the end of the bar, where the hulking bartender stood, leaning against
~~~

the counter. He noticed Knapp straighten for a moment to give him the once-over before returning to leaning on his elbows against the wooden top of the bar.

"You must be Knapp. Remember a good-looking girl who came in here the other day asking about George Hopley?" Irish went straight to the point.

The scarred face of the ex-fighter gave no hint he heard the question. Instead, he pulled a mug from the tray below his belly, sitting it on the counter.

"I only talk with customers."

"Then fill it with a decent beer," Ray told him.

Still leaning against the bar, Knapp pulled a bottle and opened it. He placed the warm bottle across from Ray, who stepped to the counter and threw a dime on the bar. He picked up the mug.

"The name of the guy who left with George Hopley the other day. You know the name, and I'm asking for it."

Knapp snorted.

"What makes you think I'll give it to you?"

Irish continued to look at his beer.

"You look like a person who wouldn't mind a little cabbage for the name."

Knapp scowled at the shamus, leaning closer to his customer. "Well, you might have it wrong."

Ray glanced at the boxer's large hands gripping the edge of the dirty counter. A disfigured right knuckle showed him the ex-fighter's primary weapon. Irish felt the weight of the hefty glass in his hand, and he sensed a growing dislike for the slob behind the bar.

"I'll tell you what I'll do," Knapp continued. "You send that sweet little dish back to my office, and she can do me a favor for the name." The bartender gave an evil grin as he licked his lips. "She looks the type."

Irish reached across the bar, grabbing the ex-fighter by his hair. He slammed the off-balanced man's face into the bar counter. Still holding Knapp's greasy hair, Ray smashed the mug into the bar and pushed the half-broken glass in front of Knapp's wide, watery eyes.

"You tell me the name, or you get accidentally blinded, that's my offer." A deep growl of rage came from Irish.

Less than a minute later, Ray left the bar with the name of Fat Louie. Hands still shaking with his receding fury, he got into the car. As the shamus drove away, he didn't notice another vehicle pull away from the curb behind him.

Ray found Arizona Campbell sitting at his desk, having a late lunch. The pastrami and rye sandwich sat half-finished on the man's desk with a cup of coffee. The shamus knocked and stuck his head in the door.

"Got time for me?" Irish asked after he saw the detective's grimace.

"No, but get in here since it saves me the trouble of tracking you down," Arizona told him.

After he entered, Ray closed the door, taking the wooden chair across from the policeman who tried to finish his lunch.

"Something I need to know about?"

"You might say that. It appears Bishop La Spina has called the DA about you." The cop took a large bite of his meal.

"And?" Ray asked, expecting the worse.

"According to the bishop, you misrepresented yourself to him, posing as a reporter. He claims you pushed past his butler to harass his wife. He also states on another occasion that you threatened his wife. At this point, he says he is seriously considering the idea of pressing charges against you." Arizona glared at Irish.

"What do you think?" Ray asked.

The policeman wolfed down the rest of his sandwich.

"Listen, I don't care if you play footsy with his wife. Hell, a lot of guys already have. But I can tell you this: go anywhere near that woman now, and the DA will slap you in the slammer and put you in front of a grand jury. After that, there will be enough charges against you to send you to the pen for several years. You got that?"

"I get it." Irish smiled unexpectedly. "With her husband suddenly involved, Greye is afraid of her shadow now."

"What do you mean?" Arizona became intrigued.

"You'll be the first to know when I have it," Ray assured him. "Anyway, I'm not seeing that woman, especially not by myself. I just stopped by to see if you got a match on the bullets that killed George and One-Eye."

Campbell stared at him for a long moment.

"Yes, there's a match. The same gun used in both murders."

"You have any suspects?" Ray forced himself not to say more when the detective shook his head.

"When we get the gun, we'll have our guy. But I've got other things going on right now. You still interested in Guy Young's work?" Arizona asked as he grimaced at the foul police coffee. Irish nodded carefully.

"We got a call from the county sheriff, who told us they found a stiff at the Camelot Motel this morning. Young owns that place under another name, and the sheriff is sure there is a prostitution ring going on there." The cop noticed Ray's reaction to the mention of a corpse. Arizona paused, then took a drink of his coffee.

"You been out there recently?" he asked.

"No, never heard of the place." Irish realized the conversation was getting dangerous. "Is that it?"

"Yeah, and remember to stay away from the La Spina's, or a ton of trouble will fall on you," the policeman warned again before Ray left the office.

~~~

The winter darkness settled early under the gray sky while Henry La Spina looked out the window at the large mansion of the Hopley's across the street. The fortress-like building stood tall, complete with gray stones, tall windows, turrets, and even gargoyles on the eves. Shadows from the nearby lights fell across the grotesque figureheads, briefly reminding him of his childhood fear of nighttime monsters. A dark limousine pulled out of the driveway, turning into the street for the mayor's nightly trip to the house of his sister. The large man turned to his desk when he saw his wife. Greye's eyes were red, and she sniffed, wiping her nose with a tissue.

"My dear, you look terrible. You should go to bed." Henry's voice carried a natural soothing tone from years of practice.

Greye shook her head. "I'll be all right; it's just, I'm having a difficult time. So many bad things are happening."

He remained in his place by the window.

"Quincannon and his associate were not of our class, so you shouldn't dwell on such things." When La Spina turned back to look out of the window, he didn't see his wife's contorted expression at his comment. "Be thankful for the things we have together. Remember, I took care of that imbecile Irish fellow who threatened you."

"I'm grateful for that. Are you expecting someone?" She noticed how unusually tense he appeared.
~~~

Henry remained silent for a moment, nodding absently.

"Yes, I received a phone call today and am expecting them to arrive anytime. Why don't you go to our bedroom and rest for a while? I'll be quite busy this evening."

She knew the tone of his voice meant for her to leave. She sighed, feeling tired and confused. Greye silently left, leaving the door open.

A few minutes later, the bishop saw his visitor pull up in a black car about half a block away. Henry watched as the person got out of the car, looking carefully around the area before walking along the sideway to the fence surrounding the house. The bishop left the window and walked to his front door. Hearing footsteps on the front steps, the cleric opened the door as the surprised visitor reached for the doorbell.

"Were you waiting for me?" Detective Howard asked as he entered the residence.

"Let's just say we have sensitive issues we must discuss," the bishop replied; his dull face showed no emotion which bothered his visitor.

Henry led the corrupt policemen to his study, closing and locking the door. Ron Howard looked around the plush room, pushing back his fedora while unconsciously licking his lips at the thoughts running through his head. He put his hand in his wool coat, pulling out something wrapped in a white cloth.

"Here's the sensitive issue, bishop," Howard stated as he confidently crossed the room, placing the object on the desktop. The lieutenant unwrapped the white handkerchief he held while Henry walked over. He displayed a gold dagger with precious embedded stones on the scabbard and handle.

"Friend of mine at the sheriff's office found this in a motel today. It appears this weapon cut a man's throat. It looks like it'll fit nicely back in your display case," he told the bishop. "However, it will come at a cost."

The bishop glanced at his collection of similar-looking daggers behind his desk. He stared at the weapon on the bureau. "It appears to be a Holbein dagger, also known as a *basler*. By the shape and design, I would estimate the late 1500s. You can see the dance of death design engraved into the gold sheath of the dagger."

"It's specific to the Swiss maker," he continued with a scholarly air. "The Nazi's copied the style, as you can see from the hilt. It is an expensive collectible, no doubt. However, I'm not sure why you have contacted me about this. It would seem to be evidence of a murder, would it not?"

The detective gave him a sidelong glance, then a smug laugh.

"All right, I'll play along, professor." He stepped to the displays on the wall, pulling a half-used cigar from his pocket and jamming it in his mouth. "Let's talk about the evidence. You collect fancy knives like these. Your so-called chauffer, Quincannon, has his throat slit wide open by a similar knife, perhaps the very one on your desk. And today, a known associate of your chauffeur, a guy named Pendexter, winds up with his throat slit in the same manner."

The bishop stepped around to sit in his leather chair, leaning back with his hands pressed together.

"Lieutenant, I'm still not sure why this should concern me. At best, your links appear to be an interesting coincidence."

Ron Howard glared at him.

"Let's just see if I can concern you, then. Just so happens, your wife frequently met with the two murdered men at a local tavern. The place is out of the way and designed for women like her. Maybe you got a little jealous and fixed the problem.

You understand what I'm telling you. If I take this to the grand jury, either you or your little whore wife could wind up sitting in an electric chair. Should I go on?"

Henry La Spina's eyes narrowed, but he gave Howard a friendly smile.

"Your manners are quite undignified. Do you believe the District Attorney would bring my family name into such a dastardly scheme with such little evidence? You realize, of course, the Smyth family is close friends with the La Spina family."

Howard began chewing on his cigar, his face revealing the corrupt man's quandary.

"Of course, I know all about the District Attorney's ties with your family. What if I said I have fingerprints on the weapon to prove my theory?"

The bishop's eyebrow rose slightly.

"Then, by all means, you should place your opinion in front of the District Attorney for his review. I would suggest you have such fingerprints before you meet with him. Having grown up with Peter Smyth, I know he is not a forgiving person."

Detective Howard silently stared for a long moment at his intended victim, his chomping mouth threatening to eat through the cigar. Finally, he went to the desk and picked up the weapon with his open hand. The cop slid the knife into his pocket while putting the white handkerchief into his shirt pocket. As he turned to leave, Henry spoke up.

"If that dagger is no longer evidence, perhaps we can come to an arrangement. Since it is such a rare piece, I might be interested in purchasing it from you."

The cop stopped, somewhat confused by the offer. Howard pulled the weapon out of his pocket and looked at Henry. "How much is it worth?"

"Oh, in the right hands, about a thousand dollars," the bishop replied with a smile. "I believe the foundation would like to add that weapon to our collection; you see some of our collection on the wall behind me."

Howard grinned.

"Funny how you religious types can collect such things. But it'll take fifteen hundred for me to forget about this thing. Cash!"

"I don't carry much money in the house. Let us say, tomorrow evening at the end of Andras Lane. I have an appointment there at about ten o'clock. Let's make it eleven," La Spina offered.

Howard frowned slightly. He didn't like the place, but the isolated area worked.

"All right, I'll be there, and I'll see myself out." The corrupt cop unlocked the door and left the room. Henry La Spina slowly turned the revolving chair around to look at his collection as he lightly whistled a hymnal.

~~~

After leaving Cat's car just down the street, Irish walked to his hotel when he heard the gruff voice address him.

"Hey, mister, you got a light?"

When Ray turned around, a large man, dressed in dark coveralls and wearing a heavy wool jacket, stepped from the shadows. He heard footsteps behind him and glanced back to see another similarly attired goon walk up close behind him.

"I take it you don't need a match." Irish slowly slid his hand into his suit pocket.
~~~

"You're a right smart cookie," the thug in front of him growled. "Come with us."

Irish slowly pulled to the side while turning his body. Suddenly, he pointed his finger, pushing his pocket out. In the dark, he hoped it was a reasonable impression of a gun.

"Before you make a mistake, I don't miss from this distance," he lied.

"You're bluffing, flatfoot," the leader growled.

"You want to bet your life on it?" Irish gave him a cocky grin. "I can show you my new gun permit after I plug you."

The two large men paused, apparently unsure, then the leader laughed.

"I'll think we'll chance it."

Ray did not wait for their next move. He turned and ran straight into the thug behind him, running over the surprised brute using a stiff arm that would make a football coach proud. His rebuilt legs pounded along the sidewalk as he raced across the street while the two men came after him. Irish turned the corner, finding the block filled with closed stores. The sounds of his pursuer's footsteps drew closer. Ray knew he wasn't going to outrun them, and his mind raced for a solution. Then he saw a neon sign flashing toward the end of the block. Becoming winded, the man pushed himself, just reaching the door as it opened. He almost ran into a uniformed beat cop leaving 13th Street Tavern.

"Whoa there, you looking to have me run you in? Say, what's your hurry?" The policemen barred the way as he looked at Ray.

"Sorry, I…I was looking for a phone," Irish lied as he looked back at his pursuers. The two men were standing a few feet away, trying to catch their wind.

The cop looked over at the men.

"Are you two planning on joining us?" he asked sharply. The leader in coveralls shook his head and walked away.

"Mister, I'd suggest you hang inside and find that phone. It looks like the rats are out tonight," the policemen told Ray as he slowly followed the thugs who had started across the street.

Irish watched the uniformed man walk away, swinging his baton while whistling. He had a sudden chill come over him. It was the uncanny feeling that someone was watching him. Then he saw a figure standing in the shadows of an alley by a nearby building. For a moment, Ray caught sight of a pale face staring at him. He blinked a couple of times and watched the figure slowly back into the dark shadow. The skeleton image he saw froze like ice, with the hairs on the back of his neck standing up. Ray hesitated, debating whether to enter the tavern. Then curiosity got the best of him, and Irish walked toward the alley, looking away as he crossed the street. When Irish reached the other side of the road, he cautiously entered the alley entrance, letting his eyes adjust to the darkness. The mysterious shadow figure was gone.

Detective Plug Howard's rugged face flashed into the light when he struck a match inside the shadows of his black sedan. The large man scowled, flicked the stub of dying flame out the open window of his car. He let out a long stream of cigarette smoke while he looked over the desolate scenery around him. It was a moonlit night. His car sat at the end of the narrow-paved road where he faced a quiet-looking mansion. In his eyes, the house looked like a haunted chateau with absurdly ornamented towers, spires, and a steeply pitched roof overlooking the road. Even more ominous, the spacious yard came, complete with white headstones and ancient trees. Andres Hill held the numerous graves and tombs of the family and their relatives.

Howard was a rookie cop on the beat when he first discovered the lonely road in the middle of Oyster City. A narrow driveway pushed through two giant oaks at the end of the road, leading to the house. He never liked the graveyard look of the area around the mansion.

The soft sounds of a whistled tune came through the vehicle's window. Opening the car door, Howard got out and cautiously looked around his motor vehicle. He noticed a person standing underneath the ancient oaks in the middle of the driveway. The cop saw the large figure wave to him.

"Damn rich people," Howard grumbled as he closed the car door and walked up the road. When he reached the start of the driveway, Howard heard nearby footsteps stealthily moving on his right side. He paused, scanning in the direction of the sound, but he didn't see anything.

"All right, La Spina, I'm here." He thundered, but only silence greeted him. Then he heard the crunching steps in front of him in the shadows. The sound came from the shadows near a large crypt that lay next to the driveway ahead. The dark figure stopped in a patch of moonlight and waved him forward before retreating into the shadows.

"All right, damn it, I'm not going any further, and you better have the money," Howard snapped, disturbed by the strange atmosphere.

He considered increasing the dagger's price when he came next to the rectangular, stone-gray crypt. The stone appeared eerily white under the moonlight.

"Get your ass out here so we can settle this, La Spina," Lieutenant Howard growled. Then he froze as the figure emerged from the tree's shadow.

Only a few paces away stood a masked man in a black robe. The smiling mask of death over the figure's face sent an icy fear through the detective as he backed up several steps. He became irritated.

"You better think twice about playing games with me," Howard growled as his hand started for the pistol inside his jacket. Intent on the figure in front of him, the policeman failed to recognize the faint sound of footsteps behind him.

Before he could turn around, Howard took a massive slap across the back of his head, which stunned him. The thick, weighted leather billy club hit him again, sending the policeman to the ground.

Almost instantly, a group of masked people fell on their quarry, binding Howard's hands and gagging him. As he pulled out of his shocked state, the large man tried to fight, but he was too late. Strong hands held fast to his legs, as the detective felt a rope twist around one ankle. Then, within a few seconds, he found himself upside down, swinging above the tomb among the shadows. Howard's struggles slowed as he tried to understand why the costumed figures gathered around him.

The figure of Death laid the golden dagger on the slab after pulling it from the lieutenant's jacket. Masked Judgment placed a gold cup next to the knife. The High Priestess giggled as she started to spin the hanging man.

"It's a perfect night for the blue moon. The master will be pleased," she stated, followed by a shrill laugh at the thought. Leaving the sluggishly spinning cop, the masked woman lit two candles and placed them next to the cup.

Judgment grunted as he replied. "Worthless foreigner will be no loss. It's about time someone from our group finally brought us a sacrifice."

The Demon picked up the dagger.

"It's a fitting end and a much better sacrifice."

With a steady hand, the person grabbed the struggling detective by his thinning hair as he wriggled around like a worm on a hook. The smiling Demon slid the sharp blade across the victim's throat, and the High Priest held the cup under the sacrifice's head. He struggled to collect the stream of blood spurting from their twisting prey's throat. Judgment dipped his finger into the cup and then drew a Goetic seal below their sacrifice as tribute to their raven-head master. While the dying man's struggles slowed, the masked figures began their chants to the ancient, banished one. Plug Howard gave one final death spasm while trying to remember a prayer from childhood.

Each member drank from the cup of human blood that passed between them while the Demon laid out cards next to hastily placed candles around the seal. While reciting an incantation passed down by generations of elders, the masked creature's trembling voice suddenly grew stronger. Those around the slab looked at each other; their eyes widen with a mixture of wonder and dread. The surrounding air abruptly grew cold, and the faint noises of the night went silent. Almost imperceptibly at first, a dark shadow rose from the marble tomb. Quickly, the mist enveloped the hanging body before it slid like a waterfall into the Demon holding the tarot cards. The demon mask figure began to shudder and tremble; then, the body became a wooden statue. An ominous poem from the depths of hell addressed the followers.

"More blood must flow, for the nights still yearn, bringing great prosperity through the power of the one greater.

"In the early night on the large bay, water will burn, fed by bodies of flames coming from the outsider.

"Sacrifice and blood from one family put into the urn; the gift of your fortune by your great provider."

The figure of the demon rose in the air as the fiend spoke. When the dark shadow wrapped around the robed person's body finished, a hideous wail came from the floating shade. Wretched howls erupted from dogs in the distance; their pitiful pleas echoed into the night. Then, the rigid statue of the hovering person suddenly fell to the ground.

After a momentary pause, the figure wearing the mask of death walked next to the unconscious body. Death stood and looked around the tomb at the followers. "You've heard the master's demands. We must decide which family will bear the coming sacrifice."

~~~

As the train from Boston rolled into the Oyster City station on a cold, overcast morning the next day, Catherine Bennett remained lost in thought. Her trip revealed much more than she anticipated, giving her additional reasons to dislike Greye La
~~~

Spina. The conversations with two reporters at the *Boston Post* revealed the dark past of the bishop's wife. It was something she intended to confront Greye about. Cat vowed she would ensure the wretched woman released her grip on Henry La Spina.

Cat stood and waited when the train lurched to a stop while an older couple moved through the aisle. Finally, she could retrieve her travel case from an overhead rack. She made her way through the nearly empty train car. Before stepping off the train, the petite woman put on a long, blue wool coat, then worked her way through the small crowd milling about the station platform.

"You going my way, sister?"

The familiar voice caught her by surprise. Standing by a water fountain was Ray Irish, his blue suit covered by a green trench coat. He smiled, taking off his hat as he stepped toward her. His face was still black and blue from his beating, but her eyes brightened.

"Well, look at you. When did you decide to play a chauffeur?"

Ray took her small case. "I just needed to make sure you got your car back. It's been kind of quiet with you out of the city." He took her by the arm and guided them to the exit. When they reached the car, both went to the driver's side. Ray grinned self-consciously before grabbing the handle and opening the door for her.

"I guess my days as chauffeur are already over," he joked as he bowed slightly. After the grinning woman slid in, he threw the leather case into the back seat, then hurried to the other side of the car.

As the couple drove through the city, an awkward silence hung around them as each person waited on the other to start the conversation. Finally, Cat broke the ice.

"Did anything happen while I was gone?"

Irish leaned against the door, looking at her, then tipped back his fedora. "Only the name Fat Louie came out. Have you heard of him?"

"Yeah, that rings a bell, but I can't remember from where. You know who he is?" She glanced at him.

"I'm not sure, but Louie walked out of that bar with George on the day your friend got killed. If I guessed correctly, Louie took him to the partner, and they murdered George that day. Either way, I would find out more about the name when I spoke with Arizona the other day, but he wasn't in a good mood. It seems Bishop La Spina made it clear to the cops that I am not welcome near him or his wife."

Cat's eyes narrowed as she took the corner, coming to a stop behind a line of cars held up in a traffic jam on Waterfront Street. She turned to look at him.

"I don't know who this Arizona is, but it's obvious Greye had her husband talk to his friends in City Hall."

"Arizona Campbell is a detective that I know. He seems like a good egg," Ray explained.

"Yeah, I've heard that last name before, but don't know much about him," Cat replied, tapping her hand on the steering wheel. "Anyway, back to your girlfriend. She must be getting nervous if she went to her husband about you. It's evil how the woman has the bishop wrapped around her finger, but not for long. You won't believe what I found out in Boston."

"I wondered when you would get to that." He gave her a sly grin. "And enough with the girlfriend routine. She's everyone's girlfriend."

Cat's eyes remained dark.

"Well, you can sure pick them. Greye La Spina is nothing more than a two-bit grifter. According to the people I spoke with, she has a history of scams and cons. They told me she worked with a guy named Sydney Green. The two of them traveled along the coast, convincing people they can bring in enormous fortunes to religious charities."

"Somehow, that doesn't surprise me," Ray conceded as he thought about the news. "I take it you think she must have married the bishop to help get her foot in the door with their scam. I wonder what she's after?"

"It's your girlfriend. You tell me." Cat gave him a scornful look.

He returned her look with a glare.

"All right, you win the point. What else did you get on Greye?"

She gave him a wicked smile, putting the car into gear as the line slowly moved. "Something even better. I got her maiden name. It's Pendexter."

Irish sat up at the news.

"Wait, you mean she's related to the dead killer at the Camelot?"

"Yeah, I couldn't find out anything more than that. The reporters I spoke with said Greye used many aliases as she ran with Green before he died. There has to be something there, like a family connection."

Irish whistled at the news. "I wonder how many people know…"

He stopped mid-sentence as several police cars and a white ambulance came into view. He assumed a wreck must have occurred, and then he returned to Catherine's information.

"Well, that blows several holes into my thoughts about Guy Young. He must have known about some of this." He shook his head. "Anyway, I have some news for you. I got word that the gun that killed George was the same as the one used on One-Eye. That means we know Pendexter murdered your friend. I remember the bastard carried the same automatic."

Cat went silent after she nodded at the information. After a moment, she sighed, then spoke. "Well, I'm glad we know who did it. Now, let's make sure that this Fat Louie gets what's coming to him."

"I'm with you, sister. But what's bothering me is the question of the mastermind trying to kill Young?" he asked.

"Does that matter? Shouldn't we focus on Greye?" she asked as she eased the vehicle by one police car which partially blocking a lane. A small army of police and reporters grouped around a black car parked on the edge of the street.

"You forget Dunn pays me for information on Young. Since I can't go near the bishop and his wife, I need to have another way to find out," Ray told her absently as he observed the group of policemen. He knew something big was happening, but one of the uniformed men came toward their slowing vehicle and waved them on. Cat pushed on the gas pedal, and they turned on Cherry Street, heading to downtown.

"Well, I still say we need to follow your girlfriend," Cat insisted. "We can bet she has a connection with the murders. It can't be a coincidence she has the same last name as one killer."

With a sign, Irish nodded.

"All right, we'll risk it," he agreed. "She's the key to getting Guy Young, and I want bitch put away." He smiled to himself. "Arizona didn't say anything about tailing her. Do me a favor, and let's stop by the newsstand. I want to get the latest from Pappy."

~~~

Later that day, J. Allan Dunn paced behind the desk inside the dingy office as he mulled over the information coming from Ray and Cat. His scowling face enhanced the number of wrinkles on his forehead after listening to the past few events.

"You're telling me that the wife of the bishop, one of the most highly regarded men in the city, is involved with a large graft scheme. But you have no evidence to back it up?" He scowled as he questioned the pair. "Is that what I'm paying you for, to find out rumors like that?"

Ray stood from his chair, leaning over the desk.

"Listen, Cat discovered a lot about Greye La Spina, who is the single tie into your racketeer on the boat," he insisted. "We know Greye has some relationship to that hood, Hugh Pendexter, who got killed last week. And I know the damn woman tried to kill me."

"What are you talking about?" J. Allan interrupted.

Irish grimaced.

"Just a slight case of my getting kidnapped by Hugh and his partner, Fat Louie. Mrs. La Spina set it up. But that doesn't matter for the moment, since it just muddies the water. But it means there are high stakes here. This morning, Pappy told us that the sheriff assumed Pendexter got killed by the Young gang in retaliation for the hit against One-Eye Cornell."

"I'll agree. It sounds like the bishop's wife has some evil seed in the family, but I don't see the connection," the director replied as he sat down in the chair. The squeaking noise from the movement filled the room.

"I told you this was a spider web, but we have enough information for the papers to ride Greye La Spina out of town," Ray told him. "And I'll bet your good bishop won't be far behind her if the papers run with it."
~~~

Dunn's eyes narrowed. "What you have are rumors and guesses, so don't go too far with your assumptions. I agree your information could cause some families with problems. But that can't get out. It would cause the mayor a major headache."

He turned to Cat, his voice turning almost fatherly in its tone.

"What else have you got on your trip?"

The young woman pulled a small notepad from her purse. Irish noticed how she acted like the reporters she watched at the *Beacon*.

"Well, I found out that Hugh Pendexter probably killed the clerk who wrote the letter to the *Beacon* about Greye La Spina. There was a holdup, but the reporters who covered the story told me the whole affair seemed rather suspicious. The masked robbers only went to the window where Robertson stood, and they took his cash, then shot him before running out of the bank. Cops picked up Hugh a few days later on another charge. Before the cops could make the case against him, Pendexter posted bond and skipped town." She looked up from her notes. "Nobody could figure out how he came up with the dough."

"Could be his criminal friends helped him out," Dunn reasoned.

Cat shook her head.

"No, I agree with Ray on this. That La Spina woman had something to do with springing the killer in Boston. You didn't see how she reacted when she saw the dead killer at the motel."

Their boss, leaning back in the chair, nearly tipped over at the news.

"Wait a minute; you were at the motel where this guy got killed? How could you be so foolish?" His anger caught Cat off guard.

"I was following Greye, and she drove straight to the motel and walked right into the room," she explained. "When I got there, she was in a panic. I don't think she even saw me when she took off as I helped get Ray out of there."

Cat glanced at Ray.

Dunn shook his head. "I can't believe you did such a thing." He looked at Irish, his eyes flashing hatred when he spoke. "Are you trying to get her killed? Cat is just a kid."

Ray held Dunn's gaze.

"Listen, Cat saved my hide, and you're missing what she's telling you. We have shady people involved in the murder of Cat's friend. We also have some scheme going apparently involves Guy Young. Maybe it affects the Mayor, who you want to protect. I'm going to figure this out using Greye La Spina, who tried to kill me."

The director leaned back in his chair. "Are you telling me or asking?"

"I'm telling you where the evidence leads," Irish stated, refusing to back down.

"Dunn, you need to listen to us," Cat interjected. "Do you want to know what's happening or not? There are several people dead, and we tied most of them back to that woman. I don't think Henry is anything but a victim. But his name carries a lot of weight in this city, including the mayor. You know the mayor will need to keep this tamped down, or he'll get roasted by Townsend. Your job is on the line as well."

After a long silence, the thin man behind the desk slowly leaned back.

"All right, but you let me know if anything starts to come back anywhere near the bishop or anyone else near him. Do you understand that?"

"I understand," Ray agreed. He started for the door as Cat scrambled to her feet. Irish stopped and turned back to the desk.

"One other thing, I need a gun permit."

"I'm not your secretary." Dunn's scowl returned.

"Yeah, but you can get things done when you want," Irish responded. "Your city has some dark roads which get uglier each time we take another step. The other night, I had two toughs trying to take me for a ride. I don't know who their boss is, but I'm pretty sure it wasn't Guy Young's people. That means I'm stepping on someone's toes. Anyway, the cops will ask why I need a gun in this fair city. I don't think you want me to try that route."

The sarcasm was clear in Ray's voice.

"You said you went to that bar for information." Dunn grew interested. "That's one of Mark Fordham's places. I don't know what you did, but it must have got his attention."

"Well, you can see why a gat comes into the picture," Ray replied.

"No promises, but I'll see what I can do," Dunn reluctantly told him. "Fordham's getting pretty outspoken about how he's going to change this city. There are some rumors about police looking the other way at things going on down along the docks, which will protect him. I think the mayor is getting nervous."

"He's not the only one," Ray told him as he opened the door, then stepped outside.

~~~

The sunlight quickly drifted into the night under the dull sky as Cat pulled into her regular parking spot beside her apartment building. She shut off the motor and waited for a moment while her partner seemed lost in thought.

"Why don't you come up for dinner?" she broke the silence.
~~~

"You must have heard my stomach." His jest was halfhearted, but he got out of the car. Irish remained quiet as he followed her inside the building. She didn't like his silence. It reminded her of the calm before the storm with his temper. She unlocked the door and entered.

"Why the silent treatment?" she asked, while taking off her coat. Ray's rugged face went blank for a moment.

"Sorry, I was thinking about my time since I woke up in this city." He walked to the couch, still wearing his trench coat, as he sat down. He watched her hang her coat and hat on the arms of a hat tree. When Cat turned around, she noticed how weary Ray looked.

"And what have you decided?" She sat next to him.

"Why do you stay here?" He leaned back.

Cat paused at the surprising question. Her face took on a bit of a pout as she considered it. Finally, she answered.

"I'm not sure, to be honest. I've lived here most of my life, so it's familiar to me. Why do you ask?"

Ray let out a deep breath.

"I don't know. Something is gnawing at me. When I first got here, I did some reading at the library about the city with all the violence and strange things that happen here. At first, I couldn't believe it, but now everything seems to fit with this damn town." He looked at her with a tired smile. "I guess I'm just trying to put things into place. It seems to be bigger than just a few hoodlums. Then again, maybe I'm just adding pieces that shouldn't be there."

Cat rose from the couch.

"You must be hungry; I'll get dinner started," she told him quickly. In the kitchen, she pulled out a pan, the clanging noise filling the apartment. "You can fix us some drinks if you want one. The bottle's still on the table."

Irish liked the idea and took off his coat before he walked to the small dining area to retrieve the nearly empty bottle of whiskey. He watched the woman pulling meat wrapped in butcher paper from the refrigerator. Despite his empty stomach, Ray's eyes followed her body's curves, accented by her white and blue dress. Ray squeezed past her along the narrow aisle between the cabinets and the stove to get the glasses.

"I hope you like steak," she moved over when he passed.

"Anything you make will be great," he told her as he poured the drinks.

She laughed.

"You've never tasted my cooking."

"I'll risk it," Ray amicably replied as he handed her the glass. She took the tumbler, and they lofted their drinks in a silent toast. He slid past her again, enjoying the scent of her perfume. He went to sit at the dining table.

"To answer your earlier question, I have always wondered if this city has a curse," Cat told him. "I heard about all the horrible history growing up, which is fascinating in a strange way. But the war started, and I was just out of high school when my mother died. I needed work, so when the job at the *Beacon* came up, I jumped at it. I guess I never decided to leave Oyster City."

"I guess I can understand that," Irish told her after a sip of his drink. "I've been drifting from place to place for a while now. When I woke in this city, well, it was just a distinct feeling. I mean, every city has something you immediately notice about its atmosphere. It's kind of hard to describe."

He paused as he tried to form the right words.

"Let me put it this way. This city was the first spot where you can feel everything pressing down on you, kind of cloudy all the time," he finally declared. "It's almost like the feeling you get when a shell lands close but doesn't explode. You wait and wait, just hoping it doesn't kill you."

Cat remained quiet, seemingly focused on the meal as she went back and forth between the cabinets and the refrigerator. After an untenable silence, she finally spoke.

"I'm worried about Henry La Spina. We need to get him away from his wife."

Irish didn't look up from staring at his glass.

"I don't think he'll be so willing to walk away. He knows something about her; nobody's that blind. I'm more interested in his daggers."

"You can't believe the bishop would have something to do with those murders." She turned down the flame of one burner.

"Why are you so sure? If I remember my scriptures correctly, he's a man, which means he can sin just like anybody else." Ray leaned back in the comfortable chair. "How do you know him?"

"That's a long story," she said, walking out of the kitchen. "Let's just say the man would be a saint if I had a vote in the matter."

As they ate, Cat opened up about some of her past to Irish. She explained how the bishop, at the time just a simple pastor, provided support to her mother, who kept finding drunken losers who often beat Cat's mom. Even though Cat was born of out wedlock, Henry La Spina always treated her family with respect. By the time they finished dinner, Ray knew much more about Catherine Bennett. The man congratulated himself on one part of his initial assessment of her; the lady was a tough spitfire. She was growing on him.

"Why the grin?" Cat asked him.

"Oh, I don't know. Just enjoying the conversation, I guess. By the way, you're not a half-bad cook. I'm getting the real husband's treatment tonight." His grin turned into a smile.

Her bright eyes faded at his comment, and a decidedly icy chill fell across the room. "Well, don't get used to it, partner. There's a lot of work to do, and I can't have you over here all the time. Now, what can we do about the bishop?"

Ray's smile dropped.

"Yeah, well, I can see your loyalty to him, but I'm not sure what we can do. Even if we tell him about what we know, what will happen? Nothing! He can't afford the scandal of it." His demeanor grew hard. "That reminds me, I just remembered where I saw that dagger before, the one on the floor in the motel where Pendexter died."

"What, you mean that fancy knife with the blood on it?" She shivered involuntarily. "I don't want to think about it."

He leaned forward.

"Yeah, there are several of those daggers on display in the bishop's house. I got a glance at them on the wall behind his desk. At least, they looked similar."

Cat's eyes grew wide. "Do you think there's a link?"

"I can't imagine there are many people collecting those things," Ray said as he latched onto the idea.

"Probably part of something that woman's involved with," she told him.

"Her reaction to her brother getting killed makes me doubt that," he replied. "You saw it yourself; Greye didn't know Pendexter was dead. If those weapons match, it changes my ideas. Those daggers look expensive, so maybe they are part of the bitch's scheme. It would do my soul good to know she's spending time behind bars if the weapons were part of their graft scheme. It all seems to come back to your idea about becoming her shadow."

Cat thought about it and finally agreed.

"I'll drop by your hotel early in the morning and pick you up. I don't believe that it will do much good to wait there overnight. Mayor Hopley's banquet at his home will go late. All the big shots in the city are there."

Ray rose from his chair, walking to the couch for his hat and coat. "Yeah, I agree. Let's start at sunrise. Since you're the one with the car, I don't have any choice in this." He put on the coat and went to the door. "Thanks for the meal." He didn't bother to look back as he closed the door behind him.

Cat watched the door for a long time, half expecting him to return and somewhat hoping he might. When it was clear Ray would not return, she cleared the table while berating herself for her reaction. She knew her frosty response to his joke about a husband sent their enjoyable evening into a tailspin. But that was all right; the woman reminded herself. No matter how awkward, she would not allow a man to break through to control her life. Cat learned from her mother about love and the perils of trusting a man to do the right thing. Catherine Bennett would be the one who decided her future, not a drunken drifter.

~~~

"My dear, I'm sorry I can't attend the reception this evening. I know it's most inconvenient, but I can't let my friend down." Greye strolled seductively in her tight-fitting dress to the desk of her husband. Henry always liked the way his wife looked in green. She came around the desk, leaning down to kiss his cheek while he remained passive.

"Are you sure? I know you've been upset for some reason," he said, his dark eyes turning sympathetic.
~~~

"Yes, I'll be all right," she promised, patting him lightly on the shoulder. "It's just a difficult time for me with all of the events going on and such." Greye had difficulty trying not to tear up.

"Which friend are you taking care of this time?" His tone remained even, almost distracted.

"Why, Mary Bird, of course!" She feigned astonishment, then explained. "I told you this morning at breakfast. You know she's been in such a state since her daughter ran away with that terrible man. She still doesn't understand why the police claim her daughter is missing."

Henry nodded.

"Of course, I'm sure it's a challenging time for her. You know I could skip this event the mayor is holding. I really should come along since I'm the bishop," he stated, knowing her reply.

"No, my dear, you have more important matters to attend. I'll pop by and make sure Mary is doing well. Hopefully, I'll be home early, but you know how she can be." Greye gave the man another peck on the cheek. "I'll be home as soon as I can."

The bishop watched her stroll across the room, and a grim look fell across his face. "I'm sure you will. Give my condolences to Mary."

Greye's car reached a parking area by the docks about an hour later. She stopped by Mary Bird's home on the way to the pier to make a quick courtesy call to the distraught woman who would probably not even remember Greye showing up. Mrs. La Spina knew Mary would turn into an incoherent lush within an hour after dinner, drowning her sorrow with sedatives and alcohol. Greye's expression turned rigid as she considered Mrs. Bird's reaction to her daughter running away. She disliked weak people.

Greye, in green, stepped from her car, suddenly finding a large man standing next to her. He wore a black, wool trench coat, and his face remained partially hidden by the shadows of his wide brim Fedora. He took her by the arm, his grip painfully tight.

"What are you doing?" She futilely tried to pull away.

The giant goon looked down at her. "Come on; the boss is waiting."

Greye was about to complain when Tweedledum stepped next to her.

"Lady, just keep your mouth shut, and you won't get hurt. Come on!" A second thug led the trio to a car that came to a stop next to them. The men pushed her inside.

While the large Cadillac drove away, Greye sat between the two silent men. The unusual and sinister way the thugs treated her filled Greye with growing apprehension. A few minutes later, the car turned into an alley, where they got out and entered the back of an unfamiliar building. Her escorts remained quiet, taking her past an open door. Fear gripped her as Greye walked with her guards to an office inside the narrow confines of a long hallway. The room was empty, and the goon pointed her to a single chair in front of a worn-out desk. Visibly nervous at the unexpected treatment, she quietly sat on the edge of the chair while her escort took a position by the door. She fumbled with her purse, looking inside before she clipped it shut.

A few minutes later, her host arrived. Guy Young watched her reactions as he whispered something to his henchmen before he approached. His lips were a cruel, thin line, nearly a smirk. His eyes were cold and dark.

"My dear Mrs. La Spina, you've been keeping important information from me."

She gave him a puzzled look, trying to force a smile.

"I'm not sure I understand."

He sat next to her.

"Oh, you're quite the grifter. It appears you've been running this scam on your husband and me. And you try to act like you don't know. I'll tell you what; I'll help your memory by bringing in a friend of yours."

Young waved to his bodyguard, who opened the door.

A rotund man in a black suit burst through the entrance, falling to the floor face-first. At first, Greye believed the man was dead. The large thug who came into the room stepped close and rolled the figure in the black suit over on his back. The beaten man looked up at her through a massively swollen and bruised head. Greye recognized him through the dried blood and sweat.

"My contacts finally found one man who tried to knock me off. You can see how upset that makes me. At first, I thought about a nice and slow death, but Fat Louie talked. It was an interesting conversation, as you probably realize by now. You see, this worthless piece of trash tells me your brother helped to kill my friend. Worse, he claims you knew about it before the hit happened."

The racketeer placed his chilly hand on her shoulder. He smiled at the shiver he felt running through her flesh.

"But it's your lucky night, baby. Louie traded all he had for his life. He told me all about the scam you've been running. Now, let's talk about those bearer bonds you have stashed away. Then, maybe you can convince me why you shouldn't be floating in the bay as fish food."

~~~

As Irish walked along the dark street a block away from Cat's apartment, he had the nagging suspicion someone was
~~~

following him. The street lamp's yellow glow made it difficult to see far on the empty sidewalk. He kept a steady pace, his ears trying to decipher every sound reaching him. Passing along a row of dark townhomes, he heard the rhythmic sound of leather footsteps striking concrete behind him. The noise picked up speed as his tail tried to close in.

Ray reached the corner at 8th and turned left, his glance behind revealing just a shadow of a movement about half a block away. The shamus continued along before he took across the quiet street, heading into an alleyway behind several buildings where he entered. Despite his racing heart, Irish tried to appear casual while walking into the alley, and worked through his limited options. Still unarmed, he decided the dark shadows would be his best defense for the moment.

There was a single light shining above the first building's back door, which Irish quickly passed. Ray slowed his pace, picking his way through the maze of containers and old equipment that dotted the confined area between buildings. The troubleshooter paused for a moment, and then Irish heard the footsteps coming into the alley, confirming his fear. Deciding the end of the lane was too far away, Ray quietly eased his body along the brick wall. He quietly followed along until he reached the closed door, where the darkest shadow swallowed his image.

The footsteps following him slowed, and Irish saw the person following him. A guy in a leather jacket and wearing a longshoreman's cap passed underneath the backdoor light before coming to a stop. Ray's follower walked a few steps into the gloom by the next building.

"Come on out, shamus, I know you're in here. I've got a message for you."

Ray remained covered inside the shadowed doorway.

"Then give it," he replied before sliding along the wall until he pulled behind the concrete steps leading to the door.

"You're not very sociable." The figure walked toward the sound of Ray's voice. There was the indistinct sound of a flashlight click, and a light beam focused toward the shadowed doorway.

Crouching down, Ray saw the faint outline of a trash bin just a few steps away, and he quietly moved to a position behind the container. He felt around the ground, looking for anything to defend himself, and all he found was a tin can.

The flashlight beam slowly scanned the area around the back door where Irish was hiding just seconds before. He could hear footsteps growing closer and giving a hollow whistle.

"Why are you hiding? I thought you carried a gun. Maybe I should tell you what I plan on doing to your little girlfriend. Yeah, I've been watching that dish." The stranger's mocking voice echoed slightly in the alley.

As the beam of light grew stronger, coming closer to his position, Ray heard a soft metal click. The flashlight beam moved toward a new sound from across the alley, and Ray took a glance at his opponent. The silver gleam of a long switchblade caught his eye.

Nearly upon the large container where Irish hid, the hoodlum in the leather coat edged carefully around the side. Fortunately, the light allowed Ray to see his hand still holding the can. Just as Irish felt his attacker getting close to the back of the steel trashcan, he flicked the tin can to the other side of the container. As the beam of light swept away to the sound source, Irish sprang up from his position. The sweeping blow from his fist glanced across his opponent's face. But the punch wasn't enough, and the goon whipped around. Ray instantly felt a sharp pain in his upper arm. Still, he struck his attacker with another blow, this time punching the man's head. Irish grabbed the forearm of his opponent's knife hand, holding off the deadly weapon while pressing hard into his opponent's flesh.

A strike from the flashlight came across Ray's forehead. The blow caused him to release his attacker's arm, but Ray pressed his weight advantage to get to his attacker's side. He pushed the thug into the wall a few steps away.

Just as the two men struck the wall, Irish felt a hot, burning pain slice across his ribs. Grabbing his opponent's hair, Irish pulled back as hard as he could, hearing the man yell in agony. Ray twisted his body around, locking his arm around his opponent's neck. With his attacker's head enclosed in the crook of his arm, he darted toward the trash container.

With the goon in tow, Irish slammed his opponent into the steel wall. He heard a sickening crunch under his arm. Ray grabbed the edge of the crate, trying to remain upright. While feeling his chest, his hand came across the sticky blood from his wound. Lightheaded dizziness washed over him as he tried to walk, only to grasp the edge of the trash bin again. Seconds later, he slid down to the ground next to his dead assailant.

~~~

Cat heard a banging noise at her apartment door just as she was getting ready for bed. Silently, she opened the table drawer by her bed, retrieving a revolver and double-checking her already locked windows. Cat slipped into the living room, easing to the front entrance of her apartment. There was another bump appearing to come from the lower part of the wooden door. She crept to the door, cautiously placing her ear close. Another hammer blow against the wood caused her to jump back. After a long moment, curiosity got the best of her. Keeping her gun pointed at the door, she turned the handle.
~~~

Unexpectedly, the door pushed open, and the upper body of a man fell into the room. The woman backed away in fright, nervously pointing the gun at the man. Finally, she drew closer and looked closer at the man illuminated by the pale light streaming in from the hallway. It was Ray Irish.

~~~

The sound of voices invaded the strange dreams of Ray as he woke. Immediately, Irish noticed a dull pain in his shoulder and ribcage with each breath he took. He opened his eyes and focused on two people sitting at a dining room table. Arizona and Cat were chatting amicably, each holding a cup of coffee.

"Who let the cop in?" Irish growled at the pair, and they turned to look at him. As he got his bearings, Ray realized he was lying on Cat's couch in her apartment. He remembered her helping him to the stuffed chair after he fell into the apartment. Irish also recalled her quick thinking to help stop his bleeding. His shirt was missing, and he was lying on a towel. Ray tried to sit up, but a wave of pain shot through his shoulder and ribcage.

"Lay still, Irish. Doc says you'll survive," the lieutenant replied airily before turning serious. "We need to talk."

Irish didn't like the expression on Arizona's face.

"Yeah, I guessed as much. I remember most of it until I got here." Ray let out a sigh. "Did you find the guy who attacked me?"

Arizona nodded as he pulled out a notebook from his coat pocket. "Right where you said he was. You did a hell of a job on his face. Is he the one that cut you up?"

"Damn, I would have thought that's obvious." Ray glared at him.
~~~

"If I hadn't found that knife in the dead man's hands, you might be lying in a medical cell with charges on you. Arizona raised an eyebrow. I could have considered it manslaughter. You get it?"

Ray grimaced as he tried to sit up again, then gave up the idea. "Yeah, I understand." He paused to collect his thoughts. "Here's the condensed version. I'm walking to my hotel when I discover someone following me. I try to lose him by ducking into the alley, but he tries to hunt me with that flashlight and knife you found. A fight breaks out, and he loses."

The policeman scribbled on his notepad, then looked up at the shamus. "Is that it?"

"Well, other than bleeding all over the street as I walked a couple of blocks back here, I don't have much after that. I recall talking with Cat for a bit. Also, somebody in a dark coat kept poking me, but a lot of that is a blur," he said as he shook his head.

"You were pretty out of it," Cat spoke up. "You kept telling me not to take you to the hospital. Just find a doctor. I called a physician I know and convinced him to come over. He stitched you up and left here not too long ago. He said you needed a transfusion at the clinic since you lost a lot of blood."

"Why would you ask her to keep from the hospital?" Arizona acted indifferent when he asked, but Irish wasn't buying the sham.

"Maybe because I'm an outsider who doesn't trust anyone," Ray told him directly. "Ever since I arrived in this city, only a few people have proven they aren't on the take of somebody else."

He waited for a response, but Arizona just nodded.

"Or maybe I was out of my head from blood loss," the injured man gave a half-laugh.

Arizona's face screwed up with a wry grin.

"That's more official and makes sense to me. Your story matches what my men found, so it's self-defense," he told Ray. "I doubt the District Attorney will bother you about it. But might use it to keep you away from the bishop's wife. You'll need to come down to the station to fill out an official statement."

"You mind if I give it a day or two?" Irish asked, feeling his eyelids getting heavy.

"Sure, I've got enough things on my desk. I don't need more work just because you knocked off some low life." Arizona turned serious again.

"Did you know the guy?"

"Never saw him before, but he must have been watching this building for a dupe like me to rob," Ray shook his head as he recalled what the assailant told him about Cat.

Irish looked at her as she silently walked around the apartment. She stopped to re-arrange the various knickknacks on a shelf.

"Well, that fits what we know. The guy you killed was an ex-con by the name of Woolrich, who got to Oyster City about a month or so back. Hung around a place called Anthony's," the lieutenant told them.

He didn't notice the reaction from Cat, who stopped in her tracks. Irish saw the look on her face, and he wanted to ask more, but he felt his mind drifting.

"Either you police are a damn efficient lot, or you had something on him already." Ray closed his eyes, trying to fight off a wave of nausea.

"Yeah, we're efficient in keeping tabs on ex-cons who hang out at that place. This guy was a thief and maybe a rapist, but never proved," Arizona told him, noticing something unspoken in the long glance from Ray to Cat. He disregarded his curiosity. "Anyway, I have to get going. I have bigger things to work on."

"Are you working on the death of that policeman?" Cat asked.

The detective nodded as he put his notebook into his jacket.

"Do you know who killed Detective Howard?" Her question caught the cop's interest.

"Not yet, but why are you interested?" Arizona focused on how she clasped her hands.

"I thought there was something familiar about the car when we drove past the spot where all of the police were. I saw Howard about the murder of George Hopley, who was a friend of mine," Cat replied, fighting to keep her dislike of the dead cop from showing.

"Yeah, I know all about that from your friend on the couch. The good news is we solved Hopley's case." Arizona stared at her carefully.

"What do you mean, solved?" Ray asked sleepily.

Arizona glanced over.

"Just like I said. You remember when I told you about that stiff that they found at the Camelot Motel? His gun matched up with bullets found in Hopley and Cornell."

"Not to tell you about your business, but you have the second guy who pumped slugs into Cornell. He's still running around," Irish reminded him.

Campbell scowled at him. "Yeah, shamus, we got that figured out. The partner killed Pendexter and left. The sheriff has witnesses saying there was an argument early in the morning. He probably took the money for the hit. I guess he didn't want to share."

"Do you have a name on the partner?" Cat asked.

"I doubt we'll get anything else." Arizona shook his head. "Out of our jurisdiction, anyway, it's just one crook killing another."

"Well, I've got a name for you. Fat Louie seems to match the description of the guy I saw shooting One-Eye. Cat and I found out that Louie left *Anthony's* with George Hopley. It happened on the day they killed the reporter. You might want to check if he's still hanging around," Ray told the policemen as Arizona turned to leave.

"Wait a minute," the detective growled. "Are you still working on this case?"

"Not anymore," Irish told him. "I can't say I'm sorry about that either. Remember, you just said it's closed. Word will get back to Guy Young. That will square it with him and me in my books."

"All right, but I wouldn't bet on it. Young isn't the type to let his marks payoff. Anyway, I'll let my guys know to keep an eye out for Louie. In the meantime, you call me if you hear anything related to Howard's murder. Trouble seems to follow you around."

"Yeah, you'll be my first call. I'm sorry a policeman got killed. What happened?"

"That's under wraps right now, but it was a damn bad way to go. Life of a cop, I guess," Arizona told him. He turned to Cat, who walked to the door. "Young lady, you need some sleep. I'll see you later."

Arizona tipped his derby cap as he walked past Cat. She closed the door after him and remained for a moment before turning away. The woman saw Irish struggling to rise from his resting place again.

"Where do you think you're going?" she demanded as he raced to the couch.

Straining, Ray nearly got to a sitting position.

"I've been too much of a burden on you already, so I'll go to my hotel room."

"Like hell you will," Cat flared at him, forcing him back down. "Doc told me you needed to rest, and you will do exactly that. Quit trying to be a hero. Now, lay back before I get angry!"

He stopped his effort and gave her a tired grin as he closed his eyes.

"All right, you win. Come sit down. You look about out on your feet."

Cat nodded and took a seat in the chair across from him. She stared at him for a moment. Ray felt her stare, but he kept his eyes closed.

"I guess I owe you twice now," Irish said quietly. "I'm sorry I turned up on your doorstep."

Cat leaned back in her chair.

"You are darn right you owe me." There was nothing spiteful in her voice, just a tired jest.

"I don't like how this whole thing is turning," she confessed. "I saw your expression when you spoke about the ex-con who attacked you. You think he was the one who broke into my apartment? Maybe I should thank you."

"No need. The ass told me he was planning on coming back for you after he took me out." Ray started feeling his body drifting again. "It got me mad."

She looked at him on her sofa. His long frame filled the cushions, and his feet dangled off the arm of the chair. "Get some rest. Doc told me you lost quite a bit of blood. He says those stitches will have to come out in a few days."

Irish wasn't listening.

"You know, whoever hired Woolrich to keep an eye on you might send another? That con didn't work for free. Any ideas about who the money man might be?" He couldn't turn off the questions.

Cat nodded.

"Yeah, I have an idea, but we'll talk about it later. Just get some rest, Ray."

~~~

Greye La Spina walked into her luxurious home late that Saturday morning, about the time Arizona was leaving Cat's apartment. She did not acknowledge the butler, who passed by her as she hastened through the lobby and into the dining room. Greye went directly to the small alcove behind a vertical bar. The first tumbler she took from the overhead cabinet spilled from her hand, shattering loudly on the floor. She did not look at the glass fragments all around her feet. Instead, the red-eyed woman grabbed another glass and rapidly filled it with the first bottle she found under the counter. Greye's face screwed up at the bitter taste of gin, but she finished the glass. Then she forced another drink down before she stepped around the bar to a stool on the other side. She did not hear the grating noise of the glass that she ground into the wood floor with her shoes.

Her mind remained on the last terrible hours of watching Young order his men to kill Louie in front of her. Greye stared at the mirror across from her, but all she could see was the open mouth and eyes of her partner as he gasped his last breath. He was the last of the group of ex-cons brought in by Quincannon. Now she was alone. But at least she was alive, for the moment. Greye was still shaking as she slugged down the drink, feeling the effects of the alcohol on her empty stomach. She hoped it would dull the searing memories.
~~~

Greye believed herself to be as hard as the next grifter, male or female, who came out of Boston's North End tenements. However, she was not an executioner, a butcher who enjoyed the slow killing of another person. That was what she witnessed as a human devil called Guy Young had Louie tortured to death. He forced her to hear each scream and endure the suffering of her partner, even after she told the racketeer everything concerning the scam on the church trust. The devil gave her the show to reinforce his obvious message.

"Lady, your ass and soul belong to me," Guy's voice etched into her brain. "You give me the bonds, and you live; it's as simple as that."

Visibly shaking, Mrs. La Spina reached across the bar, pulling the bottle over to refill her glass. Her future lay shattered like the glass on the floor. Her sudden laugh caught her by surprise. She could still hear Quincannon's voice when he gathered their small group to outline the scam. He told her and the others how easy it would be in this Podunk city.

The bishop and the church funds that Henry controlled would be easy pickings. Greye would use her feminine charms just like all the other times, and her husband would never be the wiser until they left town. All of them would roll in cabbage, laughing at the suckers holding the bag when they left the state.

The first feelings of lightheaded dizziness crowded into her thoughts. On Monday, when the bonds went to Young, Greye no longer carried a death sentence. The distraught woman in the mirror chuckled at the idea. Her reflection returned a grim smile, her mind telling her to be honest. She would still die a slow, painful death.

"Don't worry; your husband will forgive you since that's his business. You just do as I tell you, and he can keep that bright cathedral. And you will continue to play his loving wife. I believe your husband will cooperate with me as his new business partner. Otherwise, it'll be jail time for you and, probably, for him as well."

Young unbuttoned her dress while she watched his men drag away the body of her dead associate. Guy explained how her new world was before forcing her to lie back on the top of the filthy desk.

"Of course, I don't hold grudges. In fact, your scam has given me even more ideas. But I'll keep some of those bonds as evidence against your husband. I don't want you forgetting who is running the show."

The smile of the devil filled his face as he savagely ripped off her panties. He pushed into her without remorse. As he continued to rape her, Young told her his plans.

"Mark Fordham is going to be the next mayor. Since I have an agreement with the new mayor, I'll soon control the foundation and other such lucrative enterprises. Once we control the DA and the coppers, my legal businesses will hide the illegal stuff. I owe it all to you. Who knows what things I'll dream up for you?"

The cruel man's words echoed in her mind while Greye staggered up the stairs. There was no way to escape; Young told her that.

Near the top of the stairs, the bishop's wife looked over the railing, debating for a moment about letting herself fall over. She shook her head, knowing she was too much of a coward for suicide. Greye noticed the concerned expression on her maid's face, who stood nearby. Suddenly, maniacal laughter exploded from her as she wobbled over to the full double doors leading into her bedroom. When Greye closed the doors, the sound suddenly stopped. Mrs. La Spina walked several feet, falling on top of her bed, while silently crying.

~~~

Monday morning, the sunlight crept into the room just as a heavy knocking came from the hotel door. Irish was still painfully sore, but managed to get out of bed and slide on his pants while the next round of heavy blows hammered his door. J. Allan Dunn stood at the entrance, then stepped past the surprised shamus.

"There's no other way to put this, Ray, but you're through with all of this. I want you out of town by the end of the day." The thin man fidgeted with the brim of his hat, glancing up at Irish.

"Who the hell do you think you are?" His hand still on the half-closed door, Ray's temper flashed. "You're not big enough to make me do anything. If you want to quit paying for me to do your dirty work, that's fine; we'll call it quits. But don't you threaten me."

Dunn gave Irish a long, icy stare.

"I told you there are no other options," he said. "I've got folks screaming about you already. Then Cat tells me about the guy hanging out around her apartment who tried to kill you. They might have killed her. You've got to go."

"Dunn, there's something you are not telling me about Cat, Ray scowled at him. "Remember, I'm the one who's taken the hits, but this is the second time you mentioned the threat to her. She's not your responsibility."

He looked down at his hat again.

"She's a kid; you get paid for taking the risk."

Irish knew something else was there.

"Cat told me you helped her family out since she was a child. Most people aren't so generous with strangers."
~~~

The edgy look from Dunn was telling.

"It's none of your business. Now, are you leaving?"

Irish shook his head.

"You can go to hell. I told you I want that grifting bishop's wife in prison or dead. I've been around you enough to know you didn't make the call. Someone must be telling you to do this. Who is it?"

"I don't know what you're talking about," Dunn told him. "Now you get out of this city."

Irish placed his palm in the middle of Dunn's chest, stopping him in his tracks.

"Listen, you damn grafter," he stated, trying to ignore the pain from his injured chest. "I've had enough. You're the one who wanted to know what was happening in this damn place. Now somebody's running scared because I've found out more than you and your boss bargained for."

"Get your hand off me; you're fired," J. Allan told him. "That means stay away from Cat."

"All right, bub, we'll play it your way. But remember, I'll leave when I decide to." Irish opened the door wide for his ex-boss to leave. When he closed it, Ray stuck his hand in his pocket and retrieved a small roll of bills. A glance told him he would be looking for another place to stay by the end of the day.

About an hour later, Irish stood in the Hotel Alexander's lobby, reading the *Beacon* with a small case at his side. All of his worldly possessions, comprising two new suits and some underwear, were inside the case.

At least, it's more than I had when I arrived in Oyster City, Ray thought.

He leaned against one column, scanning through the want ads while he looked for a place he could afford. The pickings were sparse. But he was thankful since his injured ribs and shoulder were still pretty sore, so he would not be doing much walking.

"Are you heading somewhere, sailor?" Cat stepped next to him, looking down at his case.

He did not look up from his paper.

"Yeah, I'm trying to find someplace that won't bankrupt me before a week's out. Your buddy Dunn came by to fire me."

Cat went silent for a moment at the news.

"Damn, I shouldn't have told him about the bastard who broke into my apartment."

Ray glanced at her, debating on how much she realized J. Allan was shielding her.

"It was an excuse on top of a few other items," he told her. "He made it clear I was to leave town."

"What did you tell him?" She tried to remain indifferent.

"I believe, go to hell was the main point of the conversation." He gave a brief grin as he turned the page. "But it might not take long before I'm hanging out at the mission from what I see in this rag you work for."

"What about your case? Are you going to let Greye La Spina get away with what's she done?" Cat's voice was even, but Ray sensed her resolve to clear the bishop.

Ray folded the paper, turning to her.

"I have no case. We both know that I'm not a private detective, just a drifter who lived on some dirty cash for a while. I plan on getting her, but not the way we discussed. Those plans are gone. I've got to find a regular job somewhere and bide my time until she slips up. Maybe I can monitor her when I'm not working."

She suddenly hooked her arm with his, causing him to wince.

"No, we're not waiting for something that might not happen. Grab your suitcase, mister," she told him. "We've got to get over to keep an eye on La Spina's house."

As Cat drove, Ray kept looking at the black, feathered hat in the shape of a bird that she wore. While it matched her white and black polka dot blouse and black trousers, it was hardly undercover. He just smiled as she updated him on her latest news. Somehow Cat convinced one reporter, a guy name Berkley, to stake out the bishop's house over the weekend. Apparently, Greye La Spina arrived home on Saturday and had not left the house, even on Sunday morning. It forced the bishop to attend his church services alone. The reporter told her how upset the cleric appeared when Henry La Spina left the house.

"What do you owe this guy for the favor?" Ray asked as he held onto the door handle when her car took a turn. His tender ribs hurt at the effort to keep from sliding on the bench seat. He wondered if Cat secretly wanted to drive a race car.

"Oh, nothing much, just a dinner," she replied, with her attention focused on beating another car to an intersection. "Men like to do favors for me. By the way, I thought of something, so I think I'll do a favor for you."

"Let's start by not getting me killed," he told her as she sped away from a stop sign.

"Oh, you're a funny man," she frowned. "Do you want my idea or not?"

"Sure, let's hear it."

"You've still got a private investigator license. Dunn won't pull that away from you; too much trouble to bother. You just open your own business. I can see it now, Ray Irish Agency," she glanced over with a self-satisfied smile.

"Yeah, I can see it now, clients lining up by my cot inside the mission to discuss their problems." His grumpy sarcasm did not change her enthusiasm.

"I got that covered as well. What if I told you there's a Mrs. Purvey? I know who has a place that might work for you? It's on the second floor of a building on Broadway across from the *Beacon*."

Her excitement got under Ray's skin.

"Why are you so damn sure I want to stay in this place?" he asked. "Maybe I want to hightail it out of here and let the place rot to the ground?"

"Listen, Ray. I know you better than you realize," she said. "You're not going anywhere because you're stubborn as a mule. You're still on the case, but just not getting paid for the moment. Now, quit you're beefing and get with the program."

"All right, I'm with you. Just get us there alive." Irish decided Cat sounded a lot like one of his drill instructors in boot camp.

As the couple sat in Cat's car three houses down from the La Spina's, Irish focused on a dark gray Studebaker. Parked at the alley entrance across the street from the bishop's house, Ray watched the man who sat on the driver's side. The cigarette smoke exiting from the car window showed them that the stranger had no intention of leaving soon.

"We have someone else very interested in the bishop's house," Ray pointed out. "You know him?"

"No, and he doesn't look friendly," Cat squinted in the early morning sun. "What do you think is going on?"

Ray grimaced as he slid down low in the seat, trying to keep his large bulk out of sight.

"Maybe Greye's past is catching up with her. We'll just have to watch and find out. As long as the guy doesn't have a heater, we will be all right. Otherwise..." He let the thought drift.

"Are you going to be all right? You're still not healed." Cat slumped down in the seat, but she didn't remove her hat. With a smile, Irish told her he would be fine. Then he reminded her that the stranger in the car might notice a blackbird bouncing around in the driver's seat. Cat glared at him but finally removed the offending article

"Well, smart mouth, if you open my glove compartment, you'll find we're not defenseless," she told Ray, who popped open the small door in front of him. Inside, he discovered a .38 snub-nosed revolver and a box of cartridges. He flicked open the cylinder; it revealed she had loaded the weapon.

"That's a smart move; let's hope we don't need it," he told her.

"Well, your little scene in the alley the other night got me to thinking about the dangers. I drove out to a small town south of here and picked it up. Call it a present. It beats a knife." She watched him handle the weapon nonchalantly.

"Thanks, now I'm illegal as hell if I use it." Ray grimly smiled as he stuffed the items into his suit pockets. "But it makes the odds better."

"You know, I would like to see the bishop's knife collection again," he said out of nowhere.

"You keep talking about that. Why?" Cat asked as she stopped chewing on a fingernail.

"Something keeps bothering me about those guys getting their throats cut. It doesn't fit. It seems to me that a guy who helped kill Cornell using a gun would do the same with his partner. And, even weirder, why was Quincannon sitting in the parking lot at the same tavern where I met Greye? Even if he's following her, who killed him and why?"

While staring at the other car down the street, the shamus didn't see his partner's reaction to the news.

"What are you talking about?"

Ray quickly told her about the night he found Quincannon's body in the Six Jolly Squires tavern where Greye left him. He could see she grew upset, but he wasn't sure why.

"Why didn't you go to the police?" she asked.

"And tell them what? She would have left me hanging, and her husband would have protected her. Anyway, that's beside the point right now. My question is whether someone used one of those daggers on the wall in those killings." He stared at the stately manor house.

"I can't understand why you remain interested. What is it with you?" Cat shook her head in disbelief. "You like unraveling puzzles or something?"

Irish smiled at her.

"I hate puzzles; used to drive me nuts as a kid. I do like logical thinking, and we have two murders that don't fit the bill. First, the chauffeur was a big and strong guy who was in prison. You would think he would know how to defend himself. Someone nearly decapitated the guy, according to Howard. From the quick view of the murder scene I got, someone must have slipped up behind him. Second, you have a hoodlum who carries a gun, and somehow, he gets killed by a partner who is using a knife. I don't buy it. You and I both saw the dagger on the floor. A professional doesn't leave evidence like that. But Arizona told me they didn't find the weapon. How did the knife disappear, and why was it dropped?"

She was silent for a moment.

"All right, they're not logical. What does it mean?"

"I'm not sure, but it says someone went back for the dagger after we left the room. Someone wanted the weapon to remain hidden," he concluded. "The fact that both men get killed the same way makes me think they're linked."

Cat looked at the house. "One dagger used to kill Quincannon and Pendexter; then the evidence could be on the wall. But they would be clean by now."

"Exactly," he told her. "But you see why that display bothers me. Hopefully, we can find out from Greye when she decides to leave her house. Otherwise, we check with the servants. They would notice something missing."

Cat nodded, frowning at the implications.

It was close to ten in the morning when Greye La Spina exited her home. Dressed in a pair of slacks and a white top, she looked almost drab as she took the back steps to the garage. Sliding into the roadster, Greye tied a red scarf around her head to hide the undone hair, and she put on a pair of dark sunglasses to obscure the puffy, red eyes. Pulling out of the drive, the woman did not even look as she shot into the street.

The dark gray vehicle pulled into the street and followed her. Surprised by the sudden movement of the cars, Cat scrambled to get her coupe moving. She caught up with the others before Ray warned her to back off. Reluctantly, Cat complied.

"What if we lose them?" She frowned.

"Then we get to entertain each other until Greye goes back home, and we do it all over again," Irish told her casually, but he didn't believe it. The stranger in the gray car in front of them might have other plans for Mrs. La Spina.

They followed the two vehicles down Pine Street until Greye turned onto 12th and pulled up to the street's first parking spot. The gray Studebaker tailing Greye passed her Packard and stopped in a parking spot several car lengths ahead. Cat drove past both cars and turned into the alley.

"You'll need to go around the block so we can keep an eye on them," Ray grumbled when Cat brought her car to a stop.

"No, you get to go around the block." The woman opened the car door while her blue eyes danced with excitement. "I'm going to walk back and monitor things from the corner. We only met once so I can follow her. When La Spina leaves, you can come to pick me up."

While Irish winced in pain, sliding over to the driver's side, Cat made her way back to the corner of the building. After a glance, she quickly disappeared. Ray had to admit he liked Cat's idea as he drove around to 13th Street before getting back on Pine.

He pulled into a parking spot near the corner just as Greye appeared. As she stepped out in front of his car, Ray held his breath for a long moment. However, Greye remained oblivious to him. The woman hurried across the sidewalk, entering the building. Ray gingerly worked across the seat and looked up at the Morris Bank sign above the double doors. Just a few seconds later, Cat came around the corner, and Ray pointed to the building. She crossed in front of the car and went to the front window of the bank. His partner watched inside while pretending to dab at her face as she looked into a small pocket mirror.

"Well, hello there. I thought I recognized you. What a small world." Irish turned back to the passenger side to find a woman's face nearly inside the window. Initially surprised, he finally recognized the visitor.

"Hello, Pearl." He remained polite, although the chubby woman blocked his view. Pearl's low cut, bright green dress exposed her cleavage. "Have you been out to the *Stanley Rose* recently?"

The platinum blonde smiled, her cherry lipstick showing on a couple of front teeth. "Yes, and I haven't seen you out there. I've needed a dance partner."

There was a cough behind Pearl, and she pulled away from the car, turning to see Cat.

Smiling brightly, Cat slid past her. "I'm sorry, but he's waiting for me."

There was a long, pregnant pause as Cat opened the door and got into her vehicle.

"Well, aren't you going to introduce me?" Pearl came back to the open window. She asked with a tight-lipped smile.

Irish gave her a thin grin.

"Sorry, this is Catherine Bennett; she's a photographer with the *Beacon.* We're working on something."

"My husband, James, is the president and owner of the Morris Bank." Pearl gave Cat an indifferent glance. "I'm sure you've heard of him. The Morris Bank is one of the biggest banks in the city."

Cat shook her head. "I can't say that I have, but it's nice to meet you."

Pearl kept her attention on the shamus.

"I want a turn with you at the Masquerade ball. The *Stanley Rose* will be hopping this Saturday." She noticed the couple in the car looked confused.

"Oh, come now, Mr. Irish, you need to read the society pages. A man with your talent would do well with the right contacts." She leaned in the window again. "That nice Mr. Fordham is having a costume ball on the ship. There'll be lots of drinks and dancing. Everyone will be going."

Before Ray could reply, Pearl glanced at her watch.

"I'm late for the Manfred Circle meeting. Don't forget this weekend. I'll have a flapper custom on." She started walking away at a brisk clip, her purse flapping as Pearl held her green hat with the other hand. After a moment, both the driver and the passenger started laughing.

"Where did you come up with that girlfriend?" Cat's smug response caused Irish to frown.

"I needed information, and she needed a dance partner," Ray observed the heavyset woman turn the corner. "At least we know where Fordham will be that night. Now, what did you see inside the bank?"

"Greye went straight to the vault. I didn't get a good look, but it appears she's getting into a safe deposit box. Something's not right with her," she said, looking uneasy. "I wonder what she's up to?"

Irish quickly looked down, tipping his fedora low across his face.

"We'll know soon enough. She's leaving now."

After Greye left the building, she walked behind Cat's car and across the street. They waited until she turned the corner. Ray commented on the small attaché case Greye was now carrying. He pulled the car forward slowly, turning the corner at a snail's pace until they could see her get into her vehicle. Fortunately, traffic remained light that morning, and Ray stopped for a moment, waiting for the red Packard to pull into the street. As they expected, the man following Greye pulled in behind her while Irish backed off, keeping both vehicles in his sight. Soon, La Spina's car took a right on 9th, and her followers continued their pursuit.

Gradually, the buildings thinned out, replaced by two-story Victorian homes covered in gingerbread. The Packard picked up speed as the traffic lessened when the trio of vehicles turned onto State Road 66.

"I don't like this," the shamus grumbled. "I think she might be skipping town." He glanced at the fuel gauge. "I hope she doesn't have a full tank of gas."

As the cars reached the city limits, the gray coupe suddenly sped up, getting close to Greye's rear bumper. The driver attempted to whip around to pass, but Greye pushed her accelerator, cutting the gray vehicle off by using the oncoming traffic. It was apparent; the stranger following La Spina had orders to keep her from leaving town.

"Better hang on, because we're going to play this game as well," Irish warned his passenger as he gunned her coupe.

The flathead V6 screamed as they gained on the two vehicles in front of them. Greye kept speeding up, then slowing as she cut off the gray coupe trying to get past. The stranger in the coupe wasn't paying attention to the car behind him. When the thug swung into the other lane to cut off La Spina's car, Ray pressed the gas pedal to the floor. He steered directly at the back bumper of the gray coupe. The collision forced the coupe into the broad ditch next to the road. As they flew past the stranger's car, Irish glimpsed the goon trying to steer back to the road. It was a mistake. Cat turned to watch the gray car flip over several times, landing on its top at the edge of a cornfield before dust obscured the view. Glancing at her driver, she realized the deadly look in Ray's eyes had returned. He would move heaven and earth to make sure Greye would not leave the city.

As they closed on Greye's convertible, she took a sudden turn onto a dirt road, forcing Ray to slam on the brakes, nearly missing the turn. While the Packard had more power under the hood, the driver kept over-steering on the loose gravel road. While the vehicles made their way through the hills overlooking the nearby bay, Irish kept closing after each turn. Greye's car pulled away from them on the straight section of the road.

Finally, Ray decided to bump the Packard with a determined clamp of his jaw when he caught up on a curved section of the road. He let off the gas too soon, and the cars barely touched. However, Greye panicked when she saw the vehicle so close behind her. Gunning the engine, the car's rear end slid away into the soft soil by the edge of the road. La Spina over-corrected, then slammed her brakes, and turned into an open field while Ray shot past her.

By the time Irish came to a stop on the dirt road, he could see only dust flying up from the nearby field. The man slammed Cat's car into reverse and reached the small path leading into the cultivated land. Following the trail of dust, he and Cat soon came upon the stopped convertible. The driver's door hung wide open while one rear tire looked nearly shredded. Scanning the area, they noticed Greye running away, the brown portfolio case she carried flapping in one hand.

With a stone face, Ray pressed on the gas, passing the woman's disabled car and quickly coming up behind her. Greye's terrified face kept looking back at the oncoming coupe. For a moment, Cat wondered if Irish would run the woman over. Finally, he stopped as she came near the edge of a deep ravine.

"That bitch is mine," he stated in a growling whisper as he threw the car out of gear and pulled back on the handbrake.

Ray jumped out of the car, leaving the door open as he followed the bishop's wife. Greye slowed as she reached the steep drop off by an old stone fence covered with thorn bushes. Looking back, she recognized Ray steadily coming toward her.

Sprinting several feet to the wall, she broke a heel, causing her to lose the shoe. Greye looked down at the rocky face of the ravine below; tears filled her eyes. Kicking off her other shoe, she started running parallel with the fence. A glance back revealed her pursuer steadily closing on her with the look of death on his face. Desperation overcame her fear, and Greye tried to push through the small hole in the fence line. Thorns cut into her body, and she heard her blouse ripping. The tangle of roots tripped her, and she landed hard on the ledge overlooking the steep ravine.

Searching for an escape, she suddenly felt a hand grasp her collar and lift her from the ground. Immediately, Mrs. La Spina screamed in terror. Irish dragged her back through the brush and threw her to the ground. His bruised face showed the hatred as her screams for help quickly turned into uncontrollable sobs.

"Mrs. La Spina, you have a lot to answer for," Cat told Greye as she stepped next to Irish. She could see he had his hand on the gun in his pocket, but Ray had his other hand pressed against his injured chest. The pain of the recent stabbing showed through the anger.

"Don't kill me, please, I'm begging you. I can pay you," Greye sobbed. There was a slight trail of blood coming down her cheek. "It's in this case; just let me go." She hurriedly opened the attaché she carried, showing the green and white paper. "Look, see? Plenty of money. They're as good as cash."

When Ray spoke, his voice was tight and controlled.

"Lady, I don't give a damn about those things. I want to know why you tried to kill me. Then I plan on taking you back to the cops so you can explain to them about your brother and Fat Louie. Your husband can't protect you from this. I like to think that putting you into prison will make me feel better, but I doubt it."

"You can't take me back. I'm a dead woman." The distraught woman's eyes widened.

"You think I care about that? I figured you were skipping town," Ray shot back.

"Did you wear out your welcome?" Cat asked smugly. "I suppose the car following you was one of Guy Young's thugs, keeping an eye on you."

Greye buckled, her upper body leaning forward and shaking as she tried to control herself.

"He knows about the bonds, he knows everything about the grift, the setup, and now he'll take over everything."

She halted, then whispered.

"He'll kill me!"

"Sister, slow down and start making some sense. What are you talking about?" Irish glanced at Cat, who shrugged in response.

Taking a deep breath, Greye looked up, covered in streaks of dirt and tears.

"Quincannon set up this whole hoax. But now everything has spiraled out of control. Guy Young has taken over, and I have to get out of Oyster City."

"No, you're going to lay it out for us. I want the whole truth, or by God, I'll take you to Young myself. I haven't forgotten about the motel, you bitch." His venom caused Greye to stop. She stared at him for a moment before she dropped her head.

"All right, I'll tell you everything." La Spina's shoulders slumped.

"When Quincannon got out of prison, he came to Oyster City and found a job with Henry La Spina. After a while, he figured out there was a fortune tied up in the United Church Foundation that Henry runs. The foundation got all types of donations, so nobody realized how many were rare antiques and other items." She told the story like it was customary to be a crook.

"Quincannon contacted his friend in Boston, Fat Louie. They hatched this scheme to sell off the stuff and pocket the money."

"So, you're innocent in this entire scheme?" Ray's voice dripped with scorn.

"I didn't say that." Greye glared at him. "Louie decided we needed someone on the inside since they couldn't just steal it and fence the stuff locally. They had to get it out of state. Quincannon knew the bishop was going to New York for a week, so I met him and kept him occupied, making sure he didn't go back to Oyster City early. My partners hauled the most expensive stuff away from a warehouse in town." Greye paused when she saw the look of hate on Cat's face.

"Go on," the photographer told her bitterly.

"Well, Henry got serious and asked me to marry him before he left New York. I went along with the idea, thinking that I would just leave him before any wedding bells." She paused. The bishop's wife looked at Ray and Cat.

"That's when the scam went wrong. I swear to you that the guys told me the complete plan was to grab the stuff and let La Spina think Quincannon took off with them. Henry wouldn't do anything about it since it meant bad press, and the foundation could afford the loss. We would meet up in Boston and split the dough."

"What happened?" Cat asked.

"The damn Quincannon and Louie got greedy. They came up with the bright idea to go for everything. They forged a letter from the bishop's stationery to keep it all legal like for the accountant. Even better, they found some firm in New York to issue bearer bonds so there would be no questions. It would look like all the profit was going towards the construction of a new church. It was all part of their brilliant scheme. They would sell everything and turn it into these bonds. Good as gold and easier to carry was the idea."

"Let me guess; you had to marry Henry to keep the scam going for a while longer?" Cat fumed. "God, you're a worthless tramp."

Greye shook her head.

"You've never starved, looking at everything from the outside. All the money was there for the taking. So what if one guy takes the fall? It's not like the La Spinas can't afford it. Henry's family owns a good part of the city."

Irish grabbed Cat before she could pounce on her, but he lost some skin from the back of his hand during the commotion.

"Enough!" he yelled as he pulled her away from Greye. La Spina avoided the photographer's wild swings. After a couple of minutes, Ray released Cat, who continued to stare daggers at the bishop's wife.

"You two can have it out later," Irish told them.

He stepped over to Greye and crouched in front of her, his voice cold.

"Now, get back to the truth. You and your partners planned on taking the bearer bonds and skipping the state, leaving the bishop holding the bag. What happened? You could have left a while ago."

"We were going to do just that. Then, everything went south. Quincannon found out about how much my husband's weapons collection was worth, and he decided to go after that as well. Henry started getting suspicious of him when his driver started asking all these questions about the daggers. He hadn't spoken with the accounting firm yet, but I knew that was coming soon. When he did, the whole thing would blow up in our faces."

Ray stood up, his legs aching at the effort.

"Explain how Hugh Pendexter gets into this. Cat found out he killed someone back in the Boston area and somehow got out of the state. Then, he guns down One-Eye Cornell along with this Fat Louie, as you know."

"I heard all about you in Boston," Cat told her. "You ran the coast, grifting people. I suspect you had something to do with getting him out of jail there. He didn't come up with the bail on his own."

Greye looked back at Ray, teary eyes pleading. "I had to; Hugh was my baby brother. I couldn't leave him there. He'd get the chair."

"I can't imagine you could go to your husband for the cash. And it was too dangerous to sell any of the bonds you had." Irish paced around her as he worked through her motives.

He stopped and looked down.

"My guess is you got the cash from your favorite racketeer."

"It was Quincannon's idea," She nodded. "He noticed how Guy looked at me when I went to the ship occasionally. Quincannon said it was the perfect setup, and we figured we could skip town before I needed to repay him."

"Yeah, you sound like a grifter, that's for sure. What happened? Young decided you needed to make good on the money? When you couldn't pay up, he started using you as his whore, is that it?"

She barely nodded; her tears started flowing again.

"One night, out of the blue, I got a call saying I had one day to pay up. I went out to the ship that evening to ask for more time. That son of a bitch just laughed and said he'd go to my husband for the money. I couldn't let that happen, so I begged him. Then he told me he knew about my past in Boston."

"What kind of deal did you work out?" Cat asked.

"I went to work for Young. Important people came to the *Stanley Rose*. You know, the political types out of the capital that came down for a woman. I was to help him with those clients, to make sure they left happy. After I entertained them, he would make deals with them. You used that to influence those back at the capital." Greye La Spina looked up at the shamus. "I didn't have any choice."

Ray nodded, but his face remained unsympathetic.

"I bet not. What about your Boston partners? Did they go along with it?"

"Damn, Quincannon was all right with it. Bastard told Hugh that I was the perfect person. Said he should have thought of the idea first. My brother went out to *Stanley Rose* one night with Louie. At first, they promised to work a deal with Guy Young to get me out of his grip. Then, they saw all the marks coming aboard, and they came up with their crazy idea, a plan to knock Young off and take over his racket. They tried to get Quincannon to go along, but he wanted nothing to do with it. He told them it was too risky and said they were nuts. Hugh talked me into it. I wanted Young to get what was coming to him."

Ray shook his head at the news.

"God, I thought you had some brains at first. You went from the frying pan to the fire with that stupid move."

She dropped her head, going quiet for a moment.

"We were past the point of no return. I had to keep everything under wraps. I fed everything I could find out about Guy to my brother and Louie. We were so close to the jackpot, Quincannon started pushing to get the hell out of the city. Then you showed up..." She looked up at him, her eyes pleading.

"I wasn't lying about how things were that night I betrayed you. But now they're all dead, and I don't want to die." Greye's head fell into her hands, and she was sobbing. Irish glanced at Cat, and her face remained unmoved.

"My, aren't you a dutiful little woman, staying so busy with so many men? Enough of the tears, lady. Let's go." He reached down, touching her shoulder, and the bishop's wife flinched.

"Where are you taking me?" The panic in her voice was authentic.

"We'll talk about it in the car," he told her, gripping her shoulder hard.

Cat drove while Ray sat in the back seat with Greye. The bishop's wife clutched the small brown case holding the bearer bonds.

As they retraced their path back to Oyster City, the woman told them more about her past with Fat Louie. He pulled her out of the tenements of North Boston. She also talked about her brother's time in prison, where he met Quincannon.

Greye spoke quietly, almost in a trance, her accent growing thicker while she explained her experience the night Young killed Fat Louie. The bishop's wife told them about the gruesome death and Young's plans after Mark Fordham took over. She mentioned the leader of the union dockworkers had a stake in the *Stanley Rose*. Irish listened while he tried to piece together a plan which didn't involve someone dying as a result. When the bishop's wife finished, Cat brought up her friend.

"Explain why your kid brother killed my friend, George Hopley." Cat's voice remained like ice.

"I didn't know about that. You must understand that I'm not a killer, I'm not," Greye told her as she looked down at the case. "George took some money from my brother to help arrange things. Fat Louie confessed to Guy Young that he and my brother used this reporter to get to him. Then Louie told him about my part of trying to knock him off."

Irish glanced at Greye as she stared at the case in her lap.

"You cold-hearted bitch, you just said your partner got tortured to death. Of course, he told them all he knew," Ray said. "Now explain why you knocked me out and left me with your brother in that damn motel? And don't say that it was your partner's idea! I remember enough to know that plan came from you."

Greye said nothing for a moment; Ray could tell she was desperately trying to think up some fiction. He grabbed her by her hair and pulled her head back.

"I told you I want the truth. Otherwise, I'll have my partner drive us out to a lonely place, and I'll beat it out of you. I'm tired of you and your damned lies."

"Stop it, I swear I'll tell you the truth," she cried out in pain. "After my brother and Louie missed out on killing Young, they knew the gangster would be after them. Then you told me that Guy Young was putting the squeeze on you. I had to do something."

Ray released her, pulling his hand away like he was touching something dead.

"Give the rest to me straight," he growled.

"You forced me to do this," Greye pleaded. "Since you were about the same size as my brother, the idea was we would leave you in the motel. I would send a message to Guy saying it was you that set up the plan to knock him and Cornell off. When they came after you, we would get out of this place for good." Greye paused when she realized how badly her statement appeared. "I swear I was going to give you a head start; that's why I came to the motel," she quickly added, expecting a violent reaction.

Instead, he slid away from her.

"You're a worthless piece of garbage. Not too concerned about other people dying for what you're holding in your lap. By the way, who do you think killed your brother? Was it one of Young's thugs?"

She shook her head.

"I know it wasn't Guy Young or Louie. At first, I thought it was you, but I remembered they tied you up after I thought about it. But someone must have known about the place and where my brother was."

"That doesn't matter," Cat spoke up from the front seat. "We need to take this bitch to the police. She can explain all she wants. Let them sort it out."

Greye's eyes widened as she jerked up from the seat. She pleaded with Irish, grabbing his arm.

"You can't. Guy knows everything, and he's in this with Fordham. They have cops on their payroll. He had Fat Louie killed in front of me, and that bastard Young laughed. I won't last a day in jail. Give me a chance to get out of town. I was going to do that for you."

"You're pathetic," he told her as he looked back at the road. Irish noticed the city limits were getting close. Ray looked at Cat through the rearview mirror.

"Turn off the road up here, and let's find a place to park."

When the car came to a stop, Ray opened the door and nearly pushed Greye out of the backseat after taking the small portfolio she held. They parked in a sheltered, isolated area with trees all around.

"You can't just kill me and take the money?" Greye stared at her captor, expecting the worst.

"Lady, I thought mighty hard about what you did. And you deserve worse. But no, I'm not killing you, and I'm not taking this blood money. Now shut your pie hole and go sit down over there while I talk to my partner about this." Ray got in the front seat next to Cat and closed the door. He watched Greye look around the secluded area before dropping her head and slowly stepping away.

"We really should take her to the cops," Cat told him as he looked out the window.

"She's right about what will happen if we do that," he shook his head. "They'll kill her in there. Young's got too much pull with the police; we both know that. Greye is a witness to a murder, and she knows too much about Young. Plus, the story will come out about their scam to bilk the foundation, and you know that won't help your bishop. He married a witch, and he'll be paying for it. You want that on your conscience?"

"I could live with her death," she told him coldly.

"Yeah, so could I, but it's still wrong," he gave a grim smile. "Besides, I met Henry, and I don't think her husband deserves a corpse for a wife," he said as he patted the case in his lap. "However, these bonds give me an idea. Can we hide her out somewhere and make a deal with Guy Young?"

"What kind of deal?" Cat's jaw nearly dropped in amazement at the suggestion.

"Guy Young came off his ship to kill Louie. If he wants these damn bonds so bad, I'm willing to bet that he'll come ashore for these things, especially if we use Mrs. La Spina as bait. Remember, she's a witness, and Guy can't keep her alive now. He'll know pretty soon that his thug who was following her got dumped. Young will guess that she hightailed it out of the state. If we can hide her out for a day or so, he'll start getting worried. I think we can convince him to risk a meeting for the bonds. Otherwise, she'll go to the cops." Irish laid the idea out as he thought of it.

Cat stared out the window at the bishop's wife. She sat on the ground, looking off into the horizon. "All right, so he comes ashore to meet us. What then? His goons will be all over us."

"We set it up to give Young and his thugs to the police. The honest ones will jump at the chance to throw him in jail. We have a witness to the killing." Ray looked out at Greye in the field.

"I don't like it," Cat shook her head. "Greye will get off scot-free. I thought you wanted her in prison?"

"I do, but everything else I've come up with involves people getting killed," Ray replied. "Think of it this way. If I'm right, your friend the bishop gets to clean up the mess left by his wife. Don't you think the important people associated with Henry La Spina will help fix the problem? Plus, we have someone who can help us."

"Who would that be?" Cat turned to him.

"J. Allan Dunn." There was a foul grin on his face when he spoke.

"Why would he help us?"

Ray looked at her, surprised.

"He wouldn't unless we give him something he can't refuse; Mayor Hopley's re-election. You have that in your apartment."

Cat paused, transfixed at the idea forming.

"I think I understand. Once Young is in jail, Dunn takes the bonds and fixes the books with the foundation. In return, he gets the photo I have along with what we think we know about Young and Fordham."

"And they'll ship the good, little wife is out of town after a quiet divorce," Irish nodded. "Someone will probably warn her about the threat of prison if she opens her mouth. I don't like it any more than you do, but I like the other options even less."

"You could just put a bullet in her and give the bonds back to the bishop. It would be simpler and cleaner," Cat suggested coldly.

"Have you killed someone?" he glared at her.

Cat looked away and shook her head. After a moment, she finally spoke.

"I've never hated someone like that. I guess I couldn't do it."

"Once you pull the trigger, you'll always remember the face," he said. "I've seen enough death to last me a lifetime."

"Still, I'm not sure about the plan, but I can't think of anything better." Cat gazed out of the car window. "You're the one who got the worst of this so far. I guess you're looking for something more than killing someone."

"Well, I would like a little payback against Young and some others working for him." Ray agreed. "Plus, if Greye leaves town, I don't think she'll have the smarts to pull off more graft. She follows what others want her to do."

She gave him a smirk.

"By the way, you're beginning to think like everyone else in Oyster City."

His face went dark at the thought.

"I hope the hell not!"

~~~

Cat stopped by the home of Gladys Peer, telling Ray that she was picking up keys to a hideout for their passenger. He stayed with Greye in the car, watching as she tried to clean the worst of the dirt from her face using Cat's pocket mirror.

"Ray, those bonds are my ticket to staying alive. Guy knows everything. A cop will tip him off, and we'll be dead; he'll kill anyone who tries to stop him. Just let me go, and I'll be so far away, Young will never find me," Greye pleaded with him.

"No dice, lady. So far, your thinking has got your partners killed. I suggest you better line up the story you plan on giving your husband. If he's as good as everyone says, you might come out of this without going to prison," Irish told her, refusing to lay out everything he and Cat planned. She gave him a poisonous glance but went quiet. He noticed how Greye had recovered her composure, but she was correct about one thing. Young would be gunning for him. The idea he planned was risky, and there was always a chance he might miss an angle in his complex web of a plan.

"I don't know what Henry will do, or even if he can do anything," Greye leaned back in the seat. "I'm not sure how I can tell him what happened."

"You're a liar and a tramp, so using the truth might be a refreshing change." Cat slid into the driver's side, overhearing the conversation coming from the open car window. She did not bother to look at the bishop's wife.

When they arrived in front of the building at Chandler and Peach Street's corner, Greye remained sullen. Ray wondered
~~~

how much of the drama he witnessed in the field was real or just an act. She had an unusual ability to work on a guy's emotions, even when they had reason to kill her.

The trio entered a doorway between a restaurant and a dry cleaner, taking the stairs to the second floor. There were two doors at the top of the stairs. Cat unlocked the door on the left to find a nearly empty office. A single dust-covered desk and antique wood chair sat in the middle of the room. An open door in the back revealed another room with a bed.

"This will be your home until we get things set up," Cat told Greye, placing the light-colored folder holding the bonds on the desktop. "It's not the luxury, but Young won't be able to find you here. Nobody knows about the place. There's nothing to tie you to this office."

There was a frown on Greye's face as she inspected the room. She walked to the bedroom, her torn blouse barely hanging from her scratched shoulder. After a quick look around, she came back into the office. "I've seen worse," she told them, her Boston accent gone and her poise returning. She looked at her dirty clothes.

"What about clothes and food?"

"We'll come up with something," Ray told her. "Cat and I will be around to keep an eye on you." His eyes narrowed. "Don't make me bring a cop."

Slowly, Greye nodded as she looked away.

"I understand. You're running the show."

"Well, for the moment, anyway. Get cleaned up, and we'll go out and make a call to your husband. You can tell him you're staying with some friends for a couple of days. That's as close to the truth as you ever give him."

Greye looked out of the dusty window to the street. "I…I think that will work. He's very understanding."

"Yeah, with you, he'd have to be." Cat's bitter tone showed no truce. "I'll stay here with her," she turned to Ray. "You can call a mechanic about having her car towed to their house. There's nothing that Guy Young can do but watch her home."

Ray pulled the bonds from the desk, noticing Greye's eyes follow his movement. "I'll take these with me just in case our new partner forgets her agreement. When I get back, we'll get some food and make the phone call." As she stepped out of the office, he glanced back at Cat.

"Don't beat her up; we'll need her to make this thing work." There was a grin on his face.

"No promises," Cat replied.

~~~

It was the next morning when Irish walked along Main Street, heading for Pappy's newsstand. His mind remained muddled from lack of sleep and a whirlwind of thoughts. Ray spent an uncomfortable night sleeping in the old chair at the empty office, while Greye slept in a bed behind a closed door only a few paces away.

Early in the evening, after Greye got a bath and put on the clothes Cat came up with, her demeanor returned to a confident crook. Around him, Greye attempted her same sexy illusion. The trio took a ride to an isolated gas station, and Greye called her husband while Cat listened as she stood nearby. Ray could see the young woman's murderous stare as he filled up the car, and he recognized how much the photographer hated Greye. Irish shook his head, realizing his anger at the bishop's wife transformed into disgust. At least, he was not thinking of the best way to dispose of her body. Instead, he kept fine-tuning a plan which might keep all of them alive.

When they arrived back at the hideout, Cat stayed for the evening while Ray went out for their food. When he returned, Ray could feel the tension in the air. The man suspected the two
~~~

women had a bitter argument while he was gone. Ray decided he would stay overnight and let Cat get some rest.

However, during the long evening with Greye, he had learned a lot about her. If he was honest with himself, Ray could understand how a pretty woman, growing up on the rough streets of North Boston, learned to use her sex to get out of poverty. Still, Greye's lack of conscience reminded him that behind her attractive smile was a heartless snake. In some ways, he felt sorry for the man married to her. Others might take her to bed, but Henry La Spina would have to pick up the pieces from his wife's pursuit of the easy buck. He gave a grim smile.

Yeah, the easy way to an early grave!

He stepped next to the wooden structure holding magazines and newspapers.

"Well, shamus, you look out of sorts." Pappy sat on a stool, handing out the latest paper. A pork-pie hat covered his head, and he wore a brown sweater over his black vest.

"Yeah, rough night," Ray told him, pulling a Lincoln from his pocket. "Say, can you let me know if you hear anything about Greye La Spina going around? It appears she might have left town."

"Funny thing, you asking me something like that." Pappy handed him the morning paper. "I heard this morning that a lot of folks are interested in her Packard."

Ray had to force a smile away as he scanned the paper. "I'll bet, maybe like Guy Young's folks."

"Those are the ones, all right. They were interested. You have something to do with it?"

"I don't know a thing." Irish shook his head.

Then he noticed a headline about a corpse found out at the abandoned military base. From the description, he guessed it was Fat Louie. He folded up the paper, sliding it under his arm.

"Got any other good stories?"

"Nah, it's been pretty quiet around here. You got the Soviets making noises overseas in Iran. That guy Churchill is talking about some Iron Curtain falling across Europe. Oh, and Mrs. Purvey's latest article claims that dinner dresses with just one shoulder strap are a very flattering look to the female figure."

Irish gave him a sour glance at the last bit of news. Pappy returned a big grin. "You should keep up with everything in the newspaper, my mother always told me. You might learn something."

"And how will that help me?" Ray asked.

"Well, there's a big party out on the *Stanley Rose* this weekend. Find you a girl to go out there, and she'll want that dinner dress. It seems like Fordham is going all out to get the very wealthy and very corrupt to pay his way to the top."

"Yeah, I heard about that," Irish told him. "I might have to check it out. Did you go to those places with your wife? I'll bet she liked to dance."

His friend suddenly frowned and chuckled at the idea.

"Not hardly. The colored class doesn't get that type of invitation. But my Emma danced better than Ginger Rogers."

"Yeah, I always said the world's a crazy place, with people filling their heads with crap. I saw enough of that malarkey in the Navy. Well, I've got to get going. I'll see you later."

"Irish, Emma told me to thank you for coming by the other day for dinner. She said that it was really sweet of you."

"I never turn down a free meal," he said with a wink. "Besides, those were the best pork chops I've ever had. We'll do it again soon."

Heading across the street, Ray stepped to the sidewalk. A white Hudson pulled close to the curb and honked. Inside was Lieutenant Arizona Campbell, who waved him into the car.

"Irish, how are you doing? You get healed yet?"

Ray nodded. "I'll survive once I get those stitches out if I don't scratch them out first," he said. "What's a police detective picking me up for?"

"It beats hauling you into the office for a chat. Have you been staying away from the La Spina gal?" The cop's tone was light, but Irish figured he was fishing.

"Haven't been around her place, if that's what you're asking. Is something up?" Irish stared ahead as the car took the turn down 6th Avenue.

"Well, the sheriff found her in a field before the tow truck picked it up. Plus, one of Young's thugs died in an auto accident out on the highway near there," Arizona glanced at his passenger. "I thought you might know more about it. The sheriff thinks another car was involved."

"Sounds like one of those gangsters making a play," Ray replied carefully. "Maybe you should ask Guy Young?"

"You're going to play it close to the vest?" the policeman grunted. "All right, you get Young to come ashore, and I'll be happy to talk with him. I've got several unexplained deaths he and I could chat about."

"I just read in the paper about the body they found. It sure seems like an excellent description of Fat Louie. You get a positive ID on it?" Ray told him, noticing the policeman turn by the courthouse.

Arizona remained quiet as he drove along. Ray glanced at him, and he could tell the cop was debating something. Finally, the man came to a decision.

"Listen, Irish, you realize you're playing with fire here? Word is out that we're supposed to be looking for Greye La Spina, but they're keeping everything very low-key. If something is going on between you and her, it would be wise to spill the beans. The DA is already looking to knock you down about her."

Irish watched as the vehicle drove past the District Attorney's office and turned on Patriot Street.

"Arizona, I'll tell you what. Find out if you have the body of Fat Louie. Then, I'll offer you a gift? Fair enough?"

Arizona pulled next to the sidewalk in front of the police station.

"You've got something up your sleeve." He turned the car off. "I don't like this one-man show you're running here. If you have something, turn it over."

Ray looked at him, pointing his thumb at the building.

"Do you trust everyone in there with information someone might have about Young and his operation?"

Arizona let out a deep breath and shook his head.

"No, I don't." He paused, glaring at the shamus. "I'll play along. You were right about the body; we got it tagged down at the morgue. Now, what is this gift?"

Irish opened the door and got out of the vehicle.

"I'll call you tonight at your office with the time and place. Have your best men with you, and I'll give you Guy Young on a silver platter."

~~~

The note arrived at the *Stanley Rose* when a young messenger handed the small envelope to the club manager. The short, balding man named Pauly frowned at the interruption to his overbearing flirtations with the hat-check girl who he brought in early that day. Addressed to Guy Young, the small letter held no other information as he debated whether to disturb his boss, who seldom rose before noon. Deciding to risk it, Pauly walked across the ship to the office where his boss had made his home. Just as the manager was about to knock on the door, he felt someone behind him.
~~~

"What are you doing? Nobody wakes the boss unless he tells them," Tweedledee grumbled at the short man.

Pauly turned, looking at the chest of the bodyguard. His beady eyes blinked several times, and he held up the envelope. "You can give this to him when he wakes up. This message just came in, and I figured it might be important."

The scarred man took the paper.

"Just get out of here, you little twerp. I'll take care of it."

The manager quickly walked away, cursing the guard under his breath. Tweedledee looked at the envelope again before depositing the message into his suit pocket.

An hour later, Guy Young sat behind his pretentious desk, drinking his coffee from a delicate cup while going through his daily ritual of reading his mail. As he scanned the terse letter from Greye La Spina, a cold fury slowly filled the racketeer's face. The bitch was making a play to double-cross him. He'd already assumed she left the state, but she remained close. After his henchman's death, the mobster sent out telegrams to friends throughout the country, offering a large reward for her death. Young believed in a few months; she would turn up in a morgue. The bonds would eventually make their way back to him, no doubt minus a recovery charge from his friends.

Instead, that whore wife was telling him what to do. The letter gave instructions for the racketeer to be waiting on her call to meet. Unless he agreed to split the bonds and allow her to leave town, Greye was going to the cops to become a witness to his murder of Fat Louie. She also said she would tell the police he killed her brother and One-Eye Cornell.

He flung the letter away, then took a massive swipe with his arm across the top of the desk, scattering the dishes from his breakfast. The breaking crash of glass and pottery woke the sleeping woman in the round bed. She immediately sat up, pulling the gold cover around her naked breasts. Guy noticed the movement and glared at the lovely girl.

"Get the hell out of here before I get mad," he fumed.

~~~

J. Allan Dunn walked into the administration building just after the church bells stopped ringing across the street. It was a few minutes after twelve. The thin man remained lost in thoughts while climbing the six sets of stairs leading to his office. His wife kept harping at him for another radio in the house, like one wasn't sufficient. The argument after breakfast left him with a headache. Helen enjoyed spending money, something he should have realized, considering her family ties. However, even after all the special deals J. Allan worked out to bring in the extra cash from city contracts. He was no further ahead than when he got the job. The thought depressed him as he turned down the hallway to an office with the sign on the door: Director of Public Works. The sound of his footsteps filled the empty hall since most of the employees had already left for lunch. He went into the office, paying no attention to Madge, who was not at her desk. His secretary was a virtual time clock, entering the office precisely at nine each morning. Dunn guessed Madge was just sitting down across the street at the diner where her beau worked. Opening the next door, he halted.

"Mr. Dunn, please shut the door. We have important business to discuss," Ray Irish told him as he sat behind the desk with his feet up on the desktop. Catherine Bennett stood by the window, turning around at the sound of the door opening.

"What the hell do you think you're doing? Get out of my office before I call the police," Dunn raised his voice, his eyes ablaze.
~~~

"Well, your secretary is on a long lunch hour so that we can have a chat. That's not a friendly welcome considering all we've been through together," Ray said as he lifted his feet, placing them on the floor. He leaned forward in the chair.

"I once saved you from being pounded by Young's thugs. But that's the past, and I'm not going to hold a grudge. However, I don't think you want to miss out on the opportunity that Cat and I have come up with for you."

Dunn slid off the cashmere coat he wore, hanging it up on the wooden coat rack behind the door. He placed his derby hat on the stand.

"You don't have anything I want, Irish. Now get out of here."

"Dunn, you want to hand your buddy the mayor his re-election on a platter or not? That's what Ray's offering you," Cat stated when she stepped to the desk and laid her photo of Mark Fordham with the dead policeman.

Glaring at her, J. Allan stepped over, looking at the picture. "It's Fordham, so what?"

"He just happens to be with a corrupt cop by the name of Plug Howard, the murdered cop," she said. "Do I need to draw you a picture?"

Immediately, J. Allan shook his head.

"No, I get it. Get the dirty boys out, implying a policeman got killed because of his association with Howard." His eyes darted between the two people. "It might work, but I don't see the silver platter."

"Well, this is a two-part deal. You also get to save your boss the embarrassment of his close friend spending time behind bars. If Fordham gets this information, he'll have the election," Ray told him, observing Dunn's eyes widen, and the shamus smiled.

"No, I'm not talking about you," Irish said as he pulled out the small parcel holding the bearer bonds. He opened the case and removed one.

"One of our illustrious citizens is involved in a scam that's worth about fifty thousand dollars. If the information comes out and your boss loses the election, just think of the heads that will roll. Like rats from a sinking ship, it's about to get real messy when Fordham takes it over. Not to mention the fact that Young's gang has a deal with the union boss." Ray paused, holding out the paper. "I can always go to the mayor or the DA myself. Here's one of the bearer bonds issued for the construction of a non-existent church."

"I don't trust you, Irish. You're getting too bright." Grudgingly, Dunn looked over the paper in his hand. The bond showed the name United Church Foundation, and he greedily licked his lips. Then his eyes grew wide.

"Are you telling me Henry La Spina's involved in this?"

"His name's all over it, whether he's involved or not." Ray nodded. "I'm just trying to clean up all the loose ends of the web you stuck on me. Now, I'm driving you to the end of the rainbow, so it's your choice if you want the pot of gold or not."

Irish stood.

He stepped close to Dunn, pulling the bond from his hands.

"We're going to give your mayor both Guy Young and Mark Fordham," Cat told him with a smile as she picked up her photo. "But it's going to cost you."

"How much are you talking about?" Dunn asked as he eyed them suspiciously.

"First, you'll give me and Cat two thousand each for doing your dirty work. The money will be in our hands by the end of the day," Ray stated as he stuffed the bond back into the folder, then put it inside his coat. His grim smile showed his enjoyment as his former boss nearly choked on the price.

"What the hell are you talking about? I can't come up with that kind of cash so quickly," J. Allan stammered, staring at the coat pocket holding the bonds.

"Then you need to get with your boss and come up with enough money. No cash, then no photo and no bonds," Cat replied. "Think what Fordham might pay for it."

There was a long pause as Dunn's narrowed eyes kept darting between them.

"All right, I'll have it by tonight."

"Meet us at that out of the way office you use at five o'clock. By the way, I'm telling you not to let your friends in City Hall know about this. Otherwise, you can kiss the deal goodbye," Ray warned Dunn. "Any tidbits back to Fordham or Young will throw a wrench into the whole thing. That'll make it dangerous for Cat and you." Ray started for the door while Dunn's scowl followed him.

"Don't worry, we've got this worked out," Cat told the thin director. She patted him on the shoulder as she went to the door.

"Irish, it appears this city is rubbing off on you." J. Allan Dunn's mocking tone came as the troubleshooter opened the door.

Ray refused to look back.

"Don't ever say that to me again if you want to keep your teeth."

~~~

Ray was silent as Cat drove them back to Greye's hideout. She took many turns and a couple of back alleys to ensure no one was following them. After a while, she glanced at the silent man.

"Why did you tell Dunn this setup is dangerous for me?" she asked. "You're in as deep as I am."

Ray tipped back his hat, coming out of his thoughts.
~~~

"In his eyes, I'm expendable; you're not. I was making sure he would keep his mouth shut until I figure out who his partners are."

She turned into another alley, looking back in her mirror. "Dunn wouldn't sell us out. He's greedy, but not a fool."

"Yeah, but he'll be more careful since you're involved with this," he replied.

Cat frowned. "What are you saying?"

"Nothing," Ray told her firmly as they came to a stop close to the building. "I'm trying to keep this plan on track. Now, let's figure out how to tell Greye that she'll be the bait for Guy Young tonight."

Several minutes after the couple entered the room, they laid out the plan to the bishop's wife. It surprised Irish at Greye's calmness when she reluctantly accepted her role as the carrot to bring Guy Young into Oyster City. He told her that.

"I've been around cons all my life," she explained. "It didn't take a genius to figure out your plan when you asked me to write that note." Her strained face scowled. "You don't belong in this place if you're too honest to run with the money. What about my husband?"

"Once we get Young taken care of, then sort that out with him on your own," he replied. "We'll point out you've been cooperating with the authorities."

"Ray's already gave you an out since some people will clean up your mess with the foundation," Cat interrupted. "You might take it as a path for you to get the hell out of the city."

Panic filled Greye's hazel eyes at the news.

"You mean Henry already knows?"

"Maybe not yet, but that doesn't matter at the moment," Irish told her. He didn't understand why she appeared so upset.

"The cops will be there tonight, so you should be safe," his confident claim made Greye turn and walked to the back of the room as she considered the plan. Cat looked at her watch and stepped close to Irish.

"I'll get us some lunch. Don't let the damn woman out of your sight," Cat warned him. Ray absently nodded as he watched her standing in the sparse bedroom.

Not long after Cat left the building, Greye wandered back into the office. She quietly watched Irish for a long moment. He acted like he didn't notice as he leaned back in the chair. With his feet propped on top of the windowsill, Ray stared at the building across the street.

"You won't admit it, will you?" Greye said, interrupting his thoughts.

"Admit what?" he asked.

"You know there's something good between us. You've known it since the first time we met. I'm not the devil; I'm a survivor."

Irish remained quiet, continuing to stare out the window.

"That little girl isn't your type," she came closer to Ray, taking a seat on the edge of the desk. "Cat's still young and naïve. I could tell by the way she worships my husband. Your girlfriend can't see the forest for the trees." Greye shook her head.

"I pity her."

"I don't know about that; she's pretty sharp and tough. Grew up in this rotten place." Ray almost explained how the young woman saved his hide.

"You might be right. It is a corrupt city; I hate it here." She shivered.

"The problem is your little girlfriend worships icons, and there are no such things. Henry's a pretty good guy, but behind those puppy dog eyes, he has his secrets, like the rest of those in control of this town. But nobody gets behind the masks they put on."

"Well, Cat's someone I can trust. That's something you'll never know. Such ideas won't get past your greed." Irish looked at her finally. "You're only loyal to the cash you have."

Greye dropped her head.

"Greed isn't all I'm about." She paused, then looked at him. "But I can bet she'll never make you happy the way I can. Will you be content knowing that?"

Ray went quiet again. In the afternoon sun, she wasn't quite as attractive as he recalled the morning they met. Without the eyeshadow, the false lashes, and makeup covering the few emerging wrinkles, she would look like a thousand other everyday girls. But her eyes held a hypnotic fire, which drew him in for a moment. Full lips smiled as she leaned closer to him.

"Think about what's in that attaché you have. Fifty thousand could take you a long way. You could go anywhere and do anything. You and I could be happy together," she said, a mixture of hope and anxiety in her words.

He looked down at his suit, pulling the small portfolio from his jacket, his mind mildly entranced by the idea. Then Ray glanced at Greye, whose eyes followed the package in his hand.

"You told me you don't want to die," he said. "You think nobody hunts down this fifty thousand in blood money?"

"We could cash those in New York and disappear. No one could find us," she insisted. "I know people who can make it happen, new papers and a new life. That little girl will be a distant memory I'll make you forget. What do you say?" She licked her lips, eyes following the folder he placed on the desk near her.

Irish let out a long sigh as he let his feet fall to the floor. He stood, picking up the portfolio and putting it back in his pocket. When he opened the office door, Ray looked back.

"You didn't answer my question," she replied, gracefully sliding off the desk and stepping toward him.

"Yes, I gave you the answer."

He walked into the hall and closed the door.

With his trap in place, Ray Irish walked out of Dunn's anonymous storage office. The day was too cold for spring, but the sunlight felt good. All he needed now was the timing to fall into place, as expected.

Cat and Greye were still inside the office, where J. Allan had begrudgingly handed his photographer four thousand dollars. He got the incriminating picture of Fordham and the dead cop. Ray noticed the smirk directed at him from the bishop's wife while she witnessed the exchange. Ray glared at her for a moment, then nodded to the phone on the desk. Greye frowned and hesitated before she went to the desk and lifted the handset from the cradle. After taking a deep breath, she called the number to a diner by the docks where Young would be waiting.

As Irish slid into the coupe's passenger side, he considered the timing of their plan again. He had already called Arizona with the layout and timing, but he kept Greye's role a secret. The detective was less than thrilled with Ray's idea.

"You're taking a big gamble," Arizona warned him. "If you get someone killed, they'll throw away the key after you go to prison."

"Just make sure you arrive on time. We'll be in a gray coupe, getting there ahead of everyone. Any car that's coming into the place after that won't be on our side. When you hear the full story, you'll see that I don't have much choice. I can't have any police seen; otherwise, he'll never show up." Irish grimly smiled when he remembered Arizona's grunted disapproval, followed by a curse before he hung up.

Cat came out of the building, her brown wool coat covering her white blouse and tan slacks. Greye walked close behind, trying to keep warm in her thin red jacket, which covered her gray dress suit. Both women were silent, each person dealing with their concerns behind worried expressions. Ray guessed if he looked in a mirror, his face would show the same anxiety. In his pocket was the .45 auto he purchased that day, insisting Cat keep the snub-nose revolver she gave him.

"You better have the police there; Young is on his way," Greye told Ray as she climbed into the back seat. "The bastard had his man take my message, said he wouldn't talk to a person like me."

"I expect he didn't use those words." Irish flipped the seat back as she got comfortable.

"No, he didn't, but I don't care what they call me as long as I don't get killed by your brilliant idea," she replied to his sad smile.

Cat drove them out of the alley and followed the street toward the outskirts of the city. They were heading to the abandoned military base to make the swap. With the head start, they would be there twenty minutes before Young and his thugs. Arizona and his men would follow Guy right into the trap, cutting off any escape.

While Ray thought about any flaws in the plan, Cat interrupted his thoughts.

"What do you think our odds are coming out clean on this? Dunn tried hard to get me to stay there, even offered me more money."

"Why didn't you take him up on it?" Irish asked, staring at the nearly empty sidewalks as they drove.

Cat glanced at him, surprised.

"Are you kidding me? I want to see the look on their faces when the cops show up," she said. "Why do you think I have my camera case in the back seat? The *Beacon* will pay me a mint for the pics."

Irish groaned as he looked at her. "I'd say the odds of a picture aren't that high even when Arizona shows up. Just don't get yourself killed in the process. That camera won't stop a bullet."

"Ah, you do care." She gave him a light laugh and a wink, but he knew it was for show.

"I still don't like it," Greye complained. "You're relying on too many people who can sell us out."

"Shut up!" Cat countered before Irish could reply. "It was your scam that put all of us behind the eight ball."

After the outburst, they went silent until the car reached the abandoned base. Ray looked around when the vehicle passed by the abandoned guard shack and the gate which stood open. As expected, he did not see the hint of police. They slowly drove past the area where Greye had given the mickey to Irish. The eerily abandoned buildings on either side of the road looked ominous in the dusky evening light.

"Well, it looks like Arizona is following the plan. We'll have a few minutes, so let's head to the end of the road and turn around to face Young's men when they show up," Irish told Cat, who nodded. "The cops will follow them in, and we'll have Young in the trap."

A moment later, Cat suddenly slowed the vehicle when she noticed a car ahead, blocking their way. Almost immediately after, Greye let out a shriek as she saw two black cars speeding toward them after they emerged from between two buildings on their right.

"Gun it," Ray yelled at Cat, pulling his .45 auto while he started rolling down the passenger side window.

He didn't hear the shots, but the window next to him shattered as two bullets narrowly missed him. Cat pressed on the accelerator, pushing her car forward. She headed for a narrow opening between the blocking vehicle and a cement dock leading to a large building. Just as she reached the incline ramp, a car struck her gray coupe in the rear. Before they realized what had happened, their coupe flipped over on the driver's side.

Metal on the vehicle screeched loudly while the passengers slid down into the doors of the car. The two speeding vehicles attempting to ram Cat's car futilely tried to stop, but they crashed hard into the larger blockade car. The wrecks sent pieces of metal and glass across the area, as Cat's coupe stopped against the side of the raised dock.

Irish landed on Cat in the crash, and his survival instinct took over. He immediately pulled himself up to the passenger door and pushed the heavy steel door upward until it fell open. Greye scrambled forward, trying to get out of the car, but Irish stood in her way. Gun in hand, Ray climbed on top of the vehicle, quickly sending two bullets into the stunned driver of the blockade vehicle, only a few paces away. The driver died while he clutched the steering wheel of the car.

"Come on," Irish yelled down into the coupe, catching a glance of Greye's pale face, bleeding from a cut on her forehead.

He slid down to the ground, keeping the vehicle between himself and the thugs who scrambled out of their cars. Bullets peppered the bottom of the gray coupe as Greye struggled to haul herself out. She pulled herself from the car, tumbling headfirst onto the ground.

Firing another couple of rounds at one thug trying to move in closer, Irish felt something pushing into his ankle. Cat's feet hammered at the partially detached front windshield. He leaned down and grabbed the window's edge, helping her rip it away from the car. As Cat slid her body out of the vehicle, more rounds struck the bottom of her car. She scrambled through the window, yelling out in pain as the shattered glass pieces in the window frame cut into her leg. Cat pulled her revolver from her coat and crouched next to Ray.

While the trio remained protected on one side by the concrete dock and the car on their side, there was an open area on their right. Two men in long trench coats came toward them, using abandoned construction equipment for protection as they tried to cut Irish and Greye off. Irish fired at them, forcing the attackers behind the steel gear.

"You think the cops will protect you, Irish?" Guy Young's shout came from behind the blockading car. "Hell, I own them. Now let me have the bonds and that Greye bitch, and I'll let you and that photographer live."

"I'll tell you what. You can kiss my ass, and I'll still put a bullet in your brain," Irish yelled, looking over the car and seeing the racketeer's face. He quickly sent two bullets in Young's direction, forcing Guy to crouch.

Ray looked at the two women, his mind racing.

"We've got to play for time while we get the hell out of here."

Cat directed his attention to the building. "There's a dock door going into the building behind," she said. "We could try that."

Ray gave her a thin smile. "I hope you brought plenty of shells."

A torrent of bullets peppered the surrounding metal, forcing the trio to huddle close together. Cat took several shots toward the men, trying to flank them, and the men scrambled back.

"All right, we'll get inside and work our way through the building. They won't be able to rush us so easily." He saw Greye's tentative agreement as he quickly reloaded his gun's magazine.

"Alright, when I open up, you two run like hell."

Ray lifted himself and began firing at those thugs he saw. Cat took off first. Greye hesitated, then followed her to the dock door. Bullets peppered the ground near them as the women sprinted along. Fortunately, Cat pushed through with little effort, still holding the door open. Greye flung Cat away from the door when a massive chorus of lead peppered the entrance. The bullets ricocheted off the door and the concrete block wall. Falling to her knees, the bishop's wife let out a moan and grabbed her upper arm.

Cat ran back to the entrance.

"Irish, come on!"

She pushed the door wider while trying to watch the action outside. Ray let loose with a couple of rounds and started toward the building. A man in a yellow fedora stepped out from behind a green trailer holding a Tommy gun. Cat shot at the guy, but she missed. Fortunately, the thug ducked out of sight. Ray's clumsy gait slowed him, but his adrenalin tried to make up for it. Several shots struck the wall as he passed through the door, nearly tackling a large dusty crate a few paces inside the door. Cat slammed the door closed behind him.

Ray tried to push the crate by himself, but it barely moved. Cat and Greye quickly joined him, and, together, the small group moved the screeching heavy container. He noticed the grimace on Greye's face while she used only one arm to assist them.

"Where did you get hit?" he asked before he noticed the bloodstain.

Irish stood next to her and carefully pulled back the shoulder of her coat, and she took a quick breath.

Irish did a quick inspection of the wound; he glanced over at Cat, who was using the crate top as a workbench to reload her revolver.

"You'll be all right," Ray assured Greye. "It's not bleeding badly, and the bullet just went through the meat."

"It hurts like hell." Her eyes revealed the pain. However, the same expression showed her toughness.

"I'll buy an Irish whiskey for you when we're through." Ray winked as he made a field bandage by ripping her sleeve apart and tying off the strip around the wound. When he finished, he turned back to Cat, who had just completed reloading her weapon.

"By the time we're through with this, you will be an expert," he told her with a sly grin.

"You and your bright ideas. Now what's the plan?" the woman shot back.

Ray looked around the large room, heading toward an office along one side. The walls were cinderblock and the large windows high above, near the roof. A few small, grim-covered windows dotted the walls closer to the ground.

"It's the same plan. We have to stay alive. They'll be splitting up now, trying to find a way inside this place. We can look at the other entrances and block them off."

"How can you be sure the police will come?" Cat asked. "You heard Young. Someone tipped him off."

Irish stopped, his rugged face wrinkled at the thought.

"I still trust Arizona," he replied firmly. "Either way, I'm not going down without giving Guy Young a bloody nose. If you have a better idea, let me know."

Ray's attention focused on exits and windows. The cinderblock walls were a comfort, but he noticed too many windows for them to cover from one spot. Walking over to a wooden door marked with an Army acronym he could not decipher, he heard glass breaking behind the door.

"Damn," he cursed as he scanned around for anything to barricade the entrance. Seeing nothing available, he cautiously cracked open the door. Inside, one of Young's thugs was trying to enter the room through a narrow window, his leg already inside. Ray's gun rang out twice, and the hoodlum gave a shocked grunt as he fell back outside. However, another goon poked out a Tommy gun barrel, sending a hot lead trail at Irish. He barely got his head out of the way as the .45 caliber bullets struck the door, bursting through while leaving large holes. Backing away, he met the two women behind a large container filled with rusting metal parts.

"That machine gun gives him the advantage, and we can't bar the door. Let's find another place," Irish told them.

"I noticed that the overhead door on the other wall." Greye pointed across the room. "It might lead to another part of the building."

Ray quickly nodded, his attention preoccupied with the pounding sound coming from the front entrance, blocked by the large crate.

"All right, let's head to that door," Irish said, then hurried along the concrete floor. Moving past a row of warehouse forklifts, each covered in military green paint and dust, they reached the large entry to another part of the building. Ray lifted on the bottom handle before the door suddenly stopped with a creaking protest. The opening along the floor was only a couple of feet high.

Bullets ricocheted after them when a Thompson submachine gun open up after Young's triggerman finally got through the office. After scampering under the overhead door on all fours, the trio entered a dim room filled with fifty-five-gallon drums, marked *Waste Oil*. While Greye and Cat went into the room, Ray jumped on the overhead door's bottom edge and forced the reluctant metal to the floor. He looked around the area, finding a grime-covered screwdriver on the top of one barrel. The shamus pushed the tool between the frame and the roller.

"They're coming in from over there," Cat whispered in a pant as she pointed at another large door leading to the front dock.

Outside the entrance, the trio heard Young barking orders to his men.

"Well, let's give them a nasty welcome." He moved closer, taking up a position in the middle of the room with a clear view. Next to the large overhead door for equipment was a smaller exit leading to the outside. Cat took a spot behind another barrel near him while Greye crouched down behind Ray.

There was the sound of kicks striking the door, which finally burst open. Two men stormed through the door; one immediately cut down by Ray's .45. Cat shot the other hoodlum. The thug cried out in pain as he grabbed his belly, doubling up into a fetal position. However, another hoodlum stuck his gun into the opening and started blasting away, forcing Ray and Cat to keep down.

"It won't be much longer, shamus. You should have taken my offer," Guy Young yelled into the room.

Ray responded with two shots just to make himself feel better. The thug inside the room fired again, hitting the steel drum above Ray's head.

Irish waved to Cat, pantomiming to retreat. She nodded and slowly backed away. Reaching out, he gripped Greye by her uninjured shoulder and led her down the line of barrels while Cat went down another aisle. They met up near the wall at the back of the building. The only door opened into a narrow electrical room with a large diesel motor-generator. The massive equipment nearly filled the area with various sized crates and barrels scattered along the back wall. Above them was a line of grimy windows.

"Damn it; we're cut off!" Ray glanced around. "We're not going to last long without an escape route."

"Here, you're better at this," Cat handed her gun to Ray. "Greye and I will find a way we can get up to those windows."

Ray hesitated, looking back and forth at the women. Then he moved aside for the women to enter. Irish took up a position behind a concrete pillar while glancing around for their enemies. He did not have to wait long. A big thug dressed in a familiar tight-fitting suit ran to the right of Irish. He got off a hurried shot and missed. But he knew it had to be either Tweedledee or Tweedledum. Either way, Ray looked for the others he knew were coming.

Abruptly, a machine gun spat bullets, striking the concrete next to him. The ricocheting lead hit several barrels across from Ray. Waste oil started spilling from the green cans like black blood from a wound. Irish took a quick look around the corner of the pillar, glimpsing Guy Young moving forward with two of his men in front of him. He waited until one thug, a guy in a dark blue coat, made the mistake of moving away from cover. Ray's bullet found its mark, sending the mobster to the concrete.

Damn it!

He saw one of Young's henchman grabbed the hoodlum's machine gun.

While Irish held off the men trying to kill them, Cat and Greye stacked the empty barrels on top of a large wooden box crate. The sounds of gunfire grew closer, and each woman forced themselves to keep working despite the pain of their injuries. Even though it was cold inside the room, sweat started dripping from their faces from their frantic re-arranging of the metal containers. Finally, their haphazard-looking pyramid completed, Cat went to the room entrance. A large thug turned the corner, only a few paces from Irish. Then she realized the shamus was reloading his gun.

"Ray, look out on your right!"

Irish dropped his pistol and swung around with Cat's revolver. Near-simultaneous shots rang out, but Ray's bullet struck first, causing the thug to flinch. The two men stared blankly at each other for a moment. Then Tweedledum fell over face first, while Irish hurriedly searched for a bullet hole in him. Ray grabbed his .45 auto and scrambled back into the room while gunshots from Young's men peppered the wooden walls. He pulled next to Cat, his face ashen as he tried to catch his breath.

"Thanks for the save. Tweedledum had me dead to rights," he told her between breaths.

"Luck of the Irish," Cat smirked, then she went to the wall. Ray gave a smile while he watched her help Greye up their makeshift ladder. He turned his attention back to the outside of the room, where Young's men continued to close in. He shot when they broke from cover to keep their heads down, but he knew they would soon overwhelm the small room.

Greye reached the top of the stack first and attempted to pull open the sash in the center of a sizeable steel-framed window about two stories above the floor. Her injured arm shook at the painful effort, but grudgingly, the frame creaked open toward her. Cat climbed next to her and helped widen the opening enough for Greye to crawl out on the roof edge.

"Come on," Cat whistled down before she scrambled over the top of the window edge.

Irish shot off with two more rounds, slamming the door closed before he hurried to the stack of barrels. Pocketing his guns, he hurriedly climbed the rickety pile of drums, which wobbled beneath him. Trying to balance with each step to the window, Ray slipped near the top and threw his arms up to catch the window's metal edge. The containers beneath him suddenly let go, falling to the concrete and crashing into the door. Hanging from the window, Irish struggled to pull himself over the top of the sash. A machine gun spewed bullets into the door below him, the ricocheting noise deafening inside the narrow room.

As Ray finally pulled his body through the opening, one of their attackers pushed into the area. Irish looked down at the roof of a long steel shed below him. The women waited for him on top of the shed. He was still hanging on to the metal frame when the thug pointed his machine gun up. Ray released his grip just as the gangster let loose with bullets, shattering the glass.

Landing on his shoulder and striking his head, Ray let out a loud groan, then felt dizziness envelop his vision. The roaring pain in his hand reached him. Rolling onto his back, Irish gripped his wounded hand as blood flowed from where he used to have a pinky finger. He did not notice Greye crouch next to him.

"We have to keep moving."

She shook him on his shoulder after picking up his dropped weapon. Her desperate words forced Irish to come out of his stupor. He swung his body over the edge of the shed, falling to the ground. Ray landed on his feet, staggering back into the metal wall of the shed. He helped the bishop's wife slide off the shed while he tried to get his bearings.

The trio landed behind the building in an open area with a few abandoned equipment pieces next to the shed. About a hundred paces across from the building, more structures had the familiar hallmarks of barracks. Cat had already jumped down from the hut, moving ahead to find a place to go. Soon she was racing back to them.

"Someone is coming from a door over there," she breathlessly huffed while he staunched the flow of blood from his finger using a handkerchief,

"Get your revolver from my pocket." Ray nodded at his coat. He finished binding his wound and took his .45 from Greye.

"Come on, Arizona," Irish whispered to himself before he looked at the women.

"Well, we go the other way."

Irish began a slow trot, following grass and weed-covered ground along the back of the shop building and moving away from the immediate danger. As he got close to the end of the building, Ray peered around the corner of the shop. He froze.

Guy Young and two of his men were cautiously working their way along the side of the building and coming toward them. Trying to back up around the corner, Ray took a quick shot, which went wide of the mark. However, the enemy bullets came flying back his way.

"We've got problems!"

"Damn it, think of something," Greye shot back.

He tried to remain calm as his mind raced for an answer. If the trio tried to run across the open ground, the hoodlums would cut them down before they got to the barracks. All they could do was try to hold out behind the steel trash bin. He gingerly pulled the box of cartridges from his pocket, then asked Greye to help him open the small package.

"Get down," Ray whispered, crouching down as he pulled Greye down with him. One of Young's men took up a position behind the shed. Irish fumbled for his cartridges, his hand shaking as he tried to reload the gun's magazine.

"Cat, you focus on keeping those goon's heads down," he said, as he slid the magazine into the gun's handle. "I'll try to hold off that clown with the Thompson behind us."

The lull in the gun battle left a deathly quiet over the area. Irish recalled a similar calm during fighting in the south Pacific. But now, he felt even more like the odds were against him. The setting sun was leaving long shadows that covered their position. But they were still sitting ducks. Like the two women next to him, Irish prayed for any help that might be available.

He noticed the goon carrying the Tommy gun decided to make a move. He dashed behind several large rusting engines on a crate about a dozen paces away. Ray fired three shots that missed. Seeing Young and his two men still approaching, Cat stuck her hand around the building's corner and shot several times. When she peeked back around, the enemy had ducked out of sight.

The huddled group of intended targets could not hear the distinct wail of sirens approaching while Young's hitman peppered the heavy metal bin. The bullets striking the steel forced them to press close together, each praying for the loud noise to stop. Then, the hoodlum heard the police sirens and took off after he emptied the round magazine. Irish glanced up to see him running away and put two slugs into his back, sending the goon tumbling on the ground.

Cat looked around the corner, seeing Young running for the building's front with his massive bodyguard right behind him. The last thug, quicker and smaller, soon passed the two men, getting to the building's front first. Soon, their enemies were out of sight.

"Are they leaving?" she asked her comrades, her tone a mixture of hope and disbelief.

Irish carefully scanned the area around them and drifted to the corner of the structure. The echoes coming from the front of the building told him someone was attempting to start a car. The sound of sirens grew closer to the trio. Staying close to the wall, Ray edged along, as Greye and Cat followed him. When they reached the front of the building, the trio peered over the top of the concrete, which extended into the road. They witnessed the aftermath.

Two police cars raced toward the crashed vehicles near the dock. Before the first police cruiser could stop, Young's black car spun away, trying to avoid the cop's vehicle. The second squad car intentionally struck the front fender of Young's larger car, sending it into a row of the abandoned army carts lined along the road. When both vehicles came to a sudden stop, a firefight broke out between the police and the remaining hoodlums. Irish forced his interested partners to remain crouched behind the concrete with him. He glimpsed one policeman's brutal death from a hail of bullets. The large man in the brown suit tried to point the Tommy gun at another cop, only to succumb to the rapid-fire shots coming from the allies spilling out of their cars. His dying body spun around from the bullets striking him, a grotesque half-dance before he flopped to the ground. Inside the large vehicle, the driver hesitated about surrendering, and his delay cost him. One policeman shattered the windshield with his shot, and the driver lost half of his face in a few milliseconds.

Inside the back of the large black car, they heard the cries of Young yelling out his surrender. Carefully, the men in uniform, along with Lieutenant Arizona Campbell, closed around the vehicle. In less than a minute, Guy Young cautiously stepped from the car with his hands held up. While the gore covered his finely tailored suit, the racketeer who terrorized Oyster City stood unscathed.

Irish and the women walked toward the cops with their hands in the air as two more cars of uniformed men arrived. Arizona directed his men to handcuff Guy Young and then sped him away to jail.

In the back of the squad car, the racketeer gave Irish a smug grin. Ray suddenly wondered if the gangster could bond himself out of jail and back to his ship. It was something he never considered. Before he could condemn himself further, Arizona came toward Ray, and his face was red with anger.

"Damn, I'm sorry we're late," he told him. "Are any more of Young's gang around?"

"I think a few are in there; they might still be alive, so be careful," Ray nodded to the building where the first battle started. "One out behind the building is probably dead."

The man felt the shakes coming over his body while he recovered from the adrenalin surge. He leaned against Cat's overturned car, watching the detective yelled out the information to his men. Then he ordered a man to call in for an ambulance. After Arizona finished, the cop asked for Ray's gun, and Ray held it out for him. Cat came next to the policeman and handed her revolver over as well. She noticed Arizona raised an eyebrow.

"I made a lot of noise, but I'm not sure what I hit," she confided.

Her shaky hand released the weapon, and the policeman nodded. He waved over a young uniformed policeman when he noticed bloody bandages and dried bloodstains on the women.

"You take these ladies to the hospital now," Arizona ordered.

Irish put his hand on Cat's shoulder.

"Thanks for the backup. You missed getting your pictures."

"Yeah, it was a little too close for that." She gave him a tired grin, then followed Greye and the policeman to a squad car.

After the women got in the vehicle, Arizona turned to Ray. "You can go with me. That way, we can talk."

Several minutes later, the two men were sitting in the back of a police car while a uniformed cop drove them to the hospital. Arizona cop asked about Ray's injury.

"Hurts like hell," he replied with a grimace. "I'm missing a good part of a finger, so call me stubby." He leaned back in the seat, carefully placing his bandaged hand on his lap.

"You were late."

The cop looked away for a moment.

"Why in the hell didn't you tell me that Greye La Spina was in the middle of this? You almost got her killed."

"You'll find out when you talk to her at the hospital. There are a lot of twists to this story. By the way, it wasn't supposed to be a shootout with us against Young's men." Irish leaned back in the seat, tired and emotionally drained.

"I feel like a damn fool about that. Somebody jimmied the motors in the police cruisers we were using, so we only got partway there. It took a while for me to hijack a couple of squad cars."

Ray noticed Arizona left something major unsaid, but he let it go. Young paid off someone inside to hold up the cops coming to arrest the racketeer. They both knew it, and there was no reason for Ray to rub Arizona's nose in it.

Half an hour later, Irish sat inside a room at the Oyster City hospital. Arizona had the full story and the bearer bonds by the time they arrived. Irish told him about Greye's scam and the United Church Foundation books. Ray also explained someone from City Hall would smooth over the financials to keep the bishop's name out of any potential scandal.

Arizona did not appear surprised at the news, although he reminded Ray that the police should have handled the problem. Irish nodded with tired politeness.

"Maybe so, but in a less corrupt city," he said.

A uniformed policeman stood outside the hospital room, but Irish was unsure whether the cop was for protection or keeping him from leaving. He knew he broke a few laws in his scheme to trap Young. Private detective license or not, Ray considered his situation tenuous. A doctor had already patched him up, sticking a needle in his finger before cleaning and stitching up the wound. The needle hurt worse than the bullet, but it left most of his hand numbed. He was looking at his wrapped appendage when the door opened. Henry La Spina stepped inside the room.

"Mr. Irish, could you spare a moment of your time?" The big man was cordial as Ray eyed him carefully.

"I'm not going anywhere. What would you like to discuss?" Ray extended his right hand, and the bishop gave him a firm handshake.

"My wife," Henry told him quietly.

"How is she doing?" Ray asked, trying to keep the conversation from going the wrong direction.

The bishop gave a thin smile.

"The wound is painful but not of major concern, according to the doctor. But I believe you already surmised that."

"I've seen worse wounds," Irish admitted.

"Yes, I'm sure. Greye told me you fought in the war. You must be a brave man. However, your idea of handling this situation in this manner seems poorly conceived and executed." The tone from the bishop was not overly friendly.

Irish looked at Henry for a moment. "That could be. Then again, I'm new at handling another person's problem. Did your wife give you all the details?"

Henry nodded and gave him a quick summary of Greye's story, which Ray backed up at times. He noticed how the man's wife worked herself into the role of a victim with her story. It was also clear that Henry La Spina didn't believe the tale.

"So, what do you think?" Ray asked when he finished.

La Spina took a deep breath.

"I'm afraid my wife can be rash in her judgment, especially regarding her male friends. However, her scandalous exploits have come to my attention before. This entire scheme is a delicate matter, given what has occurred. You can see my problem."

"From what I heard, she got in over her head," Irish attempted to defend her. "It's not the first time in history such a thing has happened."

"I appreciate your tact, even if misplaced," the bishop gave him a half-smile. "I've heard many of the stories concerning Mrs. La Spina."

"Yeah, but you know very well that not every rumor is true," Ray reminded him. "Despite what people might say, your wife showed real grit in the battle with Young's thugs. I've seen guys take off running in the same type of fight. You're lucky that she's the kind of woman who won't fall apart on you."

Henry La Spina looked at him, his dark eyes sympathetic.

"I can tell you value bravery, Mr. Irish. However, I believe that loyalty and trust are missing in your description. The whole incident came about because of her relationship with…well, those with less breeding, shall we say." The bishop looked down at Ray's hand. "Still, despite my misgivings, it appears your efforts paid off. The police lieutenant gave me the bearer bonds, and they have put a notorious criminal behind bars. The foundation should survive, provided that I keep the newspapers from the story."

Ray shrugged his shoulders.

"I don't think anyone will talk about that. Guy Young and the shootout will be good headlines for a day or two, then, on to the next big item in Oyster City." An awkward silence filled the room.

"Thank you for your explanation and for keeping my wife alive. Good evening to you, sir." With that, the bishop shook Ray's hand again and left the room.

~~~

The man with the mask of the Emperor stared across the five-sided table at the large person wearing the guise of the High Priest. On the other side of the table sat Death and Judgment.

"You heard the commandment of the Master. The rest of the circle decided your family must make the sacrifice. When will this happen?" The Emperor's voice revealed the person's concern.

The High Priest looked around the table.

"You made that decision without my vote. Other candidates bleed just as easily."

"Are you forgetting your duties to the circle and the city? Judgment spoke with a deep, gravelly voice, pausing for a moment. Yes, we chose the creature, but you should have offered the sacrifice. Certainly, this pathetic person is of no importance."

"Besides, as an outsider, it's the only real option," Death's voice interjected, melodic and persuasive. The masked man continued, thoroughly convinced of the righteousness of his ideas. "The other people of which you speak are distant relations to the founding members. While their sacrifice may be necessary in the future, it's certainly not needed at the moment. Our Master will display his power soon; your sacrifice is a fitting tribute."

The Emperor gazed at the High Priest.

"We will work on the arrangements for your compliment to the Master. Do you agree?"
~~~

The room was silent for a moment, each masked person watching the Priest. Finally, the person nodded slowly, and the thin figure with the Demon mask entered the room.

"You have done well, my friends. Because of this delay, we will find a substitute to bring forth the Master and rid the city of its menace. It is a fitting irony that the perfect person waits for the Emperor and Death to dispense justice."

~~~

Two days later, Irish was back in Detective Campbell's office. The door was open, and the two men talked while drinking the bitter coffee, which might have been in the pot for the week. Arizona pulled out Ray's .45 auto from the desk drawer, sliding it over to the shamus.

"You might as well have this back," the cop told him as he flicked a thin card across the desk. "It appears you already had a concealed weapons permit."

Ray raised an eyebrow at the news, then picked up the permit with his name on it.

"Interesting how things work in this town."

"Yeah, it's just great how a person can have a license suddenly show up that's backdated. You're a lucky man," he said. "By the way, I heard the District Attorney is still upset with you for withholding evidence about Young. But it seems you have someone in a prominent place who backs you. It must be nice, but don't let it go to your head."

Campbell sighed as he leaned back in the chair.

"Don't worry; I'm sure it's only temporary. I'm not from this city," Ray reminded him as he put the gun in his pocket. "Did you figure out who nearly gummed up the works the other day? I'm guessing someone must have been listening in on our phone call."
~~~

"It could have been anyone. The policeman shook his head. The garage is open on two sides, and I checked. No fresh faces were poking around that day."

"Then someone listened on the phone call, keeping an eye on what you're doing, and relayed the information to someone else, maybe a cop or maybe just inside. Is that it?" Irish showed his surprise at the tentacles that Young held around the place.

"No other way around it," Arizona told him. "Don't be calling me anymore. We'll just have coffee."

"I'll make sure of it; just find a place that makes better java," Ray replied with a grin. "What about your famous prisoner? How's he taking the news?"

Arizona just shook his head.

"He made a big stink for a lawyer who is driving down from upstate," he said. "A judge will probably set bond tomorrow."

"You don't think they'll let him out?" Irish wasn't surprised, just angry.

"Who knows?" Arizona told him. "All I know is if he gets back on that ship, we can kiss any trial goodbye. Governor won't touch him. Welcome to the wonderful world of law in Oyster City."

Ray thought about another drink of coffee and decided against it. He stood, grabbing his hat from the desk.

"Well, let me know if I need to get nervous about Young getting out of jail. And, just so you don't think I've forgotten, thanks for the rescue the other day."

"Just don't keep doing things alone next time," the cop nodded.

Putting on his fedora, Ray walked to the door.

"What do you mean alone? I had help from two lovely women." Irish gave him a wink as he walked out.

~~~
~~~

Saturday morning, Irish sat inside his new office across from the building housing the *Beacon*. It was the same mostly barren room, but it looked a bit more complete with a recently wiped down desk and two used chairs, which Cat stole from J. Allan Dunn's office. She even found an old picture of Franklin Roosevelt for him to hang on the wall. The biggest difference was the sign on the outside of the office door saying Ray Irish Agency. He used some of Dunn's cash to pay for six months' rent and a painter to do the signage. Next week, he had a phone coming, making the newest private detective agency in Oyster City complete. The room in the back held a lumpy twin mattress on a squeaky bed frame. A small closet contained one of his two suits, while an old dresser that he found at the second-hand store over by the mission sat next to the bed.

The new business owner had his feet propped up on the windowsill as he looked across to the windows of the newspaper building. Despite the shop activity below, it remained relatively quiet during the weekdays. However, on the weekend, the dead silence would make a crypt owner proud.

On the nearly empty desk next to him, a copy of the morning paper lay open. The screaming headline blazed in bold type; *RACKETEER GIVES IT UP*. Irish already read the article several times, so he knew it nearly by heart. Guy Young committed suicide overnight inside the jail. Found hanging at the twisted end of a sheet inside the most secure facility in the city, the notorious gangster somehow staged a suicide. On top of that, it went undiscovered for over eight hours. Those might have been the facts reported by officials, but he believed little in the article. Guy Young had money and power, along with friends in the capital.

Plus, Young had a ruthless survivor streak. In his heart, Irish knew the gangster didn't kill himself. Ray would bet his last penny something else happened inside the cell.

However, as Ray's foot tapped unconsciously on the edge of the window, his mind left such speculation behind. Instead, he thought about daggers, particularly a wall of ceremonial knives hanging inside Bishop La Spina's house. The weapons continued to bother him, so much so that they invaded his dreams. When he woke, the shamus held had no memories other than a wall of blades and a vague, ominous feeling. The same sense he got when entering a dark, musty basement of an ancient building where the flesh on his arm went cold and prickly. It bothered him the same way the gangster's suicide did. It made little sense.

The sound of footsteps racing up the staircase outside of his office brought Ray out of his trance. He turned his head at the noise of his door handle turning. J. Allan Dunn entered the room, his thin face looking paler than usual.

"Have you seen Cat?" he asked.

Irish dropped his feet and turned in the chair. "No, not since yesterday," he told him. "Why?"

"Damn it; it can't be true." Dunn's voice cracked, and his blue eyes widened in fear.

Ray instantly stood up; he felt his panic from across the room.

"What's going on, Dunn?"

"I…I got a call this morning at home." Dunn began pacing in front of the desk, pulling off his hat, his hands slowly crushing it between his fingers. "Some guy said that Cat had a photograph they wanted back. He told me she's a guest on the *Stanley Rose* until I get the picture to them."

While he was pretty sure of the answer, Ray asked his question.

"Let's slow down here. How did they know you had it, and who wants it back?"

"It's Mark Fordham; he's kidnapped Cat. I just went over to Cat's apartment after the phone call, and she wasn't there. The landlord told me she left with a couple of men yesterday. From the description he gave me, it must have been a couple of Fordham's guys. Now the bastard wants to trade her for the photo she gave me, the one with Howard in it. The son of a bitch found out everything. I need your help." Dunn's watery eyes were pleading.

Irish felt a knot in his stomach at the news, remembering the thug with the knife who was staking out Cat's place. "I'll help, but how could they know about you getting the picture?"

Dunn's shoulders sagged as his pacing slowed. "I'm not sure, but someone knows about Cat and me. He told me that on the phone."

"What are you talking about?" Ray asked.

J. Allan stammered under his breath for a moment, unable to say anything intelligent. Finally, he turned and faced the shamus. "Catherine is my little girl. Her mother and I were nearly married. It's a long story, but Cat doesn't even know about this. The bastard on the phone just said if I wanted my daughter back, I needed to come through with the picture of Fordham. He warned me that if I didn't come through, she would end up a drowned cat, feeding the fish."

"Have you still got the photograph they want?" Irish turned to look out the window, trying to understand their options.

"Yes, I still have it," Dunn told him as he started pacing again.

Ray came back to his desk. "All right, what else did they tell you?"

"Not much," he admitted. "The guy said that Cat would wait by the podium on the *Stanley Rose* tonight. I bring the picture, and Cat can leave."

The air was thick and still for a moment. "Do you believe Fordham will let you and Cat off that ship?" Ray asked.

J. Allan stopped pacing.

"I don't know what they will do, but I know I don't have a choice."

J. Allan Dunn, unrecognizable under his gold mask and red robe, remained silent as he and Irish sat in the water taxi heading to the *Stanley Rose*. Irish sat next to the city director, uncomfortable behind a grinning black mask. The entire get-up reminded him too much of the mysterious shadow figures he'd seen a few times in the alleys of Oyster City. At least the long, white robe covered him; he thought as he felt the .45 auto strapped to the inside of his ankle with some duct tape. He hated the improvised solution, but an ankle holster for his weapon was hard to find. Ray might lose some leg hair, but he felt safer if the thugs working for Fordham decided to remove Dunn and him permanently.

The rest of the partygoers heading to the gambling ship were an elaborately adorned collection of drunken men and women. Most of the women looked like they came out of a French painting with flashy and colorful hoop dresses and tight-fitting corsets, their masks delicately narrow to cover their eyes. Some husbands looked like terrible copies of the Founding Fathers, complete with powder wigs, which the men took off occasionally to scratch their balding heads. There was the sprinkling of traditional military uniforms among the rest of the men, while Ray's eyes landed on one lady. She had a knockout body and showed it with her tight buckskin custom. Unfortunately, Pocahontas looked nearly green from seasickness. The masquerade ball would be quite the event if she got sick in the middle of the dance floor. Irish turned his attention back to Dunn.

"Maria refused to marry me; she was in love with some bum who worked on the docks. The son of a bitch got himself killed not long after Maria sent me packing. But when I tried to do the right thing, she would have nothing to do with me. Still, I've helped them when they needed it. Her mom never turned down cash."

For some reason that Ray did not understand, Dunn suddenly appeared happy to unload his secret about Cat.

"I know I've not been a real father to her. But I didn't try to take Cat away from her mom. Maybe I should have. Maria was cute, but a high jumper. She liked to have everything if a guy didn't tie her down. I was just a clerk, going nowhere in her eyes." J. Allan sighed as he reminisced. "Of course, that meant she hooked onto every greaseball or crumb with a five-spot that came along."

"Why doesn't Cat know about you?" Ray tried to keep his voice down.

He did not need to worry with a burst of sudden croaking laughter from a fat guy looking like Ben Franklin.

J. Allan shrugged.

"I was just married when Cat started asking questions about her dad. You know, the kids at school got to her about not having a father and all. When Maria suggested letting her know the truth, I was still in a beef about it. I told Cat's mom that she made her bed. I might pay under the table, but I told Maria to leave me out of it. It was a dumb move. Don't think I don't regret it every time I see Cat."

"Nobody I know can tell the future. At least you tried; some people wouldn't." Irish failed to know why he was so sympathetic to the guy; it just seemed the right thing to do.

"But let's keep our heads here. Cat is tough; she'll be fine."

"You think they'll let us walk away?" J. Allan could have read Ray's mind.

"I'm not sure," he replied. "Fordham might be as ruthless as Young. I'm new here, if you remember?"

Dunn pulled off his mask to wipe his sweating face. "From what I know, he's not one to cross," he said. "Maybe he's just less public about what he does with those who cross him."

Irish realized their boat was closing fast on the *Stanley Rose,* and he stood.

"We'll know soon enough," he told him. "I bet Fordham will be easy to find since he's giving a speech for all these drunks."

J. Allan took a cursory look at the loud crowd behind them.

"He's using the ship to pad his pockets and win the election."

"Free food and booze are good ways to win your voters. Do your friends have a backup plan without your photo?" Ray noticed the fake Pocahontas now leaned over the edge of the water taxi. The girl puked up her guts as the little craft rocked back and forth in the deeper water.

"The mayor and his people always have a plan," Dunn assured the shamus with confidence. "But that won't help us here. I'm on my own. I couldn't even tell them about this thing."

The boat pulled up to the floating dock alongside the *Stanley Rose.* The passengers quickly spilled out to join with other revelers already taking part in the festivities. Two robed men held back, slowly following the group, which headed to the main deck where a small stage stood. Campaign posters and painted canvas banners covered the ship. Above the crowd, hundreds of red, white, and blue silk streamers flickered in the light breeze. Large theater lights flooded the open deck at the top of the vessel, giving a surreal daylight effect to the colorful display of customs.

Irish noticed a line forming at the side of the stage and soon saw the unmasked Mark Fordham, who stood like an emperor receiving his subjects' accolades. The guests slowly filed past the party host, giving their thanks and compliments. Electric and celebratory, the atmosphere felt like the night of the election. And the union boss stroked the egos of those passing by.

Dressed in a black tuxedo, Fordham displayed a powerful broad chest and shoulders from his years as a dock worker. His ample girth made him look like a professional wrestler. The host had gray around the temples of his thick, black hair, while his sunken gray eyes gave him a sleepy appearance. But Ray perceived an underlying menace behind the unassuming expression.

Irish and Dunn joined the line and soon noticed Cat nearby. The young woman, dressed as a flapper with a little mask covering her eyes, stood behind the stage. The clothes Cat wore, low cut and tight-fitting, highlighted her body. In another setting, the shamus would have liked the look. However, his attention quickly focused on the thug holding her arm. The lean gunman next to Cat sported a cowboy costume, and his gun belt displayed two revolvers.

"What do you want to bet those guns are real and loaded?" Ray whispered to J. Allan. "How about I pull back and start moving over to cover Cat? You can make the trade."

"That bastard acts like he's already won," Dunn replied bitterly, then nodded to Irish. "All right, I'll show my face to that union bum and make him go back to the stage. That way, you can cover both of us."

Ray started to leave the line when he felt a gun barrel pushing against his spine.

"Don't be stupid, shamus. We saw you coming with Dunn. You should have put on your costumes before you got to the dock. Just head to the stage, and we'll take you to the boss." The ominous growl was next to Ray's ear. Irish glanced behind to see two large men wearing military outfits from the First World War. The thugs didn't bother with masks.

At the same time, J. Allan Dunn felt a heavy hand on his shoulder, looking back to see one of Fordham's thugs who pushed him forward. Ray followed along, a gun poking into his back until they reached the end of the stage. Telling the two robed men not to move, one of the soldier goons went over to his boss. The cowboy escorted Cat until she stood across from Dunn. Soon, Fordham came to the back of the stage. Nodding to the man standing by Cat, the cowboy left and took up a position near the front of the stage to keep any onlookers away. Out of sight from most of the party-goers, Mark Fordham's manner changed. A spiteful gaze replaced the sleepy expression.

"I'm glad you could make it out to my victory party tonight," he addressed Dunn after the director took off his mask. "Now, let's just get this transaction completed so I can get back to my guests."

Dunn reached inside his robe, and one soldier quickly pointed his gun at them. The director froze.

"You want the damn picture or not?" he asked.

Fordham grunted, and his gray eyes remained cold.

"Go ahead."

Still in his mask, Ray walked next to Cat, taking her by the arm.

"Are you all right?"

"I'm fine," she told him, her stare remained on Fordham.

Fordham's eyes grew dark when he looked over.

"I don't like what you're implying, shamus. We treated her just fine. They just don't like people with bad attitudes.

You might remember that when my boys come by to pick you up next time."

"Yeah, I have a problem with invitations like that. Next time, send a letter," Ray told him.

"You're a lucky wise guy," the wide man smirked. "I thought about having my men take you down below to teach you some manners. But I'm in a forgiving mood tonight. Once the election is over, I'm sure we'll talk again unless you get smart and leave town." The boss turned back to Dunn. "Now give me that damn picture. I've already got the negative."

Dunn pulled an envelope from his robe and handed the letter to the union boss.

"Don't think you've got it won yet, Fordham. It's known that strangers in this town get the short straw."

"Yeah, keep telling yourself that when you're on the unemployment line," Fordham sneered as he took the picture. "Lots of changes are coming to those who backed the wrong horse." The union boss stuffed the photo in his jacket.

Ray started to walk with Cat, keeping his eyes focused on Fordham's hoodlums. Dunn joined them at the front of the stage.

Terrified screams erupted from the bow of the *Stanley Rose*. Almost immediately, a massive fireball exploded, rocking the entire ship and sending people to the deck. Chaos swept through the crowd as the blast knocked over displays and tables. Panic filled the air as the costumed crowd pushed toward the stern. Then another fireball shook the gambling ship, sending fires into the night sky like rockets. Flames shot out of the open vents across the bridge, quickly catching the hanging paper and canvas displays on fire. The wind sent thick smoke and debris over the milling crowd as they reacted like cattle in a stampede.

Irish slammed his fist into a man standing in his way as he desperately pushed to get to the edge of the ship. He heard agonized shrieks from above and caught a glimpse of two people in costume suddenly jumped in desperation from the balcony area. After they struck the metal deck nearby with a sickening thud, their broken bodies continued to burn. Ray pushed forward, trying to guide his companions away from the floating dock where many people rushed toward.

As they fought through the crowd, Cat desperately held onto Ray's robe while using her shoulder to push through those standing in her way. She witnessed more horrific scenes as the wind sent flaming streamers raining down on a massed group near a stairway. Flimsy costumes quickly caught fire, giving the place an appearance of Hell. The flame-covered bodies spasmodically danced and twisted in fear and agony while she watched, then turned away.

Near the ship's railing, the photographer saw a woman dressed like Pocahontas trying to climb over the stairway rails. However, a beefy man grabbed the lady, pulling her away to take her place. The costumed woman tumbled down the stairs to the deck, where frenzied people stomped her in their panicked escape. Cat glimpsed the unmoving body, and she noticed the woman's one open eye blankly staring from a half-crushed skull.

J. Allan Dunn stayed right behind Cat, using his fists and feet to keep people from pushing him away from his daughter. His fearless need to keep his only child alive made him mean and ruthless. At the railing, a hysterical man and his wife tried to push past Dunn, screaming about their children at home. J. Allan used his elbow to smack down the terrified woman who pulled on his robe from behind. Dunn lashed out with his foot, striking the husband in the groin. The couple fell in the wave of crushing bodies as the trio finally reached the edge of the ship.

Pulling Cat next to him at the guardrail, Irish used his strength to hold off others grappling with him. He straddled the rail. Cat looked down, and fear filled her eyes.

"The water's too cold; we'll die." Cat's trembling yell suddenly turned into a scream as the *Stanley Rose* unexpectedly tilted forward when the ship's bow dropped.

Irish grabbed Cat and dragged her over the rail with him, letting their bodies fall into the water below. When they struck the cold water, the shock nearly caused him to inhale the liquid. Almost out of breath, somehow Ray got to the surface, coughing and spitting out the water that tried to drown him. The freezing, dark water held screaming and struggling victims around him. Still, Irish heard Cat's voice calling out to him. He got her attention with a yell.

Several yards away, he caught sight of Dunn landing in the water while the shamus struggled to remove his costume. His Seabee training snapped on as the man flipped the end of the robe up in the air and used one end to create an enormous bubble under the wet fabric. He tied the ends of the makeshift life vest off and yelled for Cat to join him. Irish reached out and drew her close to him. Soon Dunn joined them, and Irish had him create a similar temporary life vest. After J. Allan finished, Ray brought them together.

While the ship's flames illuminated the night sky, the shivering trio called out for one of the few water taxis circling the area. However, *Stanley Rose*'s stern finally lifted high into the air. The screeching of the twisting metal combined with the screams of those still aboard remained etched into the survivors' minds. Within a few minutes, the gambling ship went to the bottom of the bay.

The morning came, and most of those who survived the *Stanley Rose's* sinking finally left. The survivors spent the night wrapped in wool blankets while sitting in hastily erected tents. Police officers interviewed many passengers, then released them to be accosted by reporters. The newshawks listened to the sad tales of loss and persistence while families came to the dock to retrieve the survivors.

Sunshine revealed the few passengers who remained. Huddled next to open fires burning inside large barrels on the pier, they watched the small vessels milling about the harbor. Many waited for news of loved ones. However, the boats that pulled next to the dock only offloaded the bodies found floating in the bay.

Irish stood next to the open fire in damp clothes, still quivering from the cold. Dunn and Cat had already left, taking advantage of the general disorder to avoid conversations with the police and reporters. Cat told Ray about her experience aboard the ship over the past two days during their brief time together. Fordham's men kept her locked up in a room for the time. He noticed the way Cat acted around J. Allan, so Ray assumed the woman heard Dunn and her mother's truth. He decided what the father and daughter would do from that point on was none of his business.

The shamus could have left earlier, but Irish hung around the dock out of curiosity. He listened in on the conversations and responses to the reporter's questions. When one newsman from *Beacon* came by, he recognized Ray.

"Say, aren't you a friend of Cat? I'm Stevens." The young man appeared just out of his school, but he already had the sagged, weary look of a reporter. "You came with the other passengers. What can you tell me?"

"Not much to tell; a fire broke out on the stern and bow, forcing everyone to take to the water," Irish shrugged his shoulders. "If it were two years ago, I would have said a torpedo struck the ship twice. You got a count on the dead yet?"

"No, they're still finding them in ones and twos, taking the bodies for the coroner. He'll be a busy man for the next few days," Stevens told him, thumbing toward a warehouse across the street. "Can you confirm the fires started at the same time?"

"The bow went up in flames first, followed by the stern," Ray explained. "The wind sent the flames into the decorations, which made it worse. Pretty damn suspicious, if you ask me."

"Yeah, I hear that as well," Stevens agreed, his attention suddenly on another small boat coming to the dock. The voice coming from the vessel was excitedly yelling that they found Fordham's body.

"I gotta go," the reporter said, then quickly left.

"Well, that answers my question," Ray said to himself as the troubleshooter started walking to the road. With luck, he hoped he might find a taxi.

~~~

Three weeks later, on a Friday, it was a quiet mid-morning as Irish sat in his office. His feet were back at their usual place plopped on the windowsill while he gazed at the building across the street. Over the last few days, he'd been making phone calls to insurance businesses that might have an interest in a detective working for them when the need arose. Nothing turned up from his inquiries, but he sarcastically consoled himself that at least the receptionists he spoke with now knew his name.

He glanced over at a morning copy of the *Beacon* that he had just finished reading. The election came and went with no big surprise. Mayor Hopley and his gang of thieves kept power over Oyster City. A few days before the election, state investigators came down to hold an inquiry that lasted all of
~~~

two days. When they left, their official tally of the sinking reported over a hundred dead and missing. He read that the sinking also injured another fifty people. The group of politicians agreed that the fire looked suspicious. However, the board found no evidence showing who or what had started the flames. In the end, they sold a lot of papers, while endless radio reports tried to whet the public fascination about the incident. All it did was make a load of money for those papers and stations. The case closed quietly, while the public found other terrible events to satisfy their morbid curiosity.

Lost in thought, Ray did not hear the footsteps coming up to his office or the door quietly open.

"Hello, Ray." Greye La Spina's silky voice immediately got his attention.

"Hello, Mrs. La Spina." He glanced over. "What are you doing here?"

Her long red dress whispered as she swept into the room. Greye closed the office door and locked it. She came around the desk and placed her hands on his shoulders.

"No need to be so formal, Ray. I'm here in peace. I brought you a gift."

He remained quiet, keeping his attention on the window while watching her reflection as she slowly massaged his shoulders. He could feel her energy behind him.

"All right, Greye, talk to me."

She let her hands slip away, pulling a small bottle of Irish whiskey from her purse. She sat the bottle down on the desk. "I came by to tell you I'm going away. Henry and I are taking a cruise to the Mediterranean."

"So, you've settled down and are a good wife now?" Ray could not leave the sarcasm out of his voice.

"Don't treat me that way," Greye told him as she picked the bottle back up and opened it. She took a healthy slug and gave him the bottle as she slid onto the desktop next to him.

"I might deserve it, but please don't do it, not today. We have all morning to spend together."

Irish took the bottle and looked at it.

"It's a little early in the day." He took a quick drink, thinking back to his last mickey from her.

"You and I can celebrate my departure. My husband and I are leaving for Europe, so I wanted to see you before I left." She reached down and took the bottle from his hand, taking another swig. He could tell she was trying hard not to say something. Then he noticed a red welt going around her neck, partially covered by the necklace she wore.

Greye slid off the desktop, bending over to kiss him softly on the earlobe.

"I have a case for you, shamus. Something to keep your logical mind occupied while I'm gone." She pulled a wad of bills from her bra and tossed them on the desk.

"There are five hundred dollars in that roll. It's all I have left in the world. I want to hire you to find someone." Greye walked back to the bedroom door.

"Who do you want me to find?" Ray grew increasingly intrigued by Greye's actions.

The bishop's wife turned and wagged a finger at him.

"No, we can't talk about it right now. Remember, pleasure before business, Ray Irish." She strolled into the room, where she started unzipping the back of her dress. He watched her slowly undressing in the next room, and the shamus rose from his chair.

"Well, you're making this damn difficult," Ray grumbled as he began removing his tie.

<p style="text-align:center">~~~</p>

Late the same day, Irish came out of his bedroom to answer the constant knocking at his office door. He unlocked the door to find Lieutenant Arizona Campbell standing there. Ray opened the door and went to his desk.

"Saturday is quiet around here," the shamus told him as he sat behind the bureau. He uncorked the half-filled bottle of Irish whiskey left by Greye, filling a glass he pulled from his lower desk drawer.

"Yeah, well, it's my day off, and I was driving by," the policeman replied.

Ray laughed at the blatant lie, pulling out another glass.

"Then you can have a drink with me."

Arizona smiled and took a chair.

"Well, maybe just one. How's the business going?"

"Swell. I just got a case this morning. Now, what brings a policeman over on his day off?" Ray leaned across the desk, giving him a tumbler filled with whiskey.

"Something is bothering me," the detective told him candidly as he took a drink. Arizona remained quiet for a while. Irish just sipped on the whiskey.

"I still have several unsolved murders sitting in the files," he finally said. "They're driving me nuts. Somehow, there's a link, but I can't figure it out."

Ray nodded. He understood what his friend was saying.

"You said that Quincannon and Pendexter knocked each other off."

"Yeah, I know what I said. That was the people at the top telling me the official story." Arizona leaned forward, lowering his voice. "Now add in Plug Howard and Guy Young. Despite what the papers say, Fordham's people did not kill Howard, and Young damn well didn't hang himself. But that's not coming from me."

Irish sat up, his eyes alight. "What happened?"

"Both of them had their throats cut." The cop looked around the office as if someone might overhear him. "No witnesses, even in the jail, and someone drained the bodies of blood."

Ray leaned back in his chair, giving a little whistle.

"My God, what the hell is going on?"

The inspector leaned back in his chair. "Exactly my question." He downed the drink in one gulp.

~~~

Two days later, in the early morning warmth of a rising sun, Ray stood by Pappy's newsstand, chatting about the events of the day. The newsy did most of the talking as Irish scanned the headlines, his mind in a trance, unable to interject much into the conversation. His thoughts kept coming back to Greye La Spina. Leaving that evening, she would soon be on a train away from Oyster City. However, her haunting eyes filled his mind, and he couldn't get her last conversation out of his head.

After spending most of their morning enjoying themselves in unbridled passion and lust, Irish held Greye in his arms on top of his small bed. He asked her about the line of abrasion going around her neck.

"That's a present from my husband," she sighed, laying her head on his broad, hairy chest.

"A couple of nights after we escaped from Guy Young, Henry came to my bedroom to tell me about all the stories he heard about me. At first, I thought he would kill me. Instead, my husband punished me. Put a dog leash around my neck, telling me he'd use that from now on to make sure his bitch stays home."

Ray remembered how her warm tears felt as Greye told about the mistreatment she received from her husband. He told
~~~

her she needed to leave Oyster City, but she remained quiet. Finally, Greye raised her head and looked at him.

"You don't think I deserve it after how I've humiliated him along with everything else? I did worse to you." She laid her head on his chest again, looking at the recent knife scar on his chest.

"I know you'll never be able to trust me, but I'm sorry for what I did to you."

He was quiet for a moment.

"Yeah, you did me wrong. At times, you're a no-good tramp," Irish told her simply, while he stroked her hair. "You told me there was something between us. I'm not sure about anything like that, but the truth is that I can't hate you for everything that happened."

Ray let out a deep breath.

"But I'm all over the place. It's just I can't hate like so many do. I can't trust you because you were willing to let me die. You helped me when I needed it, and you also took a bullet to keep Cat alive. I consider that a fair trade between us. Not that I want to do that again."

She lightly ran her finger across his injury, then stopped.

"You're damn right I'm a no-good tramp. My first instinct is to grab the loot and run. It's all I know. We both realize that I only helped get Young because you forced me into it." Greye glanced up at him.

"Still, I had a dream that maybe you can teach me to be better. Do you think I could be like that little photographer you want?"

Ray softly ran his hand over her shoulder.

"Listen, you're more like her than you realize," he mumbled. "This damn world is full of hurt, and I think we've all seen too much death and cruelty. But I'm not the guy to teach anything to anyone. I'm just a drifter trying to forget things, whether that means staying busy or using the bottle. Hell, I'm not even sure what I'm doing here."

"I'd leave Henry if you asked me to," Greye told him. "Maybe I could learn not to care about money?"

Ray suddenly stopped moving his hand.

"I know," he replied. "You just need to leave this place and find a new start somewhere else. That would be the best idea."

"That could happen," she turned to him, giving him a brave smile. "Henry hinted I should just stay in Europe, leaving him to return alone. I could send you a telegram if that happens."

The sudden silence from Pappy brought Irish out of his thoughts. He gave his friend a quick smile.

"Sorry, lots of things are on my mind right now."

Pappy looked at him.

"I just said my wife asked me to see when you can come back over for dinner? She was pretty impressed with how much you ate. Emma keeps telling me I don't eat enough."

"Tell your wife thanks," Ray nodded. "I'll take her up on that offer real soon. By the way, do you have any books on the prior history of Oyster City?"

"Sure I do," the newsy said. "I got an entire stack from the library when they were getting rid of their old books. Some fool wanted to give them to a paper drive for the war effort. When you come over, I can bring them out."

"Swell, I'll swing by your place. I have a couple of things to finish up first." Ray waved as he left his friend to his work.

Later that evening, the shamus took a taxi to his new home. He was sitting on his bed, thinking about going to sleep, when he heard the distinctive sound of high heels coming up the wooden stairs. Since he was the only one living on the floor, Ray was pretty sure she would knock at his door.

Curious, Irish slid off his bed and started to the front door. He reached for the handle after the third tap.

It was Cat, looking quite attractive in a polka dot, white and green dress. He smiled at the silly, green hat which completed the ensemble.

"Are you lost?" he asked.

She walked in with a smirk.

"Still, Mr. Hilarious, I see. Maybe you're in the wrong business. You need to tell jokes for a living," she told him. "I spoke with Pappy today, and he told me you had dinner with him and his wife a while back. How did it go?"

"Great food and friendly conversation," Irish replied as he closed the door. "He's a good man. Now, why are you hanging around here?"

She went to his desk, picking up the open bottle of whiskey sitting there.

"I have a piece of advice for you, shamus. People in this town won't be looking for help from a guy getting drunk at his desk. The same goes for getting clients when you have a crazy black man as a best friend." Cat's tone was critical.

"You forget I met Mrs. Purvey, so you find your friends and leave me to mine." Irish scowled at her.

"Aren't you going to offer me a drink?" she asked, her face turning bright.

Ray went behind and opened the bottom drawer, giving her a tumbler he pulled out.

"All right, enough of the dance, Cat. You don't drop in without reason."

The photographer put the bottle back on the desk and took a deep breath; her face turned to a frown.

"You're a damn ass when you want to be."

"And you can be damn hard to understand. So we're even. Now tell me why you're here, kid. I don't read minds."

"I'm not a kid, you know." Cat took a seat, looking out his office window. "You should have told me about Dunn. He explained everything about him and my mom. It was quite a shock, even though one of Fordham's goons spilled the beans when they kidnapped me."

"Well, it was none of my business, and I only suspected it." He sat on the edge of his desk, looking down at her. "How are you holding up?"

"I'll be all right, but I can't work for him anymore," Cat whispered. "It wouldn't be right."

Ray watched her, feeling an urge to reach down and lift her from the chair, holding her close. Instead, he offered advice.

"Listen, I'm hardly the guy to tell you what to do, but he's trying. Sometimes that's all a person can do. Give him that much."

"I suppose you're right. We'll see what happens." Cat glanced up at him. "You're usually not so sympathetic about him. I figured you hated him for all of what's happened."

Ray paused, thinking about her comment.

"No, I don't hate him. I don't hate anyone; life's too short for that. J. Allan Dunn is not my enemy, but I don't trust him. He's a product of the city." Irish stood, placing a hand on her shoulder. Cat put her hand on top of his.

"You know I could help you with your business. I have contacts," Cat told him, her grin returning. "After all, I helped you set this whole thing up."

Ray's eyes locked on her.

"As I recall, you practically forced me into it. But why all this interest in what I do? Why act like my right-hand man? I don't get it."

He saw the petrified look suddenly cross her face. Cat removed her hand from his, then looked away.

"Don't take what I say the wrong way," she told him. "You're a good guy, someone who'll fight for people, even when they're wrong. This place needs that, and I'm willing to help you get your detective work going. But that's it. What I do otherwise is none of your concern."

Irish walked around the desk, taking a seat in the wooden chair. He contemplated her words and actions.

"You won't make anything personal in this partnership; that's the bottom line, isn't it?"

She nodded sternly, her lovely eyes now steely.

"All right, you've made it plain. I'll do the same," Ray said. "I'm willing to accept help if it doesn't cost me too much. What do you have in mind? I'm not sure I trust you much more than your father in business."

Ray leaned back in his chair.

"I'll feed you information that I find, which could become a case for you," she told him. "If you land something, then I get a finder's fee. By the way, Max Brand is going to let me write for the *Beacon*. If you get information that I can use in the article, I'll let you keep the cut. It'll be nice and straightforward that way." She leaned over to pour a drink.

"Grab a glass, and we'll drink to it."

A couple of short glasses later, Ray told his new partner about some of his conversations and thoughts. Oddly to him, she believed the city would soon revive, informing him of a rumor about a new business coming to Oyster City. She even mentioned hearing about the bishop and his wife taking a long cruise together.

"No doubt, Bishop La Spina is trying to get that woman turned into something she'll never be," Cat said sarcastically.

Her comment reminded Irish about the late train the La Spina's would take that evening, and he mentioned it to Cat.

"Well, as long as that woman stays away from Oyster City, the better for everyone." It was clear the animosity remained for the photographer. Ray looked at the glass in his hand.

"Are you so sure the presence of Mrs. Greye La Spina matters in a place like this?" he saw the look she gave him. "Yeah, she's no good, but the entire chain of events since I've been here has got me thinking."

Cat, looking very comfortable as she leaned back in the chair, suddenly gave him an edgy look.

"I'm drinking, trying to forget some of it."

"Well, I can't," Irish confided in her. "Mark Fordham, the probable next mayor, dies on the gambling ship the city doesn't want around. We were lucky to escape with our lives; you know that. Those flames were all over the place, yet the state police and various boards can't say if the fire was deliberate or not. That ship was out there for over a year, but suddenly sinks when the next potential mayor is on it."

Ray suddenly paused as he mulled over the words.

"You said it. We were lucky. Probably just a firetrap that was waiting to happen, and run by a bunch of chuckleheads," Cat offered.

"Maybe, but now the foundation has its money back from the con job created by a few grifters who drifted into the city," Ray told her. "The bishop, who is from one of the original founding families, escapes with no hint of scandal. Hell, he's going on a cruise. Young tries to kill us for those bloody bonds, and he has powerful friends in the capital city upstate. Yet we're supposed to believe he committed suicide in jail. Word I have is that didn't happen."

He glanced at her, and the girl's expression remained stoic.

"How can a place be lucky to only a select few?" Ray asked. "Something in my gut tells me there's something rotten at the top."

She shook her head.

"It's like my mom always told me, fortune smiles on good people."

Irish turned his head to look at her; his scowl deepened. "You told me once there wasn't much of a difference between the gangsters and the people running Oyster City. Who are the good people?"

Cat remained quiet, but she frowned at the question.

"Worse, I have the rotten feeling that no matter who I helped, it was the wrong people." Ray downed the last of his drink.

~~~

The thick, foggy darkness of late evening covered Oyster City when Greye and Henry La Spina got out of the taxi at the train station. Taking the last train to Boston, the couple already had their overnight room ticketed and their trunk aboard. Greye stepped from the cab wearing a green dress and black-veiled cap, briefly watching the cabbie pulling the few remaining bags from the car's trunk. Her husband waved over a porter who took the bags.

"We're on the Boston train; we have a roomette." Henry showed his tickets to the robust porter, and the couple led their helper into the station, where the elevated platforms led to their train. Soon, they were standing outside of a Pullman car.

"My dear, why don't you go to our room? I have to make a quick phone call. It's something that I forgot to tell the Smyths the other night. I won't be too long."

Greye sighed, then followed the porter onto the train. They walked along the passage to her roomette. After the porter opened the door, he halted.
~~~

"I'm sorry, ma'am. It looks like somebody done messed up."

She looked past him and saw the enormous steamer trunk. The open lid showed it was still half-filled with clothing. Some of her clothes were lying on the bed.

"Just give me a few minutes to get the clothes out," Visibly irritated, she told the porter to place the baggage he was carrying on the couch in the room. "You can get someone to come back and take it to the baggage car."

After the porter left, Greye took off her hat and began moving the clothes from the trunk to the closet, muttering under her breath. There was a knock at the door, and she slid past the open chest. Just as she turned the handle, a hard push against the wood panel forced her back. Two masked people wearing black robes burst into the room. Before the lady could react, one of the masked figures punched her savagely in the abdomen. Greye crumpled over, unable to breathe, and the intruder shoved a thick wad of cloth in front of her mouth. Pushing her upright against the wall, the intruder pressed a dagger blade against her throat.

"Don't make a sound," a male voice growled as the other intruder quickly locked the door.

Greye's eyes widened when she realized the mask showed Death's caricature. The second masked figure started giggling at the sight, then came next to Greye. They forced her face down on the bed, where they bound her wrists behind her. After ensuring the gag in the wife's mouth remained tight using a towel hanging on the wall.

The figure with the Empress mask pulled a porcelain water bowl from under the small sink in the lavatory. She placed the bowl inside the steamer trunk while Death pulled the bishop's wife from the couch and bent her over the edge of the chest.

Greye heard the two intruders chant and saw the dagger next to her face. It looked similar to those on her husband's wall. Terror took over as she lashed out with her legs in a desperate attempt to free herself, trying to rise from her kneeling position. Death rammed the handle of the dagger into the back of her head, stunning Mrs. La Spina. But the bishop's wife continued her frantic struggle. The Empress grabbed at Greye's legs. Muffled sounds of grunting and groaning filled the room as the two robed figures finally subdued the woman again. They forced her back over the trunk, placing her over the bowl.

The whispers of ancient chants began again. This time, Death moved quickly, using the dagger to cut deeply into Greye's thin neck. As the dying woman's body shuddered, bucking in a futile attempt to remain alive, the bowl underneath turned red, filling with precious blood. The Empress enjoyed Greye's body trembling in her arms, giggling as the victim's struggles slowly subsided. The foul creature behind the mask suddenly quivered with orgasmic ecstasy while her prisoner bled to death.

When the blood finally quit spurting from the victim's neck, the masked intruders removed the bowl. Together, they unceremoniously stuffed Greye's corpse into the box. The Empress went inside the lavatory to pour the blood into an empty wine bottle, already waiting for the sacrificial liquid. Death began removing the clothes from the bed and closet, laying them on top of the body.

Three taps followed by another quick three taps coming from the door caused the killers to stop their work. Quickly closing the lid, Death eased past the trunk and turned the door handle. Bishop La Spina stood outside. He looked both ways down the aisle before he entered his roomette.

The Empress came out of the lavatory carrying the bottle of blood while Death pulled an empty suitcase from the dead woman's nearly empty closet. Pulling off his mask and robe, Death placed his costume inside the open bag. His thin, hawk-like face held piercing, gray eyes that matched his gray hair. Death wore a finely tailored blue suit, adjusting his tie while the Empress pulled off her mask and robe. The woman with the giggle smiled broadly at the bishop, then wrapped her costume and put it into the small suitcase. The brunette wore a nearly identical copy of the green dress that Greye wore to the train station.

"We have the sacrificial blood for tonight. It's a shame you can't be there," the woman's husband stated as he bent over to kiss his short woman on her cheek.

She smiled and lightly patted him on the shoulder.

"Carry it carefully for the master."

With a nod, the tall man placed the bottle into the suitcase and closed it, tightening the two leather straps which encircled the leather case. He quickly left the roomette, taking the bag with him.

Henry La Spina came around the trunk and sat in the chair. He watched the killer use a towel to clean the sink and the water bowl before placing the porcelain water bowl under the sink. After one last glance around, the brunette opened the trunk again, pulling back the clothes to view the corpse. The bishop leaned forward to look as well, picking up the ornamental dagger from the box. His face remained blank as he lifted the corpse's left hand. The crackling snap of bones and tissue filled the room when he cut the ring finger away. The man took the ring and finger, wiping the blood away with the small towel, before pocketing both in his dark suit pocket.

The lady's blue eyes were still alight at the murder as she watched the bishop clean the dagger. "It was so satisfying to watch the little bitch's blood fill the pan as she struggled. It was nearly as good as sex." Her voice was breathless. "That smug little tramp deserved much more for the mistreatment of your family name. She was really beneath you." She gave a wicked little laugh.

"True, but a man can make mistakes in a moment of weakness. I'm glad the Shadows could look past this error," Henry told her gratefully. "It's fitting that our master will have her soul for his enjoyment."

There was a knock at the door, and the Empress quickly threw the bloody towel on top of the body. After she closed the lid, she put on the black hat that the dead woman was wearing.

The bishop placed his feet on top of the trunk as he slid the dagger into the elaborate scabbard, putting the rare antique on the couch beside him.

"Come in!" he ordered.

"I'm sorry to bother you, sir. I'm here to get your trunk out of the way. We'll try to get it back to the cargo car, but the train is just about to leave. I can't imagine why my men left this in your room." A conductor looked into the cabin, while two unhappy porters stood outside.

"No need to fret, my good man." Henry removed his feet and locked the case before standing up, moving closer to the veiled lady, who looked out of the train window. "My wife and I had a last-minute change of plans. Just have this taken back down to the station. I've already called a man to pick it up on the dock tonight. We won't need that trunk anyway, just extra baggage." Henry watched the porters enter and get the steamer. Nothing showed the men caught on to the fact that the box was heavier than when it came into the room.

After they left, the bishop handed the conductor a five-dollar bill. "Please have a man bring us back a bottle of your best Rothschild when you can." The conductor tipped his cap and quickly left.

The bishop smiled at his guest.

"Well, Mrs. Smyth, my family's sacrifice should ensure our city's good fortune for a while."

"I agree with you, Mr. La Spina," she replied, but her eyes grew hard. "We'll make sure no such mistake happens again. There are suitable women among the elder bloodlines for your next wife. That will keep you from such difficulty in the future. I've learned it's far better to lose a distant relation than someone you decide to care about. The master does not forgive, as you well know."

There was a knock at the door, and the porter entered with the wine. He opened the bottle, filling glasses for his train passengers before leaving.

"When you get back from your cruise, along with the news about the unfortunate disappearance of your wife, the Shadows will find you a more suitable partner." Mrs. Smyth held up her glass in a toast, and Henry La Spina smiled, raising his glass as well.

~~~

Ray Irish stood in a mortuary, looking at the unidentified corpse of a woman. Blistered from the sun, the body's greenish -black skin covered the disfigured upper body. Most of the face's soft tissue was missing, eaten by crabs and small fish. The revolting sight wasn't new to Ray; he saw many cadavers in the same condition during the war. Drinking and drifting were his attempts to force such images from his memories. The coroner pulled back the sheet on the left side of the corpse. Only four bloated fingers remained, the ring finger severed.

"The body was in the water for about a month, no fingerprints or identifying marks. The killer removed the ring," the examiner stated, his voice monotone and sterile.
~~~

He observed Irish's reaction, then continued.

"It appears a four to six-inch blade is the weapon used to cut the woman's throat, but it's difficult to determine anything more with the damage to the corpse. Do you know her?"

"No, I didn't know her." Irish shook his head. His face remained a mask, withdrawn and emotionless.

Cat had left when the coroner pulled back the sheet. She was waiting outside, unsteady after puking up her guts from the sight and smell of the corpse.

"I'll drive," he told her.

On the way back to Oyster City, the car remained quiet except for the humming engine noise and tire's droning sound.

"What do you think?" Cat finally broke the silence.

"That was Greye La Spina," Ray replied in a monotone. "I've got a new case."

She paused, then glanced over at him. "I understand you want to believe that. Since I mentioned the state police found a woman's corpse the other day, you've changed. Ray, you can't be sure that's her. The *Beacon* reported Greye fell from the ship outside of Marseilles. The wire stated there were witnesses, and her husband was drinking with other passengers at the time."

He glanced at her, and his jaw tightened.

"Yeah, I checked. The ship barely left the harbor. They didn't find a body, and only one witness claims she fell overboard. You never heard of a bribe?" He shook his head. "No, she died before they left the city. That corpse we just saw matches that timeline, and the wedding ring is missing. The body was in the water too long, so no fingerprints either."

"Why are you so sure of this?" Cat asked.

"Not long before she left, Greye came by my office and gave me five hundred dollars," he said. "She was getting pretty tipsy, but I asked her what she wanted." His thoughts went back to that day.

"Yeah, I can guess," she said smugly.

"No, you can't," Ray replied. "She wanted to hire me to solve a case."

"What case?" Cat's blue eyes examined him.

"Greye hired me to find her murderer," Irish said as he stared ahead.

The partners fell silent, each lost in unnerving thoughts. Road noise filled the cabin as the car returned to the dark metropolis known as Oyster City.

About the Author

Gordon Brewer is the pseudonym for a professional geek, history buff, and full-time dad who took up a challenge from his son to finish his first novel. As the author of over ten books, Gordon believes he's met his son's challenge in the world of writing.

Raised on a farm in Kansas, the author spent nearly five years in the US Navy, traveling to 12 different countries during this time. After his discharge, he received his BS degree with double majors in History and Political Science.

Over the next 20 years, Gordon focused on the business and IT world. His experiences left him with a need to explore wide-ranging interests in multiple genres, each with historical consideration given to the characters and settings.

Residing in Tennessee, he often uses his family and friends as unfortunate guinea pigs where they endure his tales, no matter how poorly conceived they may be.

You can find out more about the author, his upcoming books, and novellas at his website, www.gordonbrewer.com.

www.ingramcontent.com/pod-product-compliance
Lightning Source LLC
Chambersburg PA
CBHW060911210726

48293CB00006B/2053